PLAIN AND FANCY

BRIDES *of* LANCASTER COUNTY | BOOK 3

WANDA E. BRUNSTETTER

New York Times BESTSELLING AUTHOR

BARBOUR PUBLISHING

ISBN 978-1-62836-165-0

eBook Editions:
Adobe Digital Edition (.epub) 978-1-63058-500-6
Kindle and MobiPocket Edition (.prc) 978-1-63058-501-3

All scripture quotations are taken from the King James Version of the Bible.

All German-Dutch words are taken from the *Revised Pennsylvania German Dictionary* found in Lancaster County, Pennsylvania.

This book is a work of fiction. Names, characters, places, and incidents are either products of the author's imagination or used fictitiously. Any similarity to actual people, organizations, and/or events is purely coincidental.

For more information about Wanda E. Brunstetter, please access the author's website at the following Internet address: www.wandabrunstetter.com

Cover design: Müllerhaus Publishing Arts, Inc., www.Mullerhaus.net

Published by Barbour Publishing, Inc., P.O. Box 719, Uhrichsville, Ohio 44683, www.barbourbooks.com

Our mission is to publish and distribute inspirational products offering exceptional value and biblical encouragement to the masses.

Printed in the United States of America.

To my six wunderbaar *grandchildren,*
Jinell, Madolynne, Rebekah, Ric, Philip, and Richelle.
You are each one of God's special miracles.

Commit thy way unto the LORD*; trust also in him;*
and he shall bring it to pass.
PSALM 37:5

Chapter 1

Laura Meade opened her laptop, entered the correct password to put her online, and began the e-mail she had been meaning to write for the past week:

> *Dear Shannon,*
>
> *I'm finally settled in at the Lancaster School of Design. I think I'm going to like it here. Not only is the college rated in the top ten, but the area is beautiful, and the Amish I've seen are unbelievable! I haven't met any of them up close and personal, but from what I've seen, the women wear simple, dark-colored dresses, with little white hats on their heads. The men wear cotton shirts, dark pants with suspenders, and either a straw or black felt hat with a wide brim. They drive box-shaped, closed-in buggies pulled by a horse.*
>
> *Tomorrow, I'm going to the farmers' market. I hear it's a great place to get good buys on handmade Amish quilts. I may even be able to acquire some helpful decorating ideas there.*

I hope you're doing well and enjoying your new job. I'm looking forward to seeing you at Christmas and hearing about those preschoolers you teach.

Your friend,
Laura

Laura thought about sending an e-mail to her parents, but she had talked to them on the phone just an hour ago, so there wouldn't be much to write about now. Moving away from the desk, she picked up a brush from the dresser and began her nightly ritual of one hundred strokes through her long, thick tresses.

She glanced around the room with disdain. Even the smallest room at home was bigger than this dinky dorm room. Fortunately, she would only be here two years. Then she could return to Minneapolis and redecorate to her heart's content—starting with her own bedroom at home.

"It's stifling in here." Laura dropped the hairbrush onto the bed and went to open the window. A slight breeze trickled through the screen, but it did nothing to cool the stuffy room. Here it was the first week of September, and the days were still hot and humid. To make matters worse, the air-conditioning wasn't working right and probably wouldn't be fixed until later in the week, according to what she'd been told.

Fall had always been Laura's favorite time of year. Someday, she hoped to decorate her own home with harvest colors. The kitchen windows would be outlined with sheer yellow curtains. The living-room, dining-room, and bedroom floors would be covered with thick, bronze carpets. She wanted to decorate with Early American furniture and to hang plenty of paintings from that era on the walls.

Mom and Dad had allowed her to travel halfway across the country to attend the Lancaster School of Design, despite the fact that several good schools were closer to home. When Laura had heard about this one so near to the heart of Amish land, she'd known she had to come. She'd read about the interesting culture of the Plain People on a few Web sites and was sure she could gain some unique decorating ideas here in Lancaster County.

Laura glanced at the photo of Dean Carlson, set in a gold frame on top of her dresser. Dean was the newest member of her father's law firm, and he had given her the picture soon after they'd started dating three months ago. Dean hadn't been too happy about her moving to Pennsylvania, even though she had assured him it would only be for a couple of years. She wasn't sure if his reluctance to see her go was because he cared so much or if he might be worried that she would find someone else and end up staying in Pennsylvania.

A loud knock jolted Laura out of her musings. With an exasperated sigh, she crossed the room and opened the door.

A young woman with short, curly blond hair stood in the hallway. "Hi. I'm Darla Shelby. I have the room next to yours."

Laura smiled. "I'm Laura Meade."

"Nice to meet you. Where are you from?"

"Minneapolis. How about you?"

"I grew up here in Lancaster, moved to New York with my folks when I was sixteen, and came back here again to attend this school." She grinned. "But my favorite place to be is Philadelphia. In fact, since tomorrow's Saturday, I thought I'd drive into Philly and do some shopping. Would you like to go along?"

"So you must have your own car?"

Darla nodded. "It's a little red convertible—got it for my birthday last year."

Laura thought about her own car parked in the garage at home. She wished she could have driven it here, but her parents had insisted that she fly to Pennsylvania and lease a car during her stay.

"I realize we've only just met," Darla continued, "but I figure what better way to get acquainted than during a shopping spree."

Laura leaned against the door frame as she contemplated the tempting offer. "I appreciate the invitation, and I'd love to go with you some other time, but I had planned to go to the farmers' market at Bird-in-Hand tomorrow. I understand some of the Plain People go there to shop and sell some of their wares."

Darla nodded. "Those Amish and Mennonites are quite the tourist attraction around here."

"Why don't you go to the market with me, and we can do some shopping there?"

Darla wrinkled her nose. "No way! I'd rather be caught in the middle of rush-hour traffic on the turnpike than spend the day with a bunch of farmers."

Laura giggled. "Those farmers do look pretty interesting."

"Maybe so, but they're not interesting enough for me to give up a day of shopping in Philly." Darla turned toward her own room, calling over her shoulder, "Whatever you do, Laura, don't let too much of that Amish culture rub off on you."

As Eli Yoder left Strasburg, where he worked at a store that made handcrafted Amish furniture, he thought about the conversation he'd had with Pauline Hostetler after church last Sunday. He had made the mistake of telling her that he planned to rent a table at the farmers' market this Saturday to sell some of the items he'd created in his wood shop at home.

"Oh, Eli," he could still hear her say, *"I was planning to go to the market on Saturday, too. Maybe the two of us could meet at noon and eat lunch together."*

"Pauline's after me to court her," Eli mumbled, as he headed down the road toward home in his buggy.

His horse whinnied as if in response and perked up his ears.

"Are you sympathizing with me, boy?" Eli chuckled and flicked the reins to get his horse trotting a bit faster. It was fun to ride in his open buggy and go a little faster than usual. It made him feel free and one with the wind whipping against his face.

I won't be free for long if Pauline has anything to say about it. I think she's in cahoots with Mom to see me join the church so I can get married and settle down to raising a family. Eli frowned. It wasn't that he didn't want to get married someday. He just hadn't found the right woman yet, and he was sure it wouldn't be Pauline. He was in no hurry to be baptized and join the church until he felt ready to settle down. So Mom would have to learn to be patient.

"Why'd I agree to meet Pauline for lunch?" Eli fretted. "She's likely to take it to mean I have an interest in her, and then she'll expect me to start officially calling on her."

He gripped the reins a little tighter. "I'll have lunch with her on Saturday because I promised I would, but I'll have to figure out some way to let her know there's no chance of us having a future together."

A ray of sun filtered through the window, causing Laura to squint when she opened her eyes. She peeked at the small clock on her bedside table. It was nearly nine o'clock. She had slept much later than she'd planned.

Jerking the covers aside, she slipped out of bed and headed for the shower. A short time later, as Laura studied the contents of her closet, she had a hard time deciding what to wear. She finally opted for a pair of blue jeans and a rust-colored tank top. She pulled her long, auburn hair into a ponytail and secured it with a navy blue scrunchie.

"Nothing fancy, but I'm sure I look good enough to go to the farmers' market," she said to her reflection in the mirror. "Amish country, I hope you're ready for me because here I come!"

Mary Ellen Yoder had just begun supper preparations when her husband, Johnny, stepped into the kitchen, holding a pot of pansies in his hands. He grinned at her and placed the pot on the counter. "These are for you. I got 'em from the Beachys' greenhouse."

She turned from her job of cutting vegetables for a stew and smiled. "Such a thoughtful husband I have. *Danki*, Johnny."

His smile widened, and he leaned over to kiss her cheek. "I still remember the first bouquet of flowers I bought for my special girl. Do you?"

She nodded. "That was way back when you were doing everything you could to get me to allow you to come courting."

He slipped his arm around her waist and gave her a squeeze. "And it worked, too, didn't it? We not only started courting, but you agreed to marry me, and now we've got ourselves four of the finest *kinner* around."

"*Jah*, I agree." Mary Ellen smiled and resumed cutting her vegetables.

"And let's not forget that spunky little *kindsbuh* our daughter gave us a few years back."

"Now if we can just get our three *buwe* married off so they can add more grandchildren to our family," Mary Ellen said.

"I think the chances of Lewis and Jonas finding wives might be pretty good since they've already joined the church, but Eli's another matter."

Mary Ellen sighed and glanced at Johnny over her shoulder. "It's hard for me to understand why he keeps saying he's not ready to settle down when he's got a fine woman like Pauline Hostetler interested in him. Eli's twenty-three years old already and has gone through his *rumschpringe* long enough. Wouldn't you think he'd be eager to end his running-around years and start courting a pretty girl?"

Johnny shrugged. "I don't want to get your hopes up, but I heard Eli talking to Jonas last night, and he mentioned that he's got plans to meet Pauline for lunch on Saturday when he goes to the farmers' market to sell some of his handmade wooden items."

Despite her husband's warning, Mary Ellen's hopes began to soar. "Really? You heard that?"

"Heard it with my own ears, so it's not just say-so."

She smiled. "Now that is good news. Jah, the best news I've had all day."

When Laura stepped out of her air-conditioned car, a blast of heat and humidity hit her full in the face. She hurried into the market building and was relieved to find that it was much cooler than the outside air had been.

The first table Laura discovered was run by two

young Amish women selling an assortment of pies and cookies. Both wore their hair parted down the middle, then pulled back into a tight bun. They had small, white caps perched on top of their heads, and their long-sleeved, dark blue dresses were calf-length, with black aprons and capes worn over the front. One of the women smiled and asked Laura if she would like to sample something.

She stared longingly at a piece of apple pie. They did look delicious, but she'd had breakfast not long ago and didn't think she needed the extra calories.

"No thanks. I'm not really hungry right now." The truth was Laura was always counting calories, and she figured one bite of those scrumptious pastries would probably tip the scales in an unfavorable direction. She moved on quickly before temptation got the better of her.

The next few tables were run by non-Amish farmers. The items they offered didn't interest Laura much, so she found another table where an elderly Amish woman sold handmade quilts.

"Those are gorgeous. How much do they cost?" she asked.

The woman showed her each one, quoting the prices, which ranged from four hundred to nine hundred dollars.

"I'm definitely going to buy one," Laura said without questioning the price. "I don't want to carry it around while I shop, though. Can you hold this one for me?" She pointed to a simple pattern that used a combination of geometric shapes done in a variety of rich autumn colors.

"Jah, sure. I can hold it."

"Great. What's this one called, anyway?"

"It's known as 'Grandmother's Choice.' " The Amish woman's fingers traveled lightly over the material.

Laura smiled. "I like it very much. I'll be back for it before I leave, but I can pay now if you'd like."

"Pay when you come back; that'll be fine." The woman placed the quilt inside a box, then slipped it under the table.

It was getting close to lunchtime, so Laura decided to check out one more table, then look for something nonfattening to eat.

The next table was loaded with a variety of hand-carved items. Laura glanced around for the person in charge but didn't see anyone. She picked up one of the finely crafted birdhouses and studied the exquisite detailing. When a young Amish man popped up from behind the table, she jumped, nearly dropping the birdhouse. He held a box filled with more birdhouses and feeders. His sandy brown hair was cut in a Dutch-bob, and a lock of it fell across his forehead. His deeply set, crystalline blue eyes met Laura's gaze with such intensity it took her breath away. Her cheeks grew hot, and she quickly placed the birdhouse back on the table. "I—I was just admiring your work."

A hint of a smile tweaked the man's lips, revealing a small dimple in the middle of his chin. "I'm a woodcarver and carpenter, and I'm thankful God has given me the ability to use my hands for something worthwhile."

Though Laura had been to church a few times in her life, she wasn't particularly religious. In fact, the whole church scene made her feel kind of nervous. Nibbling on the inside of her cheek, she merely nodded in response to the man's giving credit to God for his abilities.

"Are you looking for anything special? I also have some wooden flowerpots and ornamental things for the lawn." He lifted one for her inspection.

Laura stared at the small, decorative windmill in his hand, and her gaze traveled up his muscular arm. Below his rolled-up shirtsleeve, his tanned arms were feathered with light brown hair. She moistened her lips and brought her wayward thoughts to a halt. "I. . .uh. . .live in a dorm room at the Lancaster School of Design, so I really don't have a need for birdhouses or whirligigs."

His dark eyebrows drew together. "Don't think I've ever heard of that school."

"I'm learning to be an interior decorator," she explained, drawing her gaze to his appealing face, then back to the items on the table.

When he made no comment, she looked up again and saw that he was staring at her with a questioning look.

"My job will be to help people decorate their homes in attractive styles and colors."

"Ah, I see. So do you live around here, then?"

She shook her head. "I'm from Minneapolis, Minnesota. I've already studied some interior design at one of our local community colleges, and I'm here to complete my training."

There was an awkward silence as they stood staring at one another.

"Eli, well, there you are! I thought we were supposed to meet for lunch. I waited outside, but you never showed up so I figured I'd better come looking."

A young, blond-haired Amish woman, dressed similarly to the Plain women Laura had seen earlier, stepped up to the table.

"I'm sorry, Pauline," he said. "I got busy talking with this customer and forgot about the time." He considered Laura a moment. "Is there anything you're wantin' to buy?"

"No. I. . .uh. . .was just looking."

"Eli, if you're finished here, can we go have lunch now?" Pauline took a few steps closer, brushing her hand lightly against Eli's arm.

"Jah, Pauline." Eli glanced back at Laura. "It was nice chatting with you, and I wish you the best with your studies and all." He turned away, leaving his wooden items unattended.

Laura shook her head. *That man is sure trusting. And how in the world could someone as simply dressed as him be so adorable?*

As Eli and Pauline exited the building, he glanced over his shoulder. The young English woman still stood beside his table. *She's sure a fancy one. Fancy and very pretty. I wonder why someone like her would be interested in birdhouses?*

"Eli, where do you want to eat lunch?"

Pauline's question and her slight tug on Eli's shirtsleeve brought his thoughts to a halt.

"I thought you carried a picnic basket," he said peevishly.

"I did, but I wasn't sure where you wanted to eat it."

He shrugged. "It makes no difference to me."

"Let's go to the picnic tables out back."

When Eli gave no response, she grabbed his sleeve again. "What's wrong? You're acting kind of *naerfich*."

"I'm not nervous. I've just got a lot on my mind."

Pauline slipped her hand through the crook of his arm. "After you've had a few bites of fried chicken, you won't be thinking about anything but my good cooking."

Eli feigned a smile. "Kissin' wears out, but cookin' don't." Truth be told, he wasn't really in the mood to eat just now, but he was sure Pauline had worked hard making the picnic lunch, and he'd promised to eat it with her. Besides, a few drumsticks and a plate of potato salad would probably make him feel a whole lot better.

Pauline smiled and set the wicker basket she'd filled with chicken, baked beans, cut-up vegetables, and chocolate cake on the picnic table. "You're right about cooking never wearing out. My *mamm* and *daed* have been married twenty-five years, and Dad's still complimenting Mom on her great cooking."

Eli's only reply was a quick shrug. Then he bowed his head, and she did the same. When their silent prayer was over, Pauline opened the basket and set out the food, along with paper plates, napkins, and plastic silverware. "I brought a jug of water for us to drink," she said. "I hope that's okay."

"Jah, sure; it's fine for me." Eli helped himself to a couple of drumsticks and some baked beans, and Pauline followed suit, only she added some cut-up carrots to her plate.

"I was sorry to learn that you hadn't taken the membership classes this summer so you could be baptized and join the church a week from Sunday," she said.

He gave a noncommital grunt and kept on eating.

"Will you take the classes next summer?"

"Maybe. It all depends on how I feel about things by then."

Pauline pursed her lips. "You're twenty-three years old already. Haven't you had enough rumschpringe by now? Don't you think it's past time for you to join the church and settle down?"

"Now you sound like my mamm." Eli frowned. "Maybe one of the reasons I haven't made the decision yet is because she's always hounding me about it."

Pauline flinched, feeling like he'd thrown cold water in her face. Eli obviously thought she was hounding him, too.

Eli reached into the plastic tub filled with chicken

and retrieved another drumstick. "Don't get me wrong. I'm not refusing to join the church because I have any ideas about leaving the Amish faith. I just can't see the need of joining when I'm not ready to get married yet."

Pauline felt as if her heart had sunk all the way to her toes. If Eli wasn't ready to get married, then he obviously had no thoughts of marrying her. But he'd taken her home from a couple of singings, and he'd agreed to meet her for lunch today. Didn't that mean anything at all? Wasn't that a ray of hope worth clinging to? Pauline knew she would have to be careful not to push Eli too hard, but if she had her way, by this time next year they'd be planning their wedding.

When Laura returned to her dorm room later that afternoon, she placed the Amish quilt she'd purchased on her bed, making it a definite focal point in the room. For some reason, the quilt reminded her of the young Amish man who had been selling wood-crafted items. As Laura sat at her desk, trying to study, she found herself wishing she had bought one of his birdhouses.

She drummed her fingers restlessly across the desktop. As ridiculous as it might seem, she'd been attracted to the man. It was stupid, because she knew they were worlds apart. Besides, the young woman he'd been with had seemed awfully possessive, and Laura figured she might be Eli's girlfriend or even his wife.

Fighting the urge to fantasize further, she forced herself to concentrate on the monochromatic swatches of material on her desk. It wouldn't be good to get behind in her studies because of a passing fancy with someone she would probably never see again.

Chapter 2

For the next several weeks, Laura was kept busy with classes and what seemed like never-ending homework. She hadn't ventured into Amish land since her trip to the farmers' market, but since it was Saturday and most of her homework was done, she had time to have fun.

Since Laura was so fascinated by the Plain People, she decided to check out a few gift shops in one of the nearby Amish communities. This time she made sure she brought her camera along.

Laura drove the small car she had leased for the months she would be living in Pennsylvania and headed to the town of Paradise. The first store she entered was a gift shop filled with excited tourists. It had numerous shelves full of Pennsylvania Dutch trinkets and a rack of postcards with photos of Amish and Mennonite farms, Plain People, and horse-drawn buggies. Laura bought several with the intent of sending them to family and friends back home.

Her next stop was a variety store, which was stocked with more gift items, groceries, and snack foods.

Laura wandered toward the back of the store. To her amazement, the shelves were lined with oil lamps, bolts of plain cotton material, women's black bonnets, men's straw hats, boxes of white handkerchiefs, and several pairs of work boots. Another section was stocked with various-sized shovels and other gardening tools, as well as a variety of flower and vegetable seeds.

The Amish must do some of their shopping here, she thought. *I wonder if I'll see any of them come into the store while I'm here.*

Laura hung around for a while, looking at various items and keeping an eye out for Amish people. She soon got tired of waiting, so she bought a few more postcards and left the store.

Outside on the sidewalk, she spotted two little Amish girls walking hand in hand behind their mother.

They're so cute–I just have to get their picture. Laura pulled her digital camera from her purse, focused it on the children, and was about to snap the picture when someone grasped her shoulder.

"Would you mind not taking that picture?"

Laura spun around. A pair of penetrating blue eyes bore down on her, and her heart skipped a beat. It was the same Amish man she'd met at the farmers' market a few weeks ago.

"I remember you. You were at the market, looking at my birdhouses, right?"

Laura nodded and offered him what she hoped was a pleasant smile. "Why did you stop me from taking those little girls' pictures?"

"The Amish prefer not to have their pictures taken."

"Oh? How come?"

"We believe it's a form of pride, and some in our church say it goes against Bible teachings reminding us not to make any graven images."

"What about all the pictures on postcards?" She withdrew one from her purse. "Isn't that an Amish man working in the fields?"

"Some folks don't care how we feel about being photographed, and they just snap pictures of us anyway," he said without even glancing at the postcard. "And some people use close-up lenses so they can take pictures without us knowing. I'm sure the man in the postcard didn't actually pose for the picture."

"Well, you don't have to worry about me offending anyone." She slipped the camera back into her purse, then held out her hand. "I'm Laura Meade."

He seemed kind of hesitant at first, but then he shook her hand and smiled. "My name's Eli Yoder."

"It's nice to meet you, Eli." She laughed, feeling suddenly self-conscious. "I guess we did meet before—just no formal introductions."

He motioned toward a wooden bench in front of the building. "Would you want to sit awhile? I'll take my birdhouses inside; then we can have a cup of cold root beer. That is, if you'd like one."

Laura nodded eagerly. Of course she would like a root beer—especially when it would give her more time to talk to this good-looking Amish man. She dropped to the bench and leaned forward with her elbows resting on her jean-clad knees, as she watched Eli head to the parking lot, where his horse and buggy stood waiting. He made two trips into the store, shouldering large cardboard boxes. When he emerged for the last time, he held two Styrofoam cups full of root beer. He gave one to Laura and sat down beside her.

"I noticed your buggy is open–sort of like a carriage," she remarked. "Most of the Amish buggies I've seen are closed and kind of box-shaped."

Eli grinned. "That's my courting buggy. My daed gave it to me on my sixteenth birthday."

"Your *daed*?"

"Jah, my dad."

"Oh. So what's a 'courting buggy'?"

"English boys get a driver's license and sometimes a car when they turn sixteen. We Amish get an open buggy so we can start courting–or dating, as you Englishers like to call it."

She smiled. "Have you been dating very long?"

"Are you wanting to know my age?"

Laura felt the heat of embarrassment creep up her neck as she nodded. She did want to know how old he was–and a whole lot more besides.

"It's okay. I don't mind you asking. I'm twenty-three, and my folks think I ought to be married already." Eli lifted the cup of root beer to his lips.

So, he's single and just a year older than me. Laura wasn't sure why, but that bit of information gave her some measure of satisfaction. "How come you're not married?" she ventured to ask.

"For one thing, I haven't joined our church

yet, and that's a requirement before marriage." Eli shrugged. "I haven't met the right woman yet, either."

Laura thought about the Amish woman who had been with Eli at the market. She'd seen the way that Plain girl had looked at him.

Eli smacked his lips. "*Umm*. . .this is sure good root beer. Thomas Benner, the store owner, makes it himself."

Laura took a sip. "Yes, it is very good." Her gaze traveled across the parking lot. "Your buggy's sure nice-looking. Does it ride well?"

Eli rewarded her with a heart-melting smile, and his seeking blue eyes mesmerized her. "Would you like to find out?"

"Oh, I'd love that!" Laura jumped up; then, thinking he might have only been teasing, she whirled around to face him. "Would it be all right? It's not against your religion or anything?"

Eli's smile widened, causing the dimple in his chin to become more pronounced. "There are some other Plain sects who offer buggy rides to tourists. So if someone should see us, they'll probably just think you hired me for a ride."

Eli helped Laura into the left side of the open buggy; then he climbed up on the right and gathered the reins. With a few clucks to his faithful horse, they were off.

A slight breeze caught the ends of Laura's golden bronze hair, whipping them around her face. Eli's chest constricted. *This English woman is sure appealing.*

Why, it's almost sinful to be so beautiful. I'm wondering why she would want to be seen with someone as plain as me.

Eli felt a twinge of guilt for allowing himself the pleasure of admiring her beauty, but he couldn't quit thinking how much fun it would be to get to know her better.

"This is so awesome! I never would have dreamed riding in a buggy could be so much fun." Laura's tone revealed her excitement, and her green eyes lit up like a sunbeam.

He glanced over at her and grinned. "Jah, it's wonderful good."

When they had gone a short distance, Eli turned the buggy down a wide, dirt path, where there were no cars, just a carpet of flaxen corn on either side.

"Where are we going?"

"There's a small lake down this way." Eli flashed her another smile. "I think you'll like it there."

Laura leaned back in her seat, breathed deeply of the fresh air, and drank in the rich colors of the maple trees lining both sides of the dirt road. "I think the temperate hues of autumn make it the most charming, loveliest time of the year," she murmured.

Eli raised his dark eyebrows. "Such fancy words you're using."

She laughed. "Should I have said it's 'wonderful good'?"

"Jah, sure." Eli pulled the horse to a stop in a

grassy meadow near the small lake. "Here we are."

"You were right. It is beautiful here."

Eli grinned like a child with a new toy. "In the summer, it's a great place for swimming and fishing. We like to skate on the lake when it freezes over in the wintertime, too."

"It looks like the perfect place for a picnic."

"My family and I have been here many times." Eli glanced over at Laura. "Would you like to get out and walk around?"

"That sounds nice, but I rather like riding in your courting buggy." She released a sigh of contentment. "Can't we just keep driving?"

"Sure, we can." Eli got the horse moving again.

As they traveled around the lake, Laura began to ply him with questions about his way of life. "Can you tell me why the Amish people wear such simple clothes?"

"We feel that wearing plain clothes encourages humility and separation from the world. Our clothes aren't a costume, like some may believe, but they're an expression of our faith."

"I see." A gentle breeze rustled the trees, and Laura's heart stirred with a kind of excitement she had never known before. She wasn't sure if it was the fall foliage, the exhilarating buggy ride, or the captivating company of one very cute Amish man that made her feel so giddy. One thing was for sure: A keen sense of disappointment overcame her when Eli turned the buggy back to the main road.

"Do you like wearing men's trousers?" he asked suddenly.

She glanced at her blue jeans and giggled. "These aren't men's trousers. They're made for a woman, and they're really quite comfortable." When Eli made no comment, she decided it was her turn to ask another question. "What's your family like?"

"I have a wonderful family. There's Pop and Mom, and I have an older sister, Martha Rose. She's married to Amon Zook, and they've got a three-year-old son. I also have two younger brothers who help Pop on the farm while I'm working at the furniture shop near Strasburg."

"I think it would be interesting if I could see where you live." The unexpected comment popped out of Laura's mouth before she had time to think about what she was saying.

When Eli's brows drew downward and he made no response, she wondered if she had overstepped her bounds. As much as she would like it, she knew she would probably never get to see Eli's house, meet his family, or have another opportunity to ride in an Amish buggy.

It seemed like no time at all before they were pulling into the variety store's parking lot. Eli jumped down and came around to help Laura out of the buggy. When his hands went around her waist, she felt an unexpected shiver tickle her spine. "Thanks for the ride," she said breathlessly. "If I live to a ripe old age, I'll never forget this day."

Laura started across the parking lot and was surprised to see Eli walking beside her. They both stopped when they reached the sidewalk, and Laura glanced at her watch. "I'd better call my friend.

We're supposed to meet for supper soon." She pulled her cell phone from her purse.

"Your friend is some lucky fellow."

She smiled. "It's not a man I'm meeting for supper. It's just a girlfriend from school."

"Ah, I see." Eli stared at the ground for a few seconds, then looked back at her. "Say, I was wondering–would you be interested in going back to the lake with me next Saturday? We could take a picnic lunch along, and if you have more questions about my way of life, I'll have a little more time to answer them."

Laura could hardly believe her ears. Had he really asked her on a date? Well, maybe not a date exactly, but at least it was another chance to see him.

"That would be nice," she said, forcing her voice to remain steady. "What should I bring?"

"Just a hearty appetite and a warm jacket. I'll ask Mom to fix the lunch, because she always makes plenty of good food."

"It's a date." Laura felt the heat of a blush creep up the back of her neck and spread to her cheeks. "I mean–I'll look forward to next Saturday. Should we meet here in front of the store, around one o'clock?"

"That'll be fine," he answered with a nod.

"Until next Saturday then." Just before Laura turned toward her car, she looked back and saw him wave as he was walking away. She lifted her hand in response and whispered, "Eli Yoder, where have you been all my life?"

Chapter 3

As Laura drove back to Lancaster, all she could think about was Eli. She pictured his twinkling blue eyes, sandy brown hair, and the cute little chin dimple that made him look so irresistible. Eli was full of humor and had a fresh, almost innocent way about him. It was something she'd never seen in Dean Carlson, who had a haughty attitude and seemed to think he was every woman's dream.

She clenched the steering wheel until her knuckles turned white. *What am I thinking here? I can't allow myself to fantasize about Eli or start comparing him to other men. He's off-limits–forbidden fruit for a modern English woman like me.* She grimaced as she pulled up to a stop sign and spotted a closed-in Amish buggy with two little towheaded boys peeking out the back. *Then why am I reflecting on the time we had together today? And why did I agree to go on a picnic with him next Saturday?*

As hard as Laura tried, she seemed unable to squelch the desire to see Eli one more time. She could learn a bit more about the Amish; they would enjoy a nice picnic lunch and soak up the beauty of the lake; and it would be over. They'd probably never see each other again. She would have pleasant memories of the brief time she'd spent with an intriguing Amish man, and her life would return to normal. It would be a wonderful story to tell her grandchildren someday. She smiled and tried to visualize herself as a grandmother, but the thought was too far removed. The only thing she could see was the face of Eli Yoder calling her to learn more about him and his Plain way of living.

All the way home, Eli thought about Laura and the conversation they'd had on their way to and from the lake. She had asked a lot of questions about his way of life, but he hadn't asked that many about hers. He would have to do that next Saturday, because there were so many things he wanted to know. How long would she be in Lancaster studying at the interior design school? How old was she? Did she have any brothers or sisters? Did she have a boyfriend? That was the one thing he wanted to know the most, and it troubled him deeply, because it shouldn't matter so much.

He could still picture Laura sitting in his buggy, her long auburn hair glistening in the sun like golden shafts of wheat. *I shouldn't be thinking about her, much less worrying over whether she has a boyfriend. Probably shouldn't have invited her to have a picnic with me next Saturday, but I just want to see her one more time. I'd like the chance to answer a few more of her questions and ask a few of my own.*

The family-style restaurant where Laura was to meet Darla seemed crowded, and after checking her watch, Laura knew she was late. She stood in the clogged entryway, craning her neck to see around the people in front of her. Was Darla already in the dining room? Sure enough, she spotted her sitting at one of the tables.

When the hostess seated Laura, she couldn't help but notice Darla's impatience as she tapped her fingernails against her place mat and squinted with obvious displeasure. "It's about time you got here."

"Sorry. I tried to call, but you must have had your phone turned off." Laura pulled out a chair and sat down.

"Were you caught in traffic, or do you just like to make people wait?"

"I went for a ride in an Amish buggy this afternoon, and I guess we lost track of time."

Darla's pale eyebrows furrowed: "I wouldn't think any buggy driver would lose track of time. I mean, they charge you a certain amount, and when the time's up, it's up."

Laura shook her head. "I didn't take a commercial buggy ride. I was with Eli Yoder."

"Who?"

"Eli's that cute Amish guy I met at the market a few weeks ago. I'm sure I mentioned it."

Before Darla could comment, Laura rushed on. "I had such a good time today. The fall colors at the lake were gorgeous." She glanced down at her purse and frowned. "I had my camera with me the whole time, but I forgot to take even one picture."

Darla stared out the window a few seconds; then she looked back at Laura. "I can't believe what I'm hearing."

"What do you mean?"

"You're obviously starstruck, and I hope you realize that you're making a huge mistake."

"What are you talking about?"

"I can see you're infatuated with this Amish guy, and you'd better not tell me that you plan to see him again, because it can only lead to trouble."

"I'm not *infatuated* with him!" When Laura noticed several people staring, she lowered her voice. "I did enjoy his company, and the buggy ride was exciting, but that's all there was to it. I hardly even know the man."

"Well, good. That means you're not planning to see him again then, right?"

"We did talk about going on a picnic next Saturday." Laura shrugged. "But it's no big deal."

"No big deal? Laura, do you have any idea of the trouble that could come from an Amish man dating an English woman?" Darla leaned across the table. "Don't do it. You need to cancel that date."

Laura's mouth dropped open. "It's not a real date. It's just an innocent picnic. Besides, I can't cancel. I don't have his telephone number, so I have no way of getting in touch with him." She grabbed her menu, hoping this discussion was finally over.

"Some Amish do have telephones now," Darla said, "but usually only those who have businesses.

Do you realize that the Plain People live almost like the pioneers used to? They don't use electricity, or drive cars—"

Laura held up her hand. "I get the picture. Can we change the subject now?"

Darla's voice lowered to a whisper. "I want to say one more thing."

Laura merely shrugged. Darla was obviously not going to let this drop until she'd had her say.

"I told you before that I used to live in this area before my folks moved to New York, so I know a little something about the Amish."

"Such as?"

"They don't take kindly to Englishers dating their children, and I'll bet Eli's folks don't know he was with you today, do they?"

Laura hated to be cross-examined. None of this was Darla's business. "I don't know what Eli told them when he went home, but today was the first time we've done anything together."

"The Amish are private people. They live separate, plain lives. They don't like worldly ways—or worldly women for their men." Darla shook her head. "You'd be smart to nip this in the bud before it goes any further."

Laura remained silent. She didn't need Darla's unwanted advice, and she knew exactly what she was doing.

❧

"Say, Mom, I have a favor to ask," Eli said, when he stepped into the kitchen and headed toward the table where Mary Ellen sat tearing lettuce leaves into a bowl.

She smiled, thinking her oldest boy looked happier than usual this evening. "Oh? What favor is that?"

"I'm going on a picnic to the lake next Saturday, and I was wondering if you'd mind packing a picnic lunch for me to take along."

"How much food did you need?"

He grinned. "As much as you want to fix, I guess."

"For how many people, Eli?" she asked with a groan. *Johnny's silly ways must be rubbing off on our son. He thinks he's a practical joker now.*

"Uh. . .there will be two of us, Mom," Eli mumbled, his face turning red.

She nodded, feeling quite pleased with that bit of news. Eli obviously had a date, and she figured it was probably Pauline, since he'd gone to lunch with her awhile ago when they'd met at the farmers' market. "Anything special you'd like me to fix?"

He shrugged. "Just the usual picnic things, I guess."

"All right, then. I'll put together something that I'm sure both you and your date will like."

The color in Eli's face deepened, and he looked away. "Danki, Mom. I really appreciate that."

When Wesley Meade entered the living room, he found his wife curled up on the couch, reading a book. "Hi, hon. How was your day?" He bent down to kiss her forehead.

"It was all right, I suppose," Irene replied without looking up from her novel.

He set his briefcase on the coffee table and took a seat in the recliner across from her. "Did you do anything special?"

"Helen and I went shopping at the mall, got our nails done, and had lunch at Roberto's. Then on the way home, I stopped at our favorite catering place and ordered the food for the hospital guild's annual charity dinner."

Wesley's gaze went to the ceiling. It seemed all his wife did anymore was shop for new clothes she didn't need and flit from one charity organization to another, planning dinners, parties, and elaborate balls. Not that there was anything wrong with charities. He knew that most of the organizations she was involved with did a lot of good for those in need. However, Irene's emphasis seemed to be more on the social side of things rather than on meeting the needs of people who were hurting or required financial or physical help.

"I got an e-mail from Laura today," he said, changing the subject to something he hoped might interest her.

"Really? What did she have to say?"

"So you didn't check your e-mail?"

Irene's hand fluttered as if she was swatting a fly. "Wesley, you know I rarely use the computer you bought me for Christmas last year."

"Why not? It's got all the whistles and bells anyone could want."

"Maybe so, but every time I go online, I end up

either getting booted off or everything freezes on me." She sighed. "I don't think that computer likes me."

He chuckled. "You just need to go on it more. Practice makes—"

"I know. I know. If I practiced more, I'd have it mastered." She swung her legs over the sofa and sat up. "So tell me. . .what did our daughter have to say in her e-mail?"

"She said she's getting settled in at the school and thinks she's going to like it in Lancaster County, where she can study the interesting Amish people."

Irene's perfectly shaped eyebrows drew together, and she reached up to fluff the sides of her shoulder-length auburn hair. "Amish people? Our daughter didn't go to Lancaster to study Amish people; she went to learn how to be an interior designer."

"Laura thinks she can get some design ideas from the Plain People."

She clicked her tongue. "That's ridiculous. From what I know of the Amish, they live very simply, without any decorations in their homes that don't serve some sort of purpose. So I don't see how studying the Amish can help Laura with her studies."

"Knowing our enterprising daughter, she'll figure out something about their way of life that she can use in her decorating classes." Wesley stretched his arms over his head and yawned. "Think I'll head upstairs and change into something more comfortable before we have dinner. It'll be a relief to get out of this suit." He undid his tie and slung it over his shoulder as he stood. "Never did like wearing a suit. Wish I could get out of putting one on every day."

She clicked her tongue again. "What kind of lawyer would you be if you didn't wear a suit?"

"A comfortable one."

Irene opened her mouth as if to say something more, but he hurried out of the room. He'd become a lawyer just to please her anyway, and if wearing a suit made her happy, then he'd probably end up wearing one until the day he died.

Chapter 4

Laura had been sitting on the wooden bench in front of the variety store for nearly an hour. Still no sign of Eli. *Where is he? Maybe he isn't coming. Maybe Darla's right and he's decided it's best not to have anything to do with a "worldly" woman. I'll give him another five minutes; then I'm leaving.*

She scanned the parking lot again. Several Amish buggies sat parked there, but they were all the closed-in type. Eli's courting buggy was nowhere in sight. She watched as an Amish family went into the store. *I wonder how those women deal with wearing long dresses all the time. If Eli ever shows up, I'll have to remember to ask him why they wear those little white caps on top of their heads.*

She glanced at her watch again—1:45.

Finally at 1:50, his buggy pulled into the parking lot. Laura felt such relief, she was no longer angry. She waved and skittered across the parking lot.

Eli climbed down from the buggy. "Sorry to be so late. I had to help my daed and brothers with some chores at home, and it took longer than expected."

"It's okay. You're here now; that's all that matters."

Eli gave her a boost up into the buggy, then went around and took his seat. He glanced up at the sky. "There's not a cloud in sight, so it should be a fine day for a picnic." He grinned at Laura, and her heart skipped a beat. "Did you bring a jacket? Even though the sun's out, it's still kind of chilly."

Laura shook her head. "I'm wearing a sweater, so I'll be fine."

Eli picked up the reins and said something in Pennsylvania Dutch to the horse.

"What'd you say just then?"

His face turned crimson. "I told him I was taking a beautiful young woman on a ride to the lake so he'd better behave himself."

Laura's heart kept time to the *clip-clop* of the horse's hooves. "Thank you for such a nice compliment."

Eli only nodded in response.

They traveled in silence the rest of the way, but Laura found being in Eli's company made words seem almost unnecessary.

The air snapped with the sharpness of autumn, and soon the lake came into view. If it was possible, the picturesque scene was even more beautiful than it had been the week before. Maple leaves lay scattered about, reminding Laura of the colorful patchwork quilt lying on her bed. The sun cast a golden tint against the surrounding hills, and a whip-poor-will called from somewhere in the trees. Laura relished the sense of tranquility that washed over her like a gentle spring rain.

As Eli helped her out of the buggy, she slid effortlessly into his arms. Raising her gaze to meet his, her breath caught in her throat at the intensity she saw on his face. Her pulse quickened, and she grabbed her camera, hoping the action would get her thinking straight again. She photographed the scenery, being careful not to point the camera in Eli's direction, but it was a sacrifice not to snap a few pictures of his handsome face. How fun it would be to download them to her laptop and send them on to her friend Shannon back home. Shannon would probably get a kick out of seeing how cute Eli looked wearing a pair of dark trousers, a pale blue shirt peeking out from a dark jacket, and a straw hat.

Eli pulled a heavy quilt and a wicker basket from under the buggy seat. After they'd stretched the quilt on the ground, they both took seats. When Eli opened the lid of the basket, Laura was shocked to discover more food than two people could possibly eat. She figured she would have to count calories for the rest of the week.

Eli spread a tablecloth over the quilt, then set out several containers that held fried chicken, coleslaw, dill pickles, wheat bread, Swiss cheese, baked beans, and chocolate cake. He smiled as he handed Laura a glass of iced tea, some plastic silverware, and a paper plate.

"Thank you."

"You're welcome." His face turned a light shade of red. "Uh. . .will you bow your head with me for silent prayer?"

She gave a quick nod, and Eli immediately

bowed his head. Having never believed much in prayer, Laura sat quietly, waiting for him to finish.

When he opened his eyes again, she smiled. "It was nice of your mother to prepare this. Especially since she doesn't know me."

Eli's face turned even redder as he reached for a drumstick. "I. . .uh. . .didn't tell Mom about you."

"Why not?"

He removed his straw hat and placed it on the quilt. "Even though I'm still going through my rumschpringe, my folks wouldn't take kindly to the idea of me seeing someone outside our faith."

"Rumschpringe? What's that?"

"Rumschpringe means 'running around.' It's a time in the life of an Amish young person before he or she gets baptized and joins the church. It's a chance for him to explore the outside world a bit if he chooses."

"Ah, I see."

"My folks think I'm too old to be running around still, and as I mentioned last week, they've been pressuring me to join the church and get married."

She gave him a sidelong glance. "If you didn't tell your mother about me, then why did she pack such a big lunch?"

"I told her I was going on a picnic, but I'm sure she thought it was with someone else." Eli reached for another piece of chicken. "Is there anything more you'd like to know about the Amish?"

Laura sighed. Apparently Eli wasn't that different from other men. If he didn't like the way the conversation was going, he simply changed the subject. "When did your religion first begin?" she inquired.

"Our church got its start in the late sixteen hundreds when a young Swiss Mennonite bishop named Jacob Amman felt his church was losing some of its purity," Eli began. "He and several followers formed a new Christian fellowship, later known as 'Amish.' So, you might say we're cousins of the Mennonites."

Laura nodded as Eli continued. "The Old Order Amish, which is what my family belongs to, believes in separation of church and state. We also expect Bible-centeredness to be an important part of our faith. A peaceful way of life and complying with all nonworldly ways are involved, and we believe it's the way Christ meant for the Church to be."

"Life among your people sounds almost idealistic."

He shook his head. "It may seem that way to outsiders, but underneath the joys and blessings of being Amish lie special challenges and the hardship of keeping separate in an ever-changing world."

"I guess that makes sense." Laura ate in silence for a time, savoring the delicious assortment of food and trying to absorb all that Eli had shared. She knew about some Protestant religions and had attended Sunday school a few times while growing up. The Amish religion was more complex than anything she knew about, but she found it rather fascinating.

"Now it's your turn to answer some of my

questions," Eli said suddenly.

"What do you want to know?"

He shrugged. "Guess you can start by telling me how old you are and whether you have any brothers or sisters."

"I'm twenty-two, and I'm an only child."

"How long will you be staying in Lancaster County?"

"Just until I finish my studies, which should take no longer than two years. Unless I mess up and flunk some classes, that is," she added with a frown.

"You seem real smart to me. I'm sure you'll do okay."

"Thanks, I sure hope so." She smiled. "Anything else you'd like to know?"

Eli's ears turned pink as he stared out at the lake. "I imagine a pretty woman like you has a boyfriend–maybe more than one, even. Am I right about that?"

Laura snickered. "You're really direct and to the point, aren't you, Eli?"

"My folks would say so." He turned back to look at her and chuckled.

She toyed with the edge of the quilt a few seconds, then stared into his seeking blue eyes. "I've dated several men, but none have ever captured my heart." *At least not until you came along.*

Was that a look of relief she saw on Eli's face? No, it was probably just wishful thinking on her part.

The wind had picked up slightly, and Laura shivered, pulling her sweater tightly around her shoulders.

"You're cold. Here, take my coat." Eli removed his jacket and draped it across her shoulders.

Laura fought the impulse to lean her head against his chest. The temptation didn't linger, because the sound of horse's hooves drew her attention to an open buggy pulling into the grassy area near their picnic spot.

A young Amish woman, wearing a dark bonnet on her head and an angry scowl on her face, climbed down from the buggy. Laura thought she recognized the girl, and her fears were confirmed when Eli called, "Pauline, what are you doing here?"

"I was looking for you, Eli. I stopped by your farm, but Lewis said you had gone to the lake for a picnic. I couldn't think who you might be with, but now I see who has taken my place." Pauline planted both hands on her hips as her frown deepened. "I'm mighty disappointed, Eli. How could you bring this Englisher here?"

Eli jumped up and moved toward Pauline. He placed one hand on her shoulder, but she brushed it aside. "She's that woman you were showing birdhouses to at the market, isn't she?"

Eli glanced back at Laura, his face turning redder by the minute. "Pauline, this is Laura Meade."

Pauline's lips were set in a thin line, and she glared at Laura as though she were her worst enemy.

Laura didn't feel much like smiling, but she forced one anyway. "It's nice to meet you, Pauline."

"You're involved in something you shouldn't be, Eli," Pauline said without acknowledging Laura's greeting. "*Wann der gaul dod is, drauere batt nix.*"

Eli grunted. "You're being ridiculous, Pauline."

"I don't think so, and you'll see what I mean if you don't wake up soon and join the church."

"That's my business, not yours."

Pauline turned away in a huff. "And to think, I came all the way out here for this! I deserve much better." She rushed back to her buggy and scrambled inside. "Enjoy your *wunderbaar schee* picnic!"

"Jah, I will," Eli called back to her.

Laura sat too stunned to speak and struggled to analyze what had just happened.

Pauline drove out of sight, leaving a cloud of dust in her wake. She was obviously Eli's girlfriend.

As Pauline drove away, she clamped her teeth together so tightly that it caused her jaw to ache. *How could Eli have made plans for a picnic with that Laura person, who isn't even of our faith? I thought Eli and I were drawing closer. After two rides home in his courting buggy following singings and having had lunch together recently at the farmers' market, I thought we were officially courting.*

She snapped the reins and got the horse moving faster. Maybe some wind in her face would help her think more clearly.

What I should do is drive over to Eli's place and see if his folks know where he is right now. I'll bet they have no idea he's having a picnic with a fancy English woman who wears sweet perfume and way too much makeup.

Pauline continued to fume as she drove down the road, but by the time she neared the cross street that would take her to Eli's place, she had calmed down enough to think things through a bit more. *If I run tattling to Eli's folks, Mary Ellen will probably say something to Eli about it, and then he'll be angry with me. If that happens, I might never have a chance at winning his heart.*

She shook her head and directed the horse to keep going past the road to Eli's house. If she was ever to win Eli over, she would have to find some other way to do it.

As Eli dropped to the quilt, Laura offered him a tentative smile. "Guess I owe you an apology."

"For what? You did nothing wrong."

"I caused a bit of a rift between you and your girlfriend."

Eli shifted on the blanket. "Pauline's not my girlfriend, although I think she'd like to be. We've been friends since we were kinner."

Laura tipped her head. "Kinner?"

"Children."

"If you've been friends that long, then it's obvious to me she was jealous."

"How do you know that?"

"You saw how upset she got. Only a woman in love shoots sparks the way she did."

Eli shrugged. "I'm sorry if she's jealous, but I've done nothing wrong, and neither have you."

"Nothing but have a picnic with an Englisher. I couldn't understand the Pennsylvania Dutch words you two were speaking. What were you saying?"

Eli fiddled with the end of the tablecloth. "Let's see. . . . She said, 'Wann der gaul dod is, drauere batt nix.' That means, 'After the horse is dead, grieving does no good.' "

"I don't get it."

"I think she meant that I made a mistake in asking you to have a picnic with me and that it will do no good to grieve once I find out how wrong it was."

Laura wrinkled her nose. "Is having a picnic with me really so wrong?"

"In Pauline's eyes it is." Eli grunted. "My folks would probably think so, too."

"She said something else I didn't understand. I think it was 'wonderbar' something or other."

He nodded. "Wunderbaar schee. It means 'wonderful nice.' "

"It's obvious that Pauline doesn't like me."

He frowned. "How can you say that? She doesn't even know you."

"That's true, but she knows you, and she's clearly in love with you. I think she's afraid I might be interested, too."

The rhythm of Eli's heartbeat picked up speed. "Are you?"

"Yes, I am interested. You're different from any other man I've ever met." Laura scooted across the quilt and stood. "I don't want to make trouble for you, so maybe it would be better if we say good-bye and go our separate ways." She took a step back and tripped on a rock. The next thing Eli knew, Laura had a face full of water.

As Laura sputtered and attempted to sit up, Eli rushed forward, reaching for her hand and helping her stand.

"I–I can't believe I did that." She stared down at her soggy, wet clothes and grimaced. "Look at me. I'm a mess!"

Eli's lips twitched as he struggled not to laugh. "You are pretty wet, and you might get sick if you don't get your clothes dried soon." He nodded toward his buggy. "How about I take you to my place so you can get dried off?"

"Are. . .are your folks at home?" Laura's teeth had begun to chatter, and goose bumps erupted on her arms.

"Probably so–at least Mom."

"How do you know your family won't disapprove of you bringing me there?"

Eli shrugged. "Guess there's only one way to find out."

Laura held her stomach and took a deep breath, as though she were having trouble getting enough air.

"Are you okay? Did you swallow some water?"

She nodded. "A little, but I'm more worried about meeting your mother than anything else. What if she doesn't like me? What if she throws me off your property or disowns you because you brought me there?"

Eli snickered. "I hardly think either of my folks would throw you off the property or disown me." He motioned to the food. "Let's put the leftovers away and head over to my place before you freeze to death."

"Okay. I–I think I do need to get warmed up a bit."

Chapter 5

As they traveled down the road in Eli's buggy, Eli explained that his father's farm was situated on sixty acres of dark, fertile land, and as they approached the fields he spoke of, he mentioned that they had been planted in alfalfa, corn, and wheat.

"They remind me of a quilt–rich, lush, orderly, and serene," Laura said, as she snuggled beneath the quilt Eli had wrapped around her before they'd left the lake.

Eli smiled. "You sure do have a way with words, you know that?"

She shrugged. "I'm just expressing the way I see things."

An expansive white house came into view, surrounded by a variety of trees and shrubs, while an abundance of autumn blooms dotted the flower beds. Laura spotted a windmill not far from the home, turning slowly in the breeze as it cast a shadow over the tall, white barn directly behind the house. There were no telephone or power lines on the property, she noted, but a waterwheel grated rhythmically in the creek nearby, offering a natural source of power. There was also a huge propane tank sitting beside the house.

Laura assumed it was used for heat or to run some of the Amish family's appliances.

"This is it," Eli said with a sweeping gesture. "This is where I live."

Laura's gaze traveled around the neat-looking farm. Sheep and goats stood inside a fenced corral, and chickens ran about in a small enclosure. On the clothesline hung several pairs of men's trousers, a few dark cotton dresses, and a row of towels pinned in orderly fashion.

"Here you go; this should help." Eli grabbed a towel from the line for Laura and led her around the house and up the steps of a wide back porch.

When they entered the kitchen, Laura's mouth fell open. She felt as if she'd entered a time warp and had stepped back in time. The sweet smell of cinnamon and apples permeated the room, drawing Laura's attention to the wood-burning stove in one corner of the room. No curtains hung on the windows, only dark shades pulled halfway down. Except for a small, battery-operated clock and one simple calendar, the stark white walls were bare.

A huge wooden table sat in the middle of the kitchen, with long benches on either side, and two straight-backed chairs, one at each end. A gas lantern hung overhead, with a smaller kerosene lamp sitting in the center of the table. Against one wall stood a tall, wooden cabinet, and a long counter flanked both sides of the sink. Strategically placed near a massive stone fireplace sat a sturdy-looking rocking chair.

Eli motioned to the stove. "Why don't you

stand over there? The heat from the stove will help your clothes dry."

Like a statue, Laura stood as close to the stove as she dared. "Do all Amish live this way?"

Eli moved across the room. "What way?"

"So little furnishings. There aren't any pictures on the walls and no window curtains. Everything looks so bare." Laura rubbed her arms briskly with the towel and then did the same with her stringy, wet hair.

"The Old Order Amish believe only what serves as necessary is needed in the home. Although I must admit that my folks live more simply than some in our community."

This home was like no other Laura had ever seen. Here was a group of people living in the modern world yet having so little to do with it.

Eli looked a bit uncomfortable when a slightly plump Amish woman entered the room. Her brown hair, streaked with a bit of gray, was parted down the middle and worn in a bun at the back of her head. A small, white head covering was perched on top of her head, just like all the other Amish women Laura had seen in the area. The woman's hazel-colored eyes held a note of question when she spotted Laura.

"Uh. . .Mom, I'd like you to meet Laura Meade." Eli motioned to Laura, then back to his mother. "This is my mamm, Mary Ellen Yoder."

Eli's mother gave a quick nod in Laura's direction. Her forehead wrinkled as she looked back at Eli. "What in all the world?"

She doesn't like me. The woman's just met me, and

she's already decided that I'm the enemy. Laura forced a smile. "It's nice to meet you, Mrs. Yoder."

Mary Ellen grunted and moved toward the stove, where she began to stir the big pot of simmering apples. "Do you live around here, Laura?"

"No, I. . .uh. . ."

"Has your car broken down, or are you lost and in need of directions?" She stared at Laura and squinted. "And why are your clothes all wet?"

"Laura's from Minneapolis, Minnesota, Mom," Eli said, before Laura had a chance to respond. "She attends a designer school in Lancaster, and she fell in the lake while we were–"

Mary Ellen whirled around to face Eli. "You know this woman?"

"We met at the farmers' market a few weeks ago. Laura was interested in my birdhouses, and I've been showing her around."

Mary Ellen's gaze went to the wicker basket in Eli's hand. "You two have been on a picnic at the lake?"

"Jah."

"It's beautiful there," Laura put in. "The lunch you made was wonderful."

Before Eli's mother could respond, the kitchen door flew open, and two young Amish men sauntered into the room. They spoke in their native tongue but fell silent when they noticed Laura standing beside Eli and Mrs. Yoder near the stove.

"These are my younger brothers, Lewis and Jonas." Eli motioned to the rowdy pair. "Boys, this is Laura Meade. We met at the farmers' market, and I took her on a picnic today, but she ended up falling in the lake."

Lewis removed his straw hat, revealing a thick crop of dark, Dutch-bobbed hair. Then he nudged Jonas and chuckled. "It looks mighty nice around here, jah?"

Jonas nodded and removed his hat as well. "It sure does."

Laura felt their scrutiny all the way to her toes, and she knew the heat of a blush had stained her cheeks. "It's nice to meet you."

Turning to his mother, Jonas said, "Pop will be right in. Have you got any lemonade? We've worked up quite a thirst out there in the fields."

Mary Ellen nodded and moved across the room to the refrigerator.

Jonas, who had light brown hair and blue eyes like Eli's, pulled out one of the benches at the table. "Why don't you set yourself down and talk awhile, Laura?"

Laura glanced at Eli to see if he approved, but he merely leaned against the cupboard and smiled at her. His mother was already pouring huge glasses of lemonade, while her two youngest boys hung their hats on wall pegs and took seats at the table.

Laura would have expected Eli's brothers to have reacted more strongly to a stranger in wet clothes standing in their kitchen, but maybe they were used to having uninvited guests show up out of the blue.

She had the distinct feeling that Mrs. Yoder would be happy to see her leave, however, and she was about to decline the invitation when Eli spoke up. "I think Laura could probably use something hot to drink, and some of those ginger cookies you made yesterday would be nice, too, Mom."

With a curt nod, Mary Ellen scooped several handfuls of cookies from a ceramic jar, piled them on a plate, and brought it over to the table. Then she poured some coffee from the pot at the back of the stove into a cup and handed it to Laura without even asking if she would like some cream or sugar.

"Thank you."

"Welcome."

Lewis and Jonas dropped to one bench, and Laura sat beside Eli on the other one. Her hair and clothes were somewhat drier now, and since the table was near the stove, she figured she would be nearly dry by the time she finished her coffee.

Eli made small talk with his brothers about the weather and their work in the fields, and occasionally Laura interrupted with a question or two. She was getting an education in Amish culture that rivaled anything she had ever read about or seen on any postcard.

They were nearly finished with their refreshments when the back door swung open, and a tall, husky man with grayish-brown hair and a full beard lumbered into the room. He slung his straw hat over one of the wall pegs near the door, then went to wash up at the sink. All conversation at the table ceased, and Laura waited expectantly to see what would happen next.

The older man dried his hands on a towel, then took a seat in the chair at the other end of the table.

He glanced at Laura but said nothing. Maybe he was used to seeing strangers in their house, too.

Eli decided he needed to break the silence. "Laura, this is my daed, Johnny Yoder. Pop, I'd like you to meet Laura Meade."

Laura nodded. "Hello, Mr. Yoder."

Pop gave a quick nod, then turned to Mom, who was now chopping vegetables at the kitchen counter. "What's to eat?"

Mom's face was stoic as she replied in Pennsylvania Dutch, "Our guest is having coffee, and the rest are having lemonade and cookies. What would you like?"

Pop grunted. "Coffee, please."

Mom brought the coffeepot and cup to the table and placed it in front of Pop.

"Danki," he muttered.

Eli turned to his father again. "Laura's from Minneapolis, Minnesota. She's attending some fancy school in Lancaster, and I've been showing her around the area."

"The wisdom of the world is foolishness," Pop grumbled in his native language.

Eli grimaced. "There's no need to be going rude on my guest."

"Ah, so the Englisher can't understand the *Deitsch*. Is this the problem?" Pop asked with a flick of his wrist.

"What kind of fancy school do you go to, Laura?" Lewis questioned.

"I'm learning to be an interior decorator."

"It's so she can help folks decorate their homes," Eli interjected.

Mom placed another plate of cookies on the table. "It wonders me so that anyone could put such emphasis on worldly things."

"As I said before, Laura and I went to the lake for a picnic," Eli said, changing the subject to what he hoped was safer ground. "It's sure beautiful there now. Some of the leaves are beginning to fall."

"I'll be glad when wintertime comes and the lake freezes over," Jonas added. "I always enjoy goin' ice-skating."

Eli noticed that Laura's hand trembled as she set her cup down. He wasn't the least bit surprised when she hopped off the bench and announced, "Eli, my clothes are drier now, so I think I should be going."

He sprang to his feet. "I'm gonna drive Laura back to Paradise so she can pick up her car. I'll be home in plenty of time for chores and supper."

When no one responded, Eli opened the back door so he and Laura could make a hasty exit. "That didn't go so well, did it?" he mumbled a few minutes later, as he helped her into the buggy.

"No, it didn't, and I'm sorry for putting you through all that. Your parents obviously don't approve of me."

"Don't worry about it. We're just friends. I'm sure they know that."

Laura twisted the ends of her purse straps, biting down on her lower lip. "Maybe it would be better if you never saw me again."

"No," Eli was quick to say. "I want to be your friend, and I'll be glad to show you around more of the area whenever you like."

"Even if your parents disapprove?"

He shrugged. "Pop and Mom are really fun-loving, easygoing folks, and since we're not courting or anything, there's nothing for them to be concerned about."

Laura looked a little disappointed. Was she hoping they could begin courting? No, that was about as likely as a sow giving birth to a kitten.

"How about next Saturday?" she asked. "Could you show me around then?"

He nodded. "Jah, I think I could."

As the door clicked shut behind Eli, Mary Ellen turned to Johnny and frowned. "This isn't good. Not good at all."

Johnny glanced at Lewis and Jonas, then nodded toward the living room, across the hall. "Why don't you two go in there awhile? Your mamm and me need to talk."

Jonas grabbed a handful of cookies and his glass of lemonade, then headed out of the room. Lewis did the same.

"Now let's talk this through," Johnny said, turning his chair to face Mary Ellen.

She moaned and let her head fall forward into her hands. "What are we going to do about Eli and that fancy English woman?"

"Since Eli's not joined the church yet, I doubt there's much we can do except look the other way."

Mary Ellen lifted her head. "We can't just stand by and let him be led astray."

Johnny reached over and took hold of her hand. "Now don't go borrowing trouble. Maybe Eli has just been showing Laura around, like he said. Might not be anything more to it than that."

"I hope you're right. It would break my heart if any of our kinner were to leave the Amish faith."

Eli returned home an hour later, just in time for supper. He was glad when neither of his parents brought up the subject of Laura, but just as they were finishing with the meal, Jonas spoke up.

"That English woman you brought home is sure pretty, Eli. Too bad she isn't Amish, because if she was, I'd be tempted to court her."

Mom let out a little squeal and pushed away from the table, and Pop just sat there with his eyes squinted, looking kind of befuddled.

"She's not trying to make you go fancy, is she, Eli?" The question came from Lewis, and it was followed by a jab to Eli's ribs.

"Of course not. Laura's just a friend who wants to know a little something about the way we live. I only brought her home after her fall in the lake so she could get dried off a bit."

"You play with fire, and you're bound to get burned," Mom mumbled from across the room, where she stood in front of a sink full of soapy water. "There's always trouble somewhere, and that Englisher had trouble written all over her pretty face."

Eli shook his head. "I'm old enough to make my own decisions, don't you think?"

Jonas grinned. "I'm thinkin' my big brother might be in *lieb*."

"I'm not in love! As I've already said, Laura and I are just friends, and I don't see how it could hurt for me to spend a little time showing her around the countryside and sharing a bit about our ways."

"Why would she need to know our ways?" Mom asked.

"She's just curious about our lifestyle, and I think–"

"A few questions here, and a few trips around the country there, and soon that woman will be trying to talk you into leaving the faith."

Eli felt his face heat up. "No way, Mom!"

"I'm sure our son is secure in his faith," Pop interjected. "He needs some time to think about what he's doing. If I know my boy right, he'll soon realize that it's time to get baptized, join the church, and find a nice Amish wife." He thumped Eli on the back. "Ain't that right, son?"

Eli swallowed the last bit of food in his mouth before he answered. "Are you forbidding me to see Laura again?"

Pop shook his head. "No, you have the right to choose, and since we haven't raised any *dummkepp*–dunces–I'm sure you'll choose wisely."

Eli pushed away from the table and stood. "I

think I'll go out to my shop awhile." He made a hasty exit out the back door before anyone could respond.

Laura collapsed onto her bed. She felt as if she hadn't slept in days. By the time Eli had dropped her off in front of the variety store where she'd left her car, all her energy had been zapped. The thrill she had felt earlier when she'd been alone with Eli at the lake had diminished some, too.

Until today, Laura had usually been able to charm anyone she met. Not only had she not charmed Eli's parents, but she was quite sure that she'd probably alienated them. If they had known that she was hoping to see Eli again and had even fantasized about asking him to leave the Amish faith and join her in the modern English world, she was sure they would have told her to leave their home at once.

Laura looked forward to her date with Eli next Saturday, but she knew she would have to take things slow and easy. She didn't want to scare Eli off by making him think there was more to their relationship than friendship. That's all there was at this point, but she was hoping for more—so much more.

Chapter 6

Saturday dawned with an ugly, gray sky and depressing, drizzling rain. Laura groaned as she stared out the window of her dorm room. She figured Eli probably wouldn't show up for their rendezvous now. If they went for another buggy ride, they would be drenched in no time, and she doubted that he would want to pass the time sitting in some restaurant or wandering through a bunch of tourist-filled souvenir shops with her. They weren't supposed to meet until two o'clock, so with any luck, maybe the rain would be gone by then.

Laura turned from the window and ambled over to her desk, fully intending to get in a few hours of study time. Her mind seemed unwilling to cooperate, however, so she pushed the books aside and painted her fingernails instead.

By noon, the drizzle had turned into a full-fledged downpour. Laura could only hope Eli wouldn't stand her up.

She hurried downstairs and was almost to the door, when Darla showed up in the hallway.

"From the way you're dressed, I'd say you're going out. What I'd like to know is where you're heading on a crummy day like this."

Laura offered a brief smile and held up her green umbrella. "I'm going to Paradise."

Darla's forehead wrinkled. "I figured you would be up in your room studying for that test we'll be having on Monday."

Laura shrugged. "I can't concentrate on schoolwork today. Besides, I'm supposed to meet Eli at the variety store."

Darla's frown deepened. "Are you chasing after that Amish fellow?"

"Of course not. Eli and I are just friends, and he's offered to show me around the area. That's all there is to it."

"Yeah, right."

"It's the truth."

"Well, do whatever you want, but don't come crying to me when you get your toes stepped on."

Laura turned toward the door. "I've got to go. See you later, Darla."

"Where are you heading?" Mary Ellen asked as Eli started for the back door. "Out to work in your shop?"

He turned to face her. "Thought I'd go to the farmers' market today."

"Did you rent a table again?"

"Nope. Figured I'd just browse a bit. See if there's anyone else selling handmade wooden items and maybe pick up an idea or two."

Mary Ellen motioned toward the refrigerator.

"We're about out of root beer. If you see some of the good homemade kind, would you pick up a couple of jugs?"

"Jah, sure. Anything else you'd like me to get?"

She contemplated a moment, then shook her head. "Guess not, but knowing me, I'll think of something after you've gone."

He chuckled and headed out the door. "I'll be home by suppertime, Mom. See you then."

Mary Ellen moved over to the sink with the last of the breakfast dishes. She would let them soak while she drank a cup of coffee and read the Amish newspaper. "Sure hope that boy of mine isn't meeting the fancy English girl he brought over here last week," she muttered as she ran water into the sink. "The last thing this family needs is for Eli to fall in love with someone outside our faith and decide to leave."

As Pauline stepped onto the Yoders' back porch, she had second thoughts about her decision to see Eli. What if he became irritated with her for coming over? Would he still be angry because she'd interrupted his picnic at the lake last Saturday? She had to know. She had to work things out with Eli. She needed to make him realize that she was right for him, not some Englisher who probably wanted to try and change him.

Drawing in a deep breath, Pauline opened the door and stuck her head inside. "Anyone to home?"

"I'm in the kitchen," Eli's mother called in return.

Pauline stepped into the kitchen and spotted Mary Ellen sitting at the table with a newspaper spread out before her and a cup in her hand. "Are you busy?"

"Just reading *The Budget* and having a cup of coffee. Come join me." Mary Ellen smiled and motioned Pauline to take a seat.

Pauline pulled out a chair across from Eli's mother and sat down.

"It's good to see you. Did you come to visit with Eli or me?"

Pauline's cheeks warmed. Apparently Mary Ellen knew she had an interest in her son. "I came to see Eli. Is he here?"

Mary Ellen shook her head. "Left a few minutes ago for the farmers' market."

"Does he have a table again today?"

"Not this time. Said he just wanted to browse around."

"I see. Did he go there alone?"

"He left here by himself, but I'm not sure what happened after that." Mary Ellen's eyebrows drew together. "I may be speaking out of turn, but I'm a bit *bekimmere* about my son, and I'm thinking maybe you can help."

Pauline leaned forward, her elbows resting on the table. "How come you're concerned, and how can I be of help?"

Mary Ellen's voice lowered to a whisper, although Pauline didn't know why, since they were alone in the kitchen. "Eli has an English friend. He brought her here last Saturday."

"Does she have long reddish brown hair and a pretty face?"

"Jah."

"Her name's Laura, and Eli met her at the farmers' market a few weeks ago. She was at his table looking at birdhouses when I went there to see if he was ready to have lunch." Pauline nibbled on her lower lip as she contemplated whether to tell Eli's mother about her encounter with Eli and Laura at the lake. As she thought it through, she came to the conclusion that if Mary Ellen had already met Laura and had some concerns, she might already know about the picnic.

Pauline sat up straight. "I saw Eli with Laura at the lake last Saturday. They were having a picnic."

Mary Ellen nodded. "He told us about that, and I wasn't pleased with the news. When I fixed a picnic lunch for him that morning, I figured he was taking you to the lake."

"I had thought Eli and I were drawing close—that we were officially courting." Pauline swallowed around the lump that had lodged in her throat. "Now I'm afraid I might be losing him to that fancy English woman."

Mary Ellen reached across the table and patted Pauline's outstretched hand. "We can't let that happen. If we work together on this, I believe we can get my son thinking straight again." Her lips curved into a smile. "Are you willing to help me?"

"Jah, sure." Pauline would walk across the country and back again if it meant getting her and Eli together.

Laura stepped out of her car just in time to witness a touching scene. Eli stood in front of the variety store, holding a black umbrella over his head. The minute he spotted Laura, he stepped forward and positioned the umbrella over her.

She smiled up at him, her heart pounding with expectation. "I'm surprised to see you."

"I said I'd meet you here."

"I thought the rain might keep you from coming."

"We Amish don't stay home because of a little rain." Eli steered her across the parking lot. "I brought one of our closed-in buggies today, but if you'd rather we take your car, that's okay, too."

Laura's heart beat a staccato rhythm, and when she felt the warmth of his hand on her elbow, she realized his touch was something she could easily become accustomed to. "The buggy's fine with me."

Eli helped her into the left side of the gray, box-shaped buggy, then went around to the driver's side.

"Where are we going?"

"The farmers' market is open today. I thought maybe we could go there."

"That sounds like fun." Laura glanced over at Eli. Her heart felt light, and she was content just being with him, so it didn't really matter where they went.

"How come you're not selling your wooden things there today?"

"Because I'm here with you." He grinned and

gathered up the reins. "I don't rent a table every week, and it will be fun just to look around."

She smiled. "Maybe I'll get some more decorating ideas, too."

When they entered the farmers' market a short time later, Laura noticed a host of people roaming up and down the aisles. "The rain didn't keep anyone at home today, did it?" she whispered to Eli.

"Nope, it sure didn't." He motioned to a table on their left. "Let's start over there."

Laura noticed several people staring at them. *What a strange-looking couple we must make: Eli dressed in his plain Amish clothes, and me wearing designer blue jeans and a monogrammed sweatshirt.* "Well, let them stare," she murmured.

"What was that?" Eli asked, as he moved close to a table where a man sold small wooden windmills.

"Nothing. I was talking to myself."

Eli let out a low whistle as he picked up one of the windmills. "Finely crafted–jah, very nice."

"It is nice," Laura agreed.

"Are you hungry? Want something to eat or drink?" he asked when they finally moved on.

"No, but if you're hungry, I'll drink a diet soda and watch you eat."

Eli gently pinched her arm. "A diet soda for someone so skinny?"

"I am not skinny. I'm merely trying to keep my figure."

Eli's ears turned red as he looked her up and down. "Your figure looks fine to me."

Laura giggled self-consciously. "Thanks for the

compliment, but for your information, this shape doesn't come easy. I have to work at staying slender, and that means watching what I eat."

Eli raised his dark eyebrows as he continued to study her. "One so pretty shouldn't be concerned about gaining a few pounds. Mom's pleasantly plump, and Pop says he likes her that way."

"You'll never catch me in any kind of plump state—pleasantly or otherwise."

"Someday you'll meet a great guy, get married, and have a whole house full of kinner. Then you probably won't even have a figure, much less have to worry about keepin' it." Eli chuckled and steered her toward the snack bar at one end of the market.

"I told you, I'm not hungry."

"Oh, sure you are." He sniffed the air. "Don't those hot dogs and sausages smell good?"

She wrinkled her nose. "They smell fattening to me."

"If you ask me, you're way too concerned about your weight."

"I don't recall asking you."

Eli jerked his head as though he'd been slapped. "Maybe today wasn't such a good idea after all. Might be better if I take you back to Paradise."

"No, I don't want to go back." Laura clutched at his shirtsleeve. "I'm sorry if I sounded snappish."

They had reached the snack bar, and Eli turned to face her. "Our worlds are so different, Laura. I'm plain, and you're fancy. I see things differently than you do, and I'm afraid it will always be so."

Laura shook her head, her eyes misting with

tears. "We're just getting to know each other. It will take some time for us to understand one another's ways." She smiled up at him. "I can teach you things about my way of life, and you can teach me more of the Amish ways."

"I already know all I need to know about the English ways, but if you're still wanting to know more about the Amish way of life, I'm willing." Eli motioned to the snack bar. "Can I interest you in a glass of root beer and a giant, homemade pretzel?"

Laura nodded and released a sigh. "Oh, all right. I guess I can count calories some other time."

Pauline wandered up and down the aisles inside the market building, searching for Eli. There was no sign of him anywhere, and she wondered if he had even come here today. Maybe he'd just told his mother he was going to the farmers' market, when in fact he'd made plans to meet that English woman again. Maybe they'd gone on another picnic at the lake.

She shook her head. No, that wasn't likely since it had been raining all morning.

"*Wie geht's*—how are you, Pauline?" Anna Beachy asked as she strolled up to her.

"I'm fine. And you?"

"Oh, fair to middlin'. Are you here alone, or did you come with your folks?"

"I'm alone. Came by to see if I could find Eli Yoder. Have you seen him around the market anywhere?"

Anna nodded. "Saw him over at Amos Hilty's

root-beer stand about ten minutes ago. He was with some English woman, which I thought was pretty strange."

"Did you speak to him?"

"Just long enough to say hello, but then before I had a chance to say anything more, Eli said he was on his way out. He grabbed two jugs of root beer and rushed off like he was in a big hurry."

Pauline felt as if her heart had sunk all the way to her toes. Not only had she missed seeing Eli, but her fears had been confirmed—he was with Laura again.

"I was just heading over to the snack bar to get a German sausage," Anna said. "If you haven't had lunch yet, maybe you'd like to join me."

Pauline shook her head. "Thanks anyway, but I'm not so hungry." She turned toward the exit door as a feeling of defeat threatened to weigh her down. At the rate things were going, she would never get Eli to marry her.

That evening, Laura lay on her bed, replaying the events of the day. As strange as it might seem, she was glad she and Eli had experienced the little disagreement about her weight. Despite the dissension it had caused, for the remainder of the day, Eli had been quite compromising.

A knock on the door stirred Laura from her musings. "Who is it?"

"Darla."

Laura crawled off the bed and opened the door.

"If you've come to give me another lecture, you can save your breath."

Darla shook her head. "I wanted to apologize and see how your day went."

Laura motioned her inside. "Actually, it went well. Eli and I drove to the farmers' market in Bird-in-Hand, and I got a few more decorating ideas while we were there."

Darla flopped onto the bed. "The Amish don't believe in fancy decorations or adornments in their homes, Laura."

"That's what makes it so unique."

"I don't follow."

Laura dropped down next to Darla, and her fingers trailed across the edge of the quilt covering her bed. "Take this, for example. It's plain, yet strikingly beautiful. A quilt such as this is in high demand, which is why it was so costly."

Darla shrugged. "To be perfectly honest, Amish decor doesn't do much for me. Neither do Amish men."

Laura clenched her jaw. She had a feeling this conversation might lead to another argument, and she wasn't in the mood for one. "It's been a long day, and I'm tired. Besides, I think it's time to end this little discussion."

"Sure, okay." Darla stood and started for the door. "Oh, I almost forgot–you had a phone call while you were out exploring Amish land."

"Who was it?"

"Mrs. Evans took the call, and she just told me it was some guy asking for you."

"Hmm. . .maybe it was Dad. But then why wouldn't he have called on my cell phone?"

"I really couldn't say, but I think Mrs. Evans left a note in your mailbox."

"I'll go check." As soon as Darla disappeared into her own room, Laura ran down the steps and found the note in her mailbox. It read:

> *A man named Dean Carlson called around two o'clock. He said he had tried to call your cell phone several times and only got your voice mail. He wants you to call him as soon as possible.*

Laura sucked in her breath. *Is Dean really missing me, or is he just checking up on me? Should I call him first thing in the morning or make him wait a few days?*

"You ought to keep your cell phone charged and check your voice mail once in a while, Laura. I tried for two days to get you and finally had to call your school and leave a message."

Laura held the cell phone away from her ear and grimaced. She knew she had made a mistake calling Dean so early in the morning. She should have remembered he was a bear before his third cup of coffee. "Well, you've got me on the phone now, so you don't have to make such a big deal of it."

"Yeah, okay."

"What did you want, Dean?" she asked, tapping her foot impatiently.

"I thought that I'd come to Lancaster to see you next weekend."

"What?" Laura's mouth went dry. "Coming here is not a good idea."

"Why not?"

"I'm busy, that's why."

"But I miss you, Laura, and I–"

Laura lifted her gaze to the ceiling. She and Dean had only begun dating a few months before she'd left Minneapolis to come here, but he acted like they were practically engaged. "It's not that I don't want you to come. It's just that–well, I'll be coming home for Christmas soon, and–"

"Christmas? That's three months away!"

Laura could almost see Dean's furrowed brows and the defiant lift of his chin. He was a handsome man with jet-black hair that curled around his ears, and eyes as blue as a summer sky, but he was way too possessive. "It would be nice to see you, Dean, but I always have a lot of homework to do on the weekends."

"Were you studying when I phoned yesterday?"

Laura knew she couldn't tell Dean about her Saturday date with Eli Yoder, but she didn't want to lie to him, either. "I went to the farmers' market."

"What's that got to do with homework?"

"I was researching the Amish culture."

"Sounds real interesting." Dean's tone was sarcastic, and it irritated her.

"Actually, it's very interesting. I've been studying their quilts and getting some ideas for my next design project." *I've been studying a fascinating Amish man, too.*

Dean cleared his throat. "How about next weekend? Can I come or not?"

Laura chewed on her lower lip. She liked Dean... or at least she had when they were seeing each other socially. So why was she giving him the runaround now? It took only a few seconds for her to realize the answer. She was infatuated with Eli and wanted to spend her free time with him. Dean would only be a distraction, and if Eli found out about her English boyfriend, it might spoil her chances with him.

"Laura, are you still there?"

Dean's deep voice drew Laura back to their conversation, and she sighed. "Yes, I'm here."

"What's it going to be?"

"I'd rather you didn't come."

"Is that your final word?"

"Yes, but as I said before, I'll be home for Christmas, so I'm sure we'll see each other then."

Dean grunted and hung up the phone without even saying good-bye. Laura breathed a sigh of relief.

Chapter 7

Over the next several weeks, Eli saw Laura as often as possible. In fact, he could hardly get her out of his thoughts. The vision of her beautiful face, smooth as peaches and cream, inched its way into his mind on more than one occasion. When he'd told his folks he was still seeing Laura, the news hadn't gone over so well, especially with Mom.

"She'll try to change you," she admonished one Saturday as Eli hitched the buggy for another trip to meet Laura. "Why, the first thing you know, that woman will be asking you to leave the faith."

"*Ach*, Mom, you worry too much. No one could ever talk me into something I don't want to do."

His mother pursed her lips. "I wouldn't be so sure about that. Love does strange things to people."

Eli's eyebrows shot up. "Love? Who said anything about love? Laura and I are just friends."

Mom gave him a knowing look. "I've seen the face of love before. Every time you come home after being with that fancy woman, I can see the look of love written all over your face, and it scares me, son."

Eli's face heated up. He would never admit it, especially not to Mom, but he was beginning to wonder if his fascination with Laura might be more than curiosity or friendship. What if he were actually falling in love with her? If she felt the same way about him, would she expect him to leave the faith? Since he hadn't yet been baptized or joined the church, the decision to stay or leave was still his to make. However, there were too many things about his way of life that he would miss if he left home and became English. Besides, there were too many things in the modern world that he didn't particularly care for.

"You have no call to be worried or scared," he said, giving her arm a quick pat. "I know exactly what I'm doing."

"I hope so."

Eli climbed into the buggy and gathered up the reins. "See you later, Mom."

"Say, Eli. . .I was wondering if you could do me a favor."

"What's that?"

"Selma Hostetler has been laid up with a bad back for the last couple of days."

"Sorry to hear that. Nobody likes back pain."

Mom nodded. "I baked some zucchini-banana bread yesterday, and I thought maybe you could drop a loaf by to her. It might help cheer her some."

"Can't Lewis or Jonas do it? I don't want to be late meeting Laura."

Mom's eyebrows drew together. "They're both out in the fields with your daed, which is where you really ought to be, don't you think?"

Eli shook his head. "This is my day off from work, and even though I sometimes help Pop on my day off, he said he didn't need me this morning."

"I see. Well, can you drop off the bread to Selma then?"

"Jah, I suppose, but–"

"I'll go get it now." Mom rushed off before Eli had a chance to say anything more.

A few minutes later, she was back wearing a smile that stretched ear to ear. She handed him the bread, which she had enclosed in some plastic wrap. "Danki, son."

"You're welcome."

As Eli clucked to the horse, his mother waved and called, "Don't be too late for supper tonight. And remember that I love you."

"I love you, too."

When Pauline heard a horse and buggy pull into the yard, she hurried to the back door, not wanting her mother to be disturbed. Mom had taken some aspirin for the pain in her back and had returned to her bed soon after breakfast was over.

When Pauline saw Eli step down from one of their closed-in buggies, her heart skipped a beat. Had he come to see her–maybe invite her to go someplace with him today? She waited on the porch with sweaty palms and shaky legs as he headed to the house. When he reached the porch, he stopped and held out a loaf of bread.

"Mom asked me to deliver this to your mamm. I hear her back's been acting up."

Pauline nodded as a sense of disappointment

flooded her soul. She took the bread and mumbled, "Danki. That was thoughtful of your mamm."

Eli shuffled his feet a few times as he stared at the ground. "Well, I–"

"Would you like to come in for a cup of coffee?" She motioned to the door. "I just made a fresh pot, and it might help take the chill out of your bones on this frosty morning."

"I. . .uh. . .appreciate the offer, but I can't stay."

"Are you working today?"

"No, it's my day off."

"Then surely you have time for a quick cup of coffee."

He shook his head. "I'm meeting a friend in Paradise, and I'm already late, so I'd better go."

Pauline clenched her teeth. *I'll bet it's that fancy English woman Eli's meeting. Should I come right out and ask?* She was about to, when Eli turned toward his buggy and started walking away.

"See you at church tomorrow," he called over his shoulder.

"Jah, see you then," she muttered as she went back into the house. *Will I ever get through to Eli? Will he ever see me as anything more than a friend?*

"I'm sorry I was late picking you up," Eli said as he helped Laura into his buggy. "I had to make a delivery for my mamm."

"That's okay. You're here now, and that's all that counts." Laura drew in a deep breath. "It feels and smells like winter is coming, doesn't it?"

Eli nodded. "It's a lot warmer inside my daed's closed-in carriage, but I sure do miss my courting buggy."

"Don't you use it in the winter months at all?"

He shrugged. "Sometimes on the milder days, but it's much nicer inside this buggy today, don't you think?"

"Jah." She giggled and flipped the end of her ponytail.

Eli grinned. "You look real schee today."

"Nice. You said I look nice today, right?"

He nodded. "You're catching on fast to the Deitsch."

Laura's heart fluttered. "Thanks for the compliment."

Eli only nodded again and made the horse go a bit faster.

"Where are you taking me today?" Laura asked.

"I thought you might like to see one of our schoolhouses."

"Schoolhouses? You have school on Saturdays?"

He chuckled. "No, but Saturday's the best day for a tour of the schoolhouse. There won't be any kinner about, and no teacher wearing a stern look or carrying a hickory switch."

"Eli Yoder, you're such a tease." Laura reached across the short span between them and touched his arm. "Maybe that's why I like you so well."

"Because I like to kid around?"

"Yes. I find your humor and wholesome view on life rather refreshing. It's like a breeze on a sweltering summer day."

Eli scrunched up his nose. "I don't believe I've ever been compared to a breeze before."

She withdrew her hand and leaned back. "I've learned a lot from you."

"Is that good or bad?"

"It's good, of course." Her voice lowered to a whisper. "I could teach you a lot about English ways, if you'd let me. We could take in a movie sometime, or—"

Eli held up his hand. "No, thanks. I think I know more than enough about the fancy life."

"How can you say that? Have you ever given yourself a chance to find out what the modern world really has to offer?"

"I'm not blind, Laura," he muttered. "I see what's out there in the world, and even though I haven't felt ready to join the church, I'm not all that interested in electrical gadgets, fancy clothes, or thinkin' I don't need God."

Laura's mouth dropped open. "Who said anything about not needing God?"

"I'm sure lots of English folks do love God," Eli said. "But I've seen many people who seem too self-centered to give Him anything more than a few thoughts, and then it's only when they're in need of something."

"Where did you hear that?" she asked, her voice edged with irritation. Was this going to turn into a full-fledged disagreement? If so, she wasn't sure it was a good idea to give her opinion. After all, she was trying to appease, not aggravate, Eli.

He shrugged. "It doesn't matter where I got the

notion. The important thing is, I'm happy to be a child of God, and I don't need any worldly things to make me complete."

"My father says religion is a crutch for weak men, and I'm inclined to believe him." The words were out before Laura had time to think, and she could have bitten her tongue when she saw the look of irritation on Eli's face.

Eli pulled sharply on the reins and eased the horse and buggy to the shoulder of the road. "Are you saying I'm a weak man, Laura?"

She turned to face him. "No, of course not. I just meant–"

"Maybe we've come too far," Eli said, his forehead wrinkling.

"Too far? You mean we missed the schoolhouse?"

He shook his head. "Too far with this friendship we probably shouldn't be trying to build."

Laura's heart began to pound, and her throat felt like she'd eaten a bunch of hot peppers. If Eli broke things off now, there would be no chance for them. She couldn't let that happen. She would not allow him to stay angry with her for something so ridiculous as a difference of opinion on religious matters.

She touched his arm and was glad when he didn't pull away. "Eli, I respect your religious beliefs, but can't we just agree to disagree on some things?"

"It's kind of hard to have a friendship with someone when we keep arguing."

She nodded. "I know, so let's not argue anymore. In fact, if it would make you feel better, I'll just sit here and listen to you narrate. How's that sound?"

He reached for the reins and gave her a sidelong glance. "You're a hard one to say no to, you know that?"

Laura smiled. "That's what my father says, too."

"Your wife called five times while you were in court today and left messages for you to call her back as soon as you could," Wesley's secretary told him when he entered the reception area of his office.

"Did she say what she wanted?"

"No, just that it was important and she wanted you to call as soon as you could."

"I can imagine how important it was," he grumbled as he headed to his office. "Probably some major crisis over a broken fingernail."

Wesley had no more than taken a seat behind his desk, when his phone rang. He picked it up on the second ring, recognizing the caller ID. "Hello, Irene. I heard you called a few times while I was in court."

"Yes, I did, and I'm very upset."

His gaze went to the ceiling. Irene was always upset about something it seemed. "What's the problem?"

"It's Laura. I got an e-mail from her today, and she's in real trouble."

Wesley's heart began to race. "Is she sick? Has she been hurt?"

"No, no. She's all right physically, but I think

she's taken leave of her senses."

He shifted the receiver to his other ear. "What's that supposed to mean?"

"Our daughter's been seeing some Amish man. She's gone out with him several times, and—"

"Whoa! Hold on a minute, and calm down. You're not making any sense."

"Laura's e-mail said she's involved with an Amish man named Eli. I think his last name is Yoder, or something like that. She said they've gone on a couple of picnics, to the farmers' market, and for rides in his buggy." After a brief pause, Irene released a shuddering sob. "We've got to put a stop to this right away, Wesley. Can you fly out to Pennsylvania and speak to her about this?"

"Me? Why can't you go? I'm tied up in court for at least another week, and then I've got—"

"I can't go, either. I'm involved with that benefit dinner I'm helping plan for the historical society, and then there's the country club luncheon I'm in charge of."

"So you're not that worried about Laura, are you?"

"Of course I am."

"Well, you needn't be. Our daughter is old enough to make her own choices about whom she sees and when. I think if we try to interfere, it will only make things worse." Wesley reached for the cup of coffee his secretary had just placed on his desk and took a drink. "Besides, Laura will be home for Christmas in a few weeks. I'll talk to her about this Amish fellow then, and if I think she's in over her head, I'll try to dissuade her."

"All right. I guess that would be best. Oh, I've got a call on the other line. I'll see you when you get home." Irene clicked off without saying good-bye.

Wesley shook his head. "Like mother, like daughter."

Chapter 8

It was only the first week of December, but Lancaster County had been hit with a heavy blanket of snow. Laura figured it would mean the end of her enjoyable rides with Eli. . .at least until spring. She would be going home for Christmas soon, so that would put an end to their times, anyway.

Leaving Eli, even for a few weeks, wasn't going to be easy. However, she had promised her parents and friends that she'd be coming home for the holidays, and she didn't want to disappoint them. Besides, even if she stayed in Pennsylvania, Eli would spend Christmas with his family, and she, the fancy English woman, would not be included in their plans.

Laura stared out her dorm-room window at the falling snow. If only she had some way to get in touch with Eli. If they could just meet somewhere for lunch before she had to leave.

She finally curled up on her bed with a romance novel, surrendered to the fact that this Saturday would be spent indoors without Eli.

Laura had only gotten to the second page when a loud knock drove her to her feet. "Who's there?"

"Darla. Are you busy?"

Laura opened the door. "What's up?"

Darla was dressed in a pair of designer jeans and a pink sweater. A brown leather coat was slung over one arm, and a furry little cap was perched on top of her short, blond curls. "I thought I'd drive into Philadelphia. I still have some Christmas shopping to do, and only the big stores will have what I want."

"You're going shopping today?"

Darla nodded. "I was hoping you'd come along."

"In this weather?" Laura gestured toward the window. "In case you haven't noticed, there's a foot of snow on the ground."

Darla shrugged. "I'm sure most of the main roads have been cleared." She nudged Laura's arm. "I'll treat you to lunch."

"I'm on a diet."

"So, order a salad."

Laura released a sigh. "Oh, all right." It wasn't the way she wanted to spend the day, but she figured it would be better than being cooped up in her room all day.

"I'm going out for a while," Eli said, as he left the kitchen table and slipped into his heavy woolen jacket.

"Where you heading?" Lewis called to him.

"I've got some errands to run. . .not that it's any of your business, *schnuppich* brother." Eli plopped his black felt hat on his head and closed the door, curtailing more comments from his snoopy sibling.

Mary Ellen clicked her tongue against the roof of her mouth and turned to face Johnny. "Seems like our oldest boy is hardly ever home anymore."

Johnny shrugged. "Guess that's his choice."

"I'll bet he's sneakin' off to see that English woman again," Jonas said as he grabbed a hunk of shoofly pie.

"Don't you ever fill up?" Johnny's eyebrows drew together. "That's your third piece now, isn't it?"

"He's probably lost count," Lewis said with a chuckle.

Jonas smacked his lips. "Shoofly is my favorite breakfast pie. Never have been able to get enough of it."

"No, but you sure have tried." Mary Ellen pushed her chair away from the table and gathered up some of the dishes. As she placed them in the sink, she glanced out the window and caught sight of Eli hitching his horse to the sleigh. She couldn't help but wonder if Jonas was right about Eli meeting Laura today. He hadn't said much about her lately, but Mary Ellen knew from her last conversation with Selma Hostetler that Eli sure wasn't courting Pauline.

On more than one occasion, Mary Ellen had tried putting in a good word for Pauline, and from what she'd heard, Pauline had made several attempts at getting Eli to invite her somewhere. So far all efforts had failed, and Mary Ellen knew all she could do was pray—and she'd been doing a lot of that lately. If enough prayers went up on Eli's behalf, he might see the light and quit spending time with Laura. Or she might get bored with him and find a nice English man to take her places. Better yet, maybe the fancy English woman would leave Lancaster County and never return.

The ride to Philadelphia went well. They took the main highway, and just as Darla had predicted, it had been plowed and treated. The bad weather hadn't kept many people home, for the stores were crowded with holiday shoppers.

Laura and Darla pushed their way through the crush of people and fumbled through the racks of clothes and stacks of gift items until they'd both purchased enough Christmas presents for everyone on their lists. Everyone except for Eli. Laura wanted to get him something special, but since he lived a much simpler life than she did and was opposed to most worldly things, she couldn't find anything that might be suitable.

They had a late lunch and left the city around four o'clock, and by the time they reached the turnpike, it was snowing again.

"I know it's a little out of the way, but would you mind stopping at the variety store in Paradise on our way home?" Laura asked Darla.

"What for?"

"I want to get a Christmas present for Eli. I couldn't find anything appropriate in Philadelphia, but I'm sure I can find something there."

Darla squinted. "I don't mind stopping, but I do mind what you're doing."

Laura looked away. "What are you talking about?"

"I can see that no matter how much I've warned you about this, you've decided to jump into the deep end of the pool without even looking."

"Huh?"

"Don't be coy, Laura. I've warned you about getting involved with that Amish man, and you've forged ahead anyway. It doesn't take a genius to realize you're head over heels in love with this Eli fellow."

"In love? Don't be ridiculous! Eli and I are just friends."

Darla gave the steering wheel a few taps with her gloved fingers. "Sure. . .whatever you say."

When they arrived at the store in Paradise, no cars or buggies were in the parking lot, and it appeared to be deserted. However, the sign in the window said they were open, so Darla parked her car, and Laura went inside.

She soon realized that choosing a gift for an Amish man, even in a Plain store, wasn't going to be easy. Shelves were full of men's black felt hats, suspenders in all sizes, and a large assortment of white handkerchiefs. Laura wanted something more special than any of these things. It had to be a gift that would cause Eli to remember her whenever he looked at it.

She was about to give up, when she spotted a beautiful set of carving tools she was sure Eli could use. She paid for them and left the store feeling satisfied with her purchase. Now if she could only get the gift to Eli before she went home for Christmas.

As Laura returned to Darla's car, her foot slipped on the walkway, and she realized the snow had begun to freeze.

"This isn't good," Darla complained as they pulled out of the parking lot a few minutes later. "I should have gone directly back to Lancaster and stayed on the main roads."

Laura grunted. "I'm sure we'll get back to the school in time for your favorite TV show."

"I wasn't thinking about TV. I'm concerned about staying on the road and keeping my car intact."

No sooner had she spoken the words than they hit a patch of ice. The car slid off the road, coming to a stop in the middle of a snowbank.

"Oh, great!" Darla put the car in REVERSE and tried to back up. The wheels spun, but the car didn't budge. She tried several more times, but it was no use. They were stuck, and it was obvious that there was nothing either of them could do about it.

"Maybe I should get out and push," Laura suggested with a weak smile.

"I'd better make a call for help." Darla reached into her purse for the cell phone and started to dial but dropped it to the seat with a moan.

"What's wrong?"

"The battery's dead. I forgot to charge it last night." Darla opened the car door and got out. Laura did the same.

"Now we're really in a fix." Darla kicked at the front tire with the toe of her boot. "I should have checked my phone before we left Lancaster this morning."

"I guess it's my fault. If I hadn't asked you to go to the variety store—"

Laura stopped speaking when she heard the *clip-clop* of horse's hooves approaching. "Do you need some help?" a man's voice called out.

She whirled around, and her heartbeat quickened as Eli stepped down from an open sleigh. "Are we ever glad to see you!"

Eli joined them right away, and Laura introduced Darla. Then, offering Eli a wide smile, she asked, "Would it be possible for you to give us a ride to the nearest town? We need to call a tow truck to get Darla's car out of that snowbank."

Eli surveyed the situation. "I think I can pull you out with my horse."

Darla shook her head. "You've got to be kidding."

"My horse is strong as an ox."

"Okay," Darla said with a shrug. "You may as well give it a try."

Laura and Darla stepped aside as Eli unhitched the horse and hooked a rope around the animal's neck, then fastened the rope to the back bumper of Darla's car. He said a few words in Pennsylvania Dutch, and the gelding moved forward. The car lurched and was pulled free on the first try.

"Hooray!" Laura shouted with her hands raised.

Darla just stood with her mouth hanging open.

"Why don't I follow you back to the main road where it's cleared?" Eli suggested. "That way I can be sure you don't run into any more snowbanks."

"Thank you," Darla murmured, as though she

could hardly believe her car had been freed by a horse.

Laura turned to Eli. "Would it be okay if I rode in your sleigh for a while? I've always wanted to ride in one." She touched his arm. "Besides, I have something for you."

His brows arched upward. "You do?"

She nodded. "I'll get it from Darla's car and be right back." Laura raced off before Eli had a chance to reply. When she grabbed Eli's gift from the car, Darla, already in the driver's seat, gave her a disgruntled look but said nothing.

Laura made her way back to where Eli waited beside the sleigh. After he helped her up, she pulled the collar of her coat tightly around her neck. "Brr. . . It's sure nippy out."

Eli reached under the seat and retrieved a quilt. He placed it across her lap, and she huddled beneath its warmth, feeling like a princess on her way to the ball.

As they followed behind Darla's car, Laura snuggled closer to Eli and said, "I'm glad you came along when you did. I'm leaving for Minneapolis in a few days, and I didn't think I'd get the chance to see you before I left."

"I went to the variety store in Paradise this morning," Eli said. "You weren't there, so I thought maybe you'd already gone home for the holidays."

Laura frowned. If she'd had any idea Eli was going to venture out in the snow just to see her, she would have moved heaven and earth to get to Paradise this morning. "I guess fate must have wanted us to meet today after all."

Eli raised one eyebrow. "Fate? You think fate brought us together?"

She nodded. "Don't you?"

He shook his head. "If anyone brought us together today, it was God."

"I have something for you," Laura said, feeling a bit flustered and needing to change the subject. She lifted the paper bag in her hands, and her stomach lurched with nervous anticipation. "Merry Christmas, Eli."

"You bought me a gift?"

She nodded and smiled.

"But, I–I don't have anything to give you."

"That's okay. I didn't buy you a present so I would get one in return."

Eli's eyebrows lifted and almost disappeared under the brim of his black hat. "What is it?"

"Why don't you open it and find out?"

"If it's a Christmas present, shouldn't I wait 'til Christmas to open it?"

She shook her head. "I'd like you to open it now, so I can see if you like it or not."

"All right then, but let's wait 'til we get to the main road and have stopped so you can get back in your friend's car again."

Laura felt a bit disappointed, but she didn't want to start an argument, so she merely shrugged and said, "Okay."

They rode in silence until Darla's car slowed and came to a parking lot. Eli guided his horse and sleigh in behind her.

"Here you go." Laura handed the sack to him.

Eli opened it and pulled out the carving set. He studied it a few seconds before he spoke. "It's a nice gift–much better than the carving set I use now." He fidgeted kind of nervously, and Laura was afraid he was going to hand it back to her.

"What's wrong? Don't you like it?"

"It's very nice, but I'm not sure I should accept such a gift."

"Why not?" she asked, looking deeply into Eli's searching blue eyes.

"It doesn't seem right, since I have nothing to give you in return."

Laura reached for his hand and closed her fingers around his. "Your friendship is the only present I need this Christmas. Please say I'm one of your special friends."

Eli swallowed so hard she saw his Adam's apple bob up and down. Several seconds went by; then he finally nodded and offered her a smile that calmed her fears and warmed every inch of her heart.

Chapter 9

Laura's first few days at home were spent visiting with her parents and thinking about Eli. When she closed her eyes, she could visualize his friendly smile, little chin dimple, and those clear blue eyes calling her to him.

Ever since Laura had returned, her mother had been trying to keep her occupied. "Why not join me for lunch at Ethel Scott's this afternoon?" she suggested one morning.

Laura was lying on the couch in the living room, trying to read a novel she had started the day before. She set it aside and sat up. "I need to get my Christmas presents wrapped."

Mom took a seat next to Laura. Her green eyes, mirroring Laura's, showed obvious concern. "I'm worried about you, dear. You haven't been yourself since you came home for the holidays." She touched Laura's forehead. "Are you feeling ill?"

Laura shook her head. "I'm fine. Just a bit bored. I'm used to being in class every weekday."

"That's precisely why you need to get out of the house and do something fun while you're here." Mom tipped her head, causing her shoulder-length auburn hair to fall across one rosy cheek. Even at forty-five, she was still lovely and youthful looking.

"Ethel's daughter, Gail, is home from college, and I'm sure she would be thrilled to see you," Mom continued. "In fact, she'd probably enjoy hearing about that boring little town you're living in now."

Laura moaned. "Lancaster isn't little, and it sure isn't boring."

"The point is you've been cooped up in this house ever since you got home. Won't you please join me today? It will be better than being home by yourself."

"I won't be alone," Laura argued. "Foosie is here, and she's all the company I need." She glanced at her fluffy, ivory-colored cat sleeping contentedly in front of the fireplace. "After I'm done wrapping gifts, I thought I might try to call Shannon again."

Mom stood. "I would think it would be Dean Carlson you'd be calling." She shook her finger at Laura. "Dean's called at least four times in the past two days, and you always find some excuse not to speak with him."

Laura drew in her bottom lip. How could she explain her reluctance to talk to Dean? She sure couldn't tell her mother that she had been comparing Dean to Eli. "I'll be seeing him on Christmas Day. That's soon enough."

Mom finally shrugged and left the room.

Laura puckered her lips and made a kissing sound. "Here, Foosie, Foosie. Come, pretty lady."

The ball of fur uncurled, stretched lazily, and plodded across the room. Laura scooped Foosie into her lap and was rewarded with soft purring when the cat snuggled against her. "I've missed you. Too bad cats aren't allowed in the dorm rooms at school. If they were, I would take you back with me."

The telephone rang and Laura frowned. "Just when we were getting all cozy." She placed the cat on the floor and headed for the phone that was sitting on a table near the door. "Meade residence."

"Laura, is that you?"

"Yeah, it's me, Shannon."

"When did you get home?"

"Last Saturday. I've tried to call you a couple of times, but you're never home."

"I've been busy planning my preschoolers' Christmas party and the program they'll put on for their parents. My answering machine isn't working right now, either, so I'm sorry you couldn't leave a message."

"That's okay. I've been busy, too." *Busy thinking about Eli and wishing I could spend the holidays with him.*

"Is it all right if I come over?"

"Sure, I'd like that."

After Laura hung up the phone, she headed for the kitchen. She had two cups of hot chocolate ready by the time her friend arrived.

"Have a seat, and let's get caught up," Laura said, handing Shannon a mug.

Shannon sniffed her drink appreciatively. "Do you have any marshmallows?"

Laura went to the cupboard to look, while her friend placed her mug on the table, then took off her coat.

"I think it's going to be a white Christmas," Shannon commented. "We usually have some snow by now, but I'm sure it's not far off, because I think I can actually smell snowflakes in the air."

Laura tossed a bag of marshmallows on the table and took the seat across from Shannon. "We've already had a good snowstorm in Lancaster."

"Really? Were you able to get around okay?"

"Oh, sure. In fact, I–"

"Say, you haven't said a word about my new hairstyle." Shannon pulled her fingers through her bluntly cut, straight black hair. "Do you like it?"

Laura feigned a smile as she searched for the right words. "You. . .uh. . .look different with short hair."

Shannon blew on her hot chocolate, then reached inside the plastic bag and withdrew two marshmallows. She dropped them into the mug and grinned. "I like my new look, and so do my preschool kids."

"I'm surprised you cut your hair. I thought you would always keep it long."

Shannon shrugged, then took a sip of her drink. "Long hair is too much work, and it takes forever to dry." She set the cup down and snapped her fingers. "Why don't you get your hair cut and styled while you're home for Christmas?"

"I don't think I could ever cut my hair. It took me too long to grow it."

Shannon poked at the marshmallows with the tip of her finger. "Have you met any cute guys out there in Lancaster County?"

"Eli Yoder. I sent you an e-mail about him."

"You mean that Amish fellow?"

"He's the one."

"I thought that was just a passing fancy. Surely you're not seriously interested in this guy."

Laura felt the heat of a blush creep up the back of her neck and spread quickly to her face. "I've been fighting my attraction to Eli, but I'm afraid it's a losing battle." She drew in a deep breath and let it out in a rush. "To tell you the truth—and I can't believe I'm actually saying this out loud—I think I might be in love with him."

Shannon nearly choked on her hot chocolate. "You can't be serious!"

"I am."

"Does he know how you feel?"

"I don't think so. We've agreed only to be friends, and I don't see how it could work for us to have a romantic relationship."

Shannon nodded. "Makes sense to me."

"Eli's family is really religious, and we're worlds apart, with him being a plain kind of guy and me being a fancy English woman." Laura laughed dryly. "At least that's how Eli sees me."

Shannon drummed her fingers along the edge of the table. "Hmm. . ."

"What?"

"Maybe he will leave the Amish faith and become fancy."

"I've thought about that—even hoped for it," Laura admitted. "Eli's religion and his plain lifestyle seem very important to him. I doubt he would be willing to give it up, though I might ask–when I get up the nerve."

Shannon reached across the table and patted Laura's hand in a motherly fashion. "This is a fine fix you've gotten yourself into. Maybe you'll end up going over to the other side before it's all said and done."

Laura's eyebrows furrowed. "Other side? What are you talking about?"

"I was thinking you might join the Amish faith. People have done a lot stranger things in the name of love."

Laura's frown deepened. "I don't think I could do that, Shannon. It would be hard to give up everything I've become used to, and–"

The kitchen door opened just then, and Laura's father entered the room, carrying an overstuffed briefcase. From the way his shoulders sagged and the grim look he wore, Laura figured he must either be exhausted or agitated about something.

Her father was a small, thin man, with dark brown hair and a matching mustache. His mahogany eyes looked unusually doleful as he shuffled across the room and collapsed into a chair.

"Dad, is something wrong?" Laura asked, feeling concern. "You look so tired."

"It's just this fast-paced world we're living in," he answered, lowering his briefcase to the table. "On days like today, I wish I could pull a magic handle and make everything slow down. Maybe the pioneer days weren't so bad. Life in the fast lane is pretty hectic, but I suppose I'll survive." His forehead wrinkled as he looked at Laura. "Whatever you do, young lady, never let 'all work and no play' become your motto."

"I'll try not to, Dad."

"By the way, your mother mentioned that you've become friendly with an Amish man, and I've been meaning to talk to you about it."

Laura nodded and swallowed hard. Was her father going to give her a lecture about Eli in front of Shannon?

Dad smiled. "Well, if you ever see that fellow again, be sure to tell him that I envy his simple lifestyle." He glanced over at Shannon then. "Nice to see you."

"It's good to see you, too, Mr. Meade."

He turned his attention back to Laura. "Where's your mother?"

"She was supposed to have lunch with her friend Ethel today, and I think they planned to do some shopping afterward." Laura released a sigh of relief. Maybe Dad wasn't opposed to her seeing Eli. Maybe there would be no lecture.

"I can only imagine what kind of unnecessary things she'll bring home this time." He shook his head. "Your mother spends more time shopping than any other woman I know."

Laura nodded. "She does like to shop—when she's not busy with all her charity functions."

"There's nothing wrong with helping out, but the kinds of things she does make me wonder if she's more interested in making herself look good rather than helping others." He grunted. "I doubt that your mother knows how to relax anymore, she's so busy flitting from one charity benefit to another. What we both really need is a vacation from the rat race of city life."

"Maybe you should take a trip to Hawaii or go on a cruise to the Bahamas," Laura suggested.

"Maybe so." He moved across the room toward the door leading to the hallway. "Guess I'll head out to the living room and unwind a bit before your mother gets home."

"Okay."

"Your dad seemed pretty uptight, didn't he?" Shannon said after Laura's father had left the room.

"Yes, he did, and I was surprised he didn't lecture me about seeing Eli."

Shannon laughed. "Parents. Who can figure them out?"

"Not me." Laura took a drink of her hot chocolate as she reflected on her father's words. The things he'd said about wanting to slow down had made her think of Eli and his Amish family. They worked hard, but they weren't really a part of the fast-paced world. From all Eli had told her, she knew that he and his family took time out for fun and relaxation. She wondered if Dad were given the chance, whether he might trade in his briefcase for a hoe and the quiet life among the Plain People. She chuckled softly. *No, that could never happen.*

Wesley wandered into the living room, leaving his briefcase in the kitchen, along with his cares of the day. He had a splitting headache and wanted to spend the rest of his day relaxing and not thinking about anything that pertained to his latest court case.

Wesley discovered Laura's lazy cat lying in front of the fireplace, but the minute he took a seat in his recliner, the cat was in his lap.

"You've got life made, you know that, Foosie?"

The cat responded with a quiet *meow*.

He reclined the chair and closed his eyes as he allowed his mind to wander back to the days when he'd been a boy growing up on his dad's farm in Montana. Life had been so much simpler then. They had worked plenty hard on the farm, but they'd always taken the time to enjoy the simple things in life, and their focus had been on family and friends, not "things."

Wesley had given up that life to please Irene, and now he felt as if he were caught in a trap from which there was no escape. Someday when he retired, maybe he would sell this place and move to the country again, where he could raise some chickens, a few pigs, and some cats. . .lots of cats.

Eli meandered toward his woodworking shop at one end of the barn. He didn't know why, but he wasn't in the mood to carve or build a single thing.

When he reached his workbench, he looked down at the woodworking set Laura had given him and groaned. He wished she hadn't presented him with such a fine, expensive gift. In fact, he wished she hadn't bought him anything. He'd given her nothing in return, and accepting Laura's present only made it that much harder to distance himself from her, which he knew he must do if he was ever going to join the church.

He thought about Pauline and wondered if he could have been content to court her if Laura hadn't come along when she did. It was hard to explain, but being with her made him feel alive and whole.

Eli sank to the metal folding chair by his workbench and leaned forward until his head rested in the palms of his hands. "If only I hadn't started seeing her. If I could just stop the feelings I have whenever we're together. It just isn't right."

"What isn't right?"

Eli jerked upright at the sound of his younger brother's voice. "Jonas, what do you think you're doing, sneakin' up on me that way?"

Jonas chuckled and sauntered over to the workbench. "I thought you came out here to work on a Christmas present, not talk to yourself." He gave Eli's shoulder a couple of thumps.

Eli frowned. "I was planning to finish up the planter box I'm making for Martha Rose, but I can't seem to get in the mood to work on it right now."

Jonas pushed a bale of straw over to the bench and plopped down on it. "Christmas is only a few days away. How do ya think our big sister will feel about not gettin' a gift from you?"

Eli grabbed the planter in question, along with a strip of sandpaper, and began sanding it with a vengeance. "It'll be done on time."

Jonas touched Eli's arm. "Take it easy. Now

you're gettin' all worked up."

"I'm not worked up," Eli snapped, as he continued to run the coarse paper over the edges of the wooden box.

Jonas eyed him intently. "Is that so? Well, ya sure could've fooled me."

"Quit your staring."

"I was just checkin' to see if my big brother is in lieb."

Eli slapped the sandpaper down on the bench and stood, nearly knocking over his wooden stool. "I'm not in love! Now, if you don't have anything sensible to say, why don't you go bother someone else?"

"It's that fancy English woman, isn't it? You're all worked up over her, I'm guessing."

Eli's forehead beaded with sweat, and he knew it wasn't from heat, for there was at least a foot of snow on the ground. If only he could get Laura out of his mind.

"You're not denying it, so it must be true," Jonas persisted. "She's gotten under your skin, huh?"

Eli whirled around to face his brother. "Laura and I are just friends." His right eyelid began to twitch. "Even if I wanted it to be more, it could never happen."

"How come?"

"She's English."

"I know, but–"

"There are no buts." Eli felt his patience begin to wane. "I don't want to leave our faith, and I sure couldn't ask Laura to become one of us."

"Why not?"

Eli folded his arms and drew in a deep breath. He was getting frustrated with this ridiculous conversation. "Let's put it this way—would you throw a newborn *bussli* into the *seischtall*?"

Jonas tipped his head and looked at Eli as if he'd gone daffy. "Huh? What's a little bitty kitten and a pigpen got to do with Laura Meade?"

Eli shook his head. "Never mind. You're probably too *verhuddelt* to understand."

"I'm not confused! Just say what ya mean, and mean what ya say!" Jonas's forehead now dripped with sweat.

"Calm down. This is a dumb discussion we're having, and I say we drop it."

Jonas stuck out his chin. "Want to know what I think?"

Eli blew out his breath and lifted his gaze toward the rafters. "No, but I'm sure you won't scram 'til you've told me."

"I think you're in love with Laura, but you know she's not good for you. I'm thinkin' the best thing for everyone is for you to hurry and get baptized, and then join the church so you can marry Pauline Hostetler."

Eli clenched his fists. If Jonas didn't leave soon, he couldn't be sure what he might do. "Just go now before I drag you outside and push your face into a pile of snow."

"Jah, right."

"I mean it, little brother."

"You think you're big enough?" Jonas planted

his hands on his hips and stared at Eli as though daring him to make a move.

Eli didn't hesitate. He lunged for Jonas, and Jonas darted for the door. When they bounded into the snowy yard, all thoughts of Laura vanished as Eli focused on catching his nosy brother and giving him a good face washing in a mound of frigid snow.

Chapter 10

Christmas Day turned out to be pretty much the way Laura had expected it to be. Her father had invited several people from his law firm to dinner, and most of them spent the whole time talking about trial dates, briefs, and who they thought might get out of going to jail.

Dean Carlson was among the guests, seated next to Laura. She studied him as he droned on about the new computer system they'd recently installed at the office. There was no denying it—Dean was one of the most handsome men Laura had ever met. The funny thing was Laura used to enjoy Dean's company. Now he seemed superficial and self-absorbed. She kept comparing him to Eli, whose warm, sincere smile could melt her heart and whose infectious laughter seemed genuine, not forced like Dean's. She didn't know why she'd never seen it before, but Dean's whole mannerism was brash, and he was certainly the most egotistical man she had ever met. Eli, on the other hand, was gentle and genuinely humble.

"Laura, are you listening to me?" Dean nudged her arm.

She managed a weak smile. "I think Dad may have mentioned the new computer system."

"You *weren't* listening. The computer system was not the last thing I said."

She blinked. "It wasn't?"

"I was asking if you'd like to go to the New Year's Eve office party with me."

Laura stared at Dean. How could she even consider dating a man like him? Oh, sure, he had money, a good education, great looks, and a prestigious job, but he simply wasn't Eli Yoder.

"I want to take you to the party," Dean said again. "Will you go with me or not?"

Every fiber of Laura's being shouted *no*! She reached for her glass of water and took a few sips, hoping to buy some time.

When Dean began tapping the side of his glass with the tip of his spoon, she finally answered. "I appreciate the offer, but I hadn't planned on going to the party."

"Why not?"

Laura wasn't sure how to respond. She really had no legitimate reason for staying home. "I. . . uh. . .I'm leaving for Pennsylvania the day after New Year's, and I need to get packed."

Dean leaned his head back and roared. It was the first genuine laugh she'd heard out of him all day, but it didn't make her smile. "You have a whole week between now and the party. Surely that's time enough to pack a suitcase."

When Laura made no reply, he reached for her hand. "Come on, honey, please say you'll go with me. After all, I do work for your dad, and I'm sure he would approve."

Laura inwardly groaned. She knew she was losing this battle, and she didn't like it one bit.

Dean leaned closer, and she could feel his warm breath against her ear. "If you don't have a wonderful time, I promise never to ask you out again."

She finally nodded in defeat. "Okay, I'll go."

All during dinner, Wesley kept glancing across the table at Laura. She looked uncomfortable, as if she would rather be anyplace else but here. Didn't she enjoy being with her family and friends? She'd always seemed to before. Surely she wasn't anxious to get back to her studies in Pennsylvania. Maybe she was just tired.

He looked over at his wife, sitting so prim and proper at the other end of the table. She seemed to be in her glory—chatting, smiling, soaking up every compliment that had come her way. He didn't know why. She really couldn't take credit for any of it. The meal had been catered. The house had been cleaned by their housekeeper. Irene's flowing, peach-colored dress had been bought at one of the most expensive shops in town. Her hair and nails had been done by her beautician. She hadn't done much of anything to prepare for this meal except tell others what to do.

Wesley inwardly groaned. It was all superficial. There probably wasn't a person sitting at this table who gave a lick about the person next to them. Except maybe Dean, who kept nuzzling Laura's neck and whispering in her ear. Could Dean be the reason Laura seemed so fidgety today?

"Wesley, did you hear what I said?"

He looked over to his wife again. "What was that, dear?"

Irene smiled sweetly. "I asked if you were still planning to host your office's New Year's Eve party at the country club. Ethel wanted to know."

"Yes, it will be there again this year." Wesley forced a smile. He would never have admitted it to his wife, but the truth was, he would much rather stay home on New Year's Eve and watch TV or read a good book instead of dishing out the money for a party that no one would remember the following day. But he knew it was expected of him, and the gleam in Irene's eyes was a reminder that at least one of them was looking forward to the gala affair.

"What are you doing out here in the cold?" Eli's sister, Martha Rose, asked, as she stepped out the back door and joined him on the porch.

Eli shrugged and leaned against the railing. "It was getting kind of stuffy in the house, so I decided to get some fresh air."

Martha Rose shivered and pulled her heavy shawl around her shoulders. "This air is downright frigid—that's what it is."

He smiled. "So what are you doing out here in it?"

"Same as you—getting some fresh air." She nudged him playfully with her elbow, but then her face sobered. "You've been quiet all day, and I was wondering if there's something bothering you."

Eli pulled his fingers through the back of his hair. Of course there was something bothering him. Ever since he'd met Laura, he had been bothered. He'd been thinking about her off and on all day, wondering how she was spending her Christmas, wishing they could be together, and fretting because he was having such thoughts. He was tempted to share his feelings with Martha Rose, because the two of them had always been close, but he wasn't sure she would understand. She might even reprimand him, the way Mom had done when she'd learned he was seeing Laura—a fancy Englisher.

"I'm feeling kind of down today," he finally mumbled.

"On Christmas?"

He nodded, keeping his focus on the snowy yard, because he knew if he looked right at Martha Rose, he was likely to give himself away.

"Mom's worried about you, Eli."

"I'm fine. A little chilly weather never hurt anybody."

She touched his arm. "She's not worried about you being out here in the cold."

His only reply was an exaggerated shrug.

"She's worried that you might be thinking about leaving the Amish faith."

Eli bristled and whirled around to face his sister. "Did Mom send you out here to try and talk some sense into me? Is that it?"

Martha Rose shook her head. "Coming out here was my idea. I've seen how sullen you've been all day, and I was worried that it might have something to do with the English woman you've been seeing lately."

"Laura and I are just friends. Mom has nothin' to worry about."

"It might help ease her concerns if you got baptized and joined the church."

"I don't think calming Mom's fears is a good enough reason to become a member of the church, do you?"

"Well, no, but—"

"I've told Mom and Pop, too, that I'm not leaving the faith, and there's nothing serious going on with me and Laura." Eli grunted. "So everyone, including you, can quit hounding me about this."

Martha Rose winced as though she'd been slapped. "I—I didn't mean to sound as if I was trying to tell you what to do. I only want your happiness."

"Sorry. I shouldn't have snapped at you that way."

She gave him a hug. "I want you to know that if you ever need to talk, I'm willing to listen, and I promise not to be judgmental."

Eli smiled and patted her on the back. "Danki. I appreciate that."

"Are you too full from dinner to finish your dessert?" Pauline's mother motioned to the half-eaten piece of pumpkin pie on Pauline's plate.

Pauline shook her head. "Not really. I'm just not so hungry right now."

Dad wrinkled his forehead. "You barely ate any dinner. As a matter of fact, you've been actin' kind of sulky all day. What's the problem, daughter?"

"Nothing. I'm fine."

"She's probably wishing she could be with her boyfriend today," Pauline's younger sister, Susan, piped up.

"I have no boyfriend. Not anymore."

"I thought you and Eli Yoder had been courting," Dad said, reaching for another slice of mincemeat pie.

"I thought so, too, but I was wrong." Pauline couldn't keep the bitterness out of her voice.

Mom poured herself a cup of coffee from the pot sitting in the center of the table. "I was talking to Eli's mamm a few weeks back, and she seemed concerned because he's not joined the church yet."

"He hasn't joined because he's seeing some fancy English woman with long, auburn hair," Sam, Pauline's brother, interjected.

Pauline glared at him. "Can't we talk about something else?"

He shrugged his broad shoulders and smiled. "Guess we could talk about Joseph Beachy. He's had a crush on you ever since we were kinner."

Pauline wrinkled her nose. "Joseph's three years younger than me, for goodness' sake."

Dad chuckled. "So what of it? Your mamm's a whole year older than me."

Mom shook her head as she lifted her gaze to the ceiling. "And you're never gonna let me live that down, are you, Ben?"

He grinned and tickled her under the chin. "Nope, but it don't make me love you any the less."

She reached for his hand. "I love you, too, even if you are just a big kid."

Feeling the need to be alone, Pauline pushed away from the table. "I'm kind of tired, so if you don't mind, I think I'll go upstairs to my bedroom."

"Sleep well," Mom called as Pauline started out of the room.

"Danki." Pauline trudged up the stairs, and with each step she took, she felt more discouraged. Even if Eli did quit seeing the Englisher and decided to join the church, she feared he might never be interested in her. And if she couldn't have Eli, then she didn't want any man.

Chapter 11

Mom had insisted that Laura buy a new dress for the New Year's Eve party. Laura couldn't understand what all the fuss was about, but she decided she might as well enjoy the pampering. After all, she would be leaving soon. Then it would be back to the grindstone of school, homework, and. . .Eli. She hoped she would be able to see him again.

Standing before her full-length bedroom mirror, Laura smiled at the lovely young woman looking back at her. *If Eli could only see me now, maybe he'd be tempted to go "fancy."*

Mom stood directly behind her, and she smiled into the mirror, as well. "You look exquisite. I'm glad you decided to buy this beautiful silk gown. That shade of green brings out the color of your eyes so well."

Laura merely shrugged in response. She knew she looked nice, but her heart wasn't in going to the party tonight or in spending the evening with Dean.

"I'm sure your date will be impressed," her mother continued. "Dean seems like such a nice young man."

"I suppose—just not my type."

"Not your type?" Mom's eyebrows furrowed. "How can you say that, Laura? Why, Dean is nice looking, has plenty of money, and—"

Laura turned away from the mirror. "Do you think my hair looks all right this way, or should I have worn it down?"

"Your hair looks lovely in a French roll," her mother responded. She gave Laura's arm a gentle squeeze. "I'm sure Dean will think so, too."

The New Year's Eve party was already in full swing by the time Dean and Laura arrived a little after nine o'clock. He'd been nearly an hour late picking her up, which had put her in a sour mood right from the beginning.

They had no sooner checked their coats, than Dean pulled Laura into a possessive embrace. "You look gorgeous tonight. I'm glad you decided to come."

Laura wished she could reciprocate with a similar remark, but the truth was she wasn't glad to be here. In fact, she felt a headache coming on, and if it didn't let up soon, she knew she would have a good excuse to leave the party.

"Would you like something to drink before we check out the buffet?" Dean asked, pulling her toward the bar.

She merely shrugged in response.

"What can I get for you?"

"Nothing, unless they have some diet cola."

"You're not driving," Dean reminded. "And if you're concerned about me drinking and driving, you shouldn't worry your pretty little head. I won't have more than a few drinks, and I can handle those with no problem at all."

Laura gnawed on her bottom lip until it almost bled. If Dean was planning to have a few drinks, she could only imagine how the evening might end. She had to do something to get away from him now. "There's my friend Shannon," she said, motioning across the room. "I'm going over to say hello."

"Okay, I'll get our drinks. I'll meet you at the buffet table in a few minutes." He sauntered off toward the bar like he owned the place.

Laura saw Shannon carrying her plate to one of the tables, and she hurried over to her. "I'm glad to see you here." She pulled out a chair and took a seat beside her friend.

"Why wouldn't I be? Need I remind you that my boyfriend works for your dad?" Shannon glanced at the buffet table and smiled. "Clark's still loading up on food, but he'll be joining me soon."

Laura shrugged. If Shannon's comment was meant to chase her away, it wasn't going to work. "Listen, can you do me a favor?"

"Sure, if I can."

"If you see my folks, would you tell them I came down with a headache so I called a cab and went home?"

Shannon's eyebrows lifted high on her forehead. "What about your date?"

"When Dean comes looking for me, which I'm

sure he will, would you tell him the same thing?"

"You can tell him yourself. He's heading this way right now." Shannon pointed across the room, and Laura groaned.

"What's wrong? Did the two of you have a disagreement?"

"Something like that." Laura decided it would be pointless to tell her friend the real reason she wanted to get away from Dean. She wasn't just worried about his drinking. She didn't like the gleam she'd seen in his eyes when he picked her up tonight. She was sure he wanted more than she was willing to give, and her best line of defense was to leave now–alone.

"Here's your diet cola." Dean handed Laura the cold drink and nodded at Shannon. "How's it going?"

Shannon smiled. "Fine. How's everything with you?"

Laura set her glass on the table and tuned them both out as they engaged in small talk. Her thoughts turned to Eli, and she couldn't help wondering how he was spending his New Year's Eve. Did the Amish celebrate with a party, or would tonight be just like any other night for Eli and his family?

Laura cringed when Dean pulled her to his side and whispered, "Tonight's going to be a great evening." When he stroked the back of her neck with his thumb, she stood up so quickly, she knocked her soft drink over, spilling some of it down the front of her new dress. "I–I'm not feeling well, Dean. I'm going to call a cab and go home."

Obvious surprise registered on Dean's face, and his eyebrows furrowed. "You can't be serious. We just got here, and I haven't had a chance to eat yet, much less show you off to my friends."

I don't want to be shown off, and I don't want to be with you. Laura thrust out her chin and stared up at him. "I'm going home."

Dean set his drink on the table and steered her toward the coat closet. "Sure, no problem. I'll get my car."

"I'm calling a cab. There's no point in both of us missing the party. You stay and have a good time."

His eyes clouded over. "If you're dead-set on going, then I may as well collect that stroke-of-midnight kiss." Before Laura could say anything, Dean bent his head and captured her lips in a kiss that would have left most women reeling with pleasure.

Laura drew back and slapped his face.

"What was that for?" He grimaced as he touched the red mark she had left on his cheek. "I thought you wanted that kiss as much as I did. Always did before."

Laura's face was so hot she felt as though she were the one who had been slapped. She wasn't in control of her emotions tonight, and that really bothered her.

"I'm sorry, Dean," she apologized. "Your kiss took me by surprise."

Dean's eyelids fluttered, and he backed up a few steps. "I don't know what's come over you, Laura, but you haven't been the same since you returned to Minneapolis after attending that stupid school in Pennsylvania for a few months. If I were your father, I would never have allowed you to go there, and I would have insisted that you finish your design courses right here in town."

Laura's hands trembled as she held them at her sides. If Dean kept goading her, she was liable to let him have it on the other cheek. "Good night, Dean," she said through her clenched jaw. "Don't bother walking me out."

The day after New Year's, Laura said good-bye to her parents at the airport. She was more than anxious to be on her way. It wasn't that she hadn't enjoyed being with them, but she wanted to get back to her studies. . .and she hoped to see Eli again.

Mom and Dad had no idea she'd fallen in love with an Amish man, only that she'd gone out with him a few times. She had no intention of informing them, either. At least not today.

Laura hugged her parents and thanked them for the beautiful leather coat they'd given her for Christmas. Then, without so much as a backward glance, she boarded the plane, welcoming the butterflies doing a tap dance in her stomach.

Her time on the plane was spent thinking about Eli. She couldn't decide if she should be straightforward and tell him that she'd come to realize how much she loved him or if she should try to draw a declaration of love from him first.

By the time the plane landed in Harrisburg,

Laura was a ball of nerves. As soon as she picked up the car she had leased, she headed for the main road, knowing the drive to Lancaster would be slow since snow still covered the ground.

When she got back to the school, it would be dark and too late to try and find Eli's house. But come tomorrow, she hoped to see him and bare her soul.

Chapter 12

Laura awoke in her dorm room the following morning with a pounding headache. A warm shower and a cup of tea helped some, but when she knocked on Darla's door to see if her friend would like to ride with her to Eli's farm, Laura's headache worsened.

"I have other plans today," Darla said with a scowl. "Besides, I wouldn't consider being a party to you ruining your life."

"How can seeing Eli again ruin my life?" Laura had hoped Darla would be willing to go with her. She needed the added courage.

Darla opened the door wider and motioned Laura inside. "Have a seat, and I'll see if I can explain things a little more clearly."

Laura pulled out the desk chair, and Darla sat on the edge of her bed.

"I know you've got a thing for this guy, but the more you see him, the further your relationship will develop." Darla pursed her lips. "One of you is bound to get hurt, and I'm guessing that you're going to be the one."

"What makes you think I'll get hurt?"

"We've been through this before. You and Eli are from completely different worlds, and even if one of you were willing to try the other's way of life, it most likely wouldn't work."

"How do you know?"

"Trust me on this," Darla asserted. "You're living in a dream world if you think you can get Eli to leave his faith."

"Why is that so impossible? People change religions all the time."

"Has Eli joined the Amish church yet? Because if he has and he decides to leave the faith, he'll be shunned. Do you understand what that means, Laura?"

She nodded. "Eli's told me quite a bit about the Amish way of life, but this isn't a problem because he hasn't joined the church yet."

Darla's eyebrows drew together. "Even so, if he were to leave, it would be a difficult adjustment."

"I'll help him adjust."

Darla shrugged. "Whatever. But think about this: Maybe he doesn't want to leave. Then what?"

"I–I don't know. I suppose I'll have to convince him that he does want to leave." Laura stood. "So are you going to help me find the Yoder place or not?"

Darla shook her head. "I'm afraid you'll have to do this on your own."

"Fine. I will."

Laura spent the next couple of hours driving around the back roads near Paradise, searching for Eli's house. Since she'd only been there once before and hadn't paid close attention to where Eli was going, she wasn't sure she was heading in the right direction.

Suddenly, she spotted a one-room schoolhouse. It was the same one Eli had pointed out on one of their rides. *I've got to be getting close to his house.*

Laura continued up the road another mile or so until she spotted a mailbox with the name Yoder on it. She drove up the driveway, and the minute she saw the house, she knew it was Eli's. She stopped the car, turned off the engine, and stepped out.

Walking carefully up the slippery path, she headed for the Yoders' front porch. She was almost to the door when a sense of panic gripped her like a vise. What if Eli wasn't home? What if he was home but wasn't happy to see her?

She thought about turning around and heading back to Lancaster, but the desire to see Eli won out, so she lifted her hand and knocked on the door.

A few moments later, Eli's mother answered. She held a rolling pin in one hand, and with the other hand, she swiped at a wisp of hair that had fallen loose from her bun. Laura couldn't read Mary Ellen's stoic expression, but the woman's silence was enough to remind her that she was on enemy territory.

"Is. . .uh. . .Eli at home?"

Mary Ellen stood quietly a few minutes before she finally answered. "He's out in the barn in his woodworking shop."

Laura nodded and forced her lips to form a smile. "Thanks." She stepped quickly off the porch before

Eli's mother had a chance to say anything more. If the older woman's sour expression was meant to dissuade her, it hadn't worked. She was here now and even more determined than ever to speak with Eli.

Eli was bent over his workbench, hammering a nail into the roof of a small birdhouse, when he heard the barn door open. He didn't think much of it, knowing his brothers were still busy with chores, but when a familiar female voice called out to him, he was so surprised, he smashed his thumb with the hammer.

"Laura! How'd you get here?"

She moved slowly across the room until she stood directly in front of him. "I drove."

"When did you get back from Minnesota?"

"Last night."

Eli wished she would quit staring at him. It was hard to think. Hard to breathe. He swallowed a couple of times. "How. . .how was your holiday?"

"It was okay. How was yours?"

"Good." *Though it would have been better if you'd been here.* Eli shook his head, trying to get himself thinking straight again.

"I've missed you," Laura said, leaning toward him. "Did you miss me?"

A warning bell went off in Eli's head, but it was too late. Laura touched his arm, as she gazed into his eyes in a way that made his heart slam into his chest. How could he tell this beautiful woman that it wasn't right for her to be here?

Eli couldn't voice any of his thoughts. He

couldn't even think straight with her standing so close and smelling so nice. He took a step back and bumped into his workbench, knocking a hunk of wood to the floor. He bent to retrieve it, feeling more frustrated by the minute.

"So this is where you make your birdhouses, huh?"

He nodded. "And many other wooden items, as well."

She glanced around the small room, as if she were scrutinizing it. "How can you do this kind of work without the aid of electricity?"

"Some time ago, my daed installed a diesel engine that not only provides power for some of my saws and planers but also powers the compressed air pump that brings water to our house." Eli pointed to a small drill lying beside a handsaw. "Of course I do many things by hand, too."

"I see." Laura took a step closer to him. "Have you been back to the lake lately?"

"The lake's completely frozen over now." He tipped his head as an uncensored thought popped into his mind. "Say, would you like to go ice-skating?"

She pointed to her boots. "Ice-skating? Eli, in case you haven't noticed, I have no skates."

"I think my sister, Martha Rose, left her skates here in the barn when she married Amon Zook, and I'm sure she wouldn't mind if you wore them."

"If your sister's skates fit, I'd be happy to go ice-skating with you."

Eli nodded and smiled. So much for his resolve to keep Laura at a distance.

"Always trouble somewhere," Mary Ellen muttered as she returned to the kitchen, where Johnny sat at the table with a cup of coffee in his hands.

"What's the problem? Who was at the front door?"

"That English woman."

"Which English woman? There are several living nearby, you know."

Mary Ellen dropped into the chair beside her husband with a groan. "I'm talking about Laura Meade. She was looking for Eli."

"What'd you tell her?"

"Said he was out in the barn, in his shop." She pursed her lips. "Couldn't hardly lie now, could I?"

Johnny shook his head. "No, but you could have sent her packing."

"I'd like to think Eli will tell her to leave, but I'm not holding my breath on that one, either."

Johnny set his cup down and reached for her hand. "We need to keep on praying and trusting that God will open our son's eyes."

She nodded. "Jah, but that's easier said than done."

When Eli pulled his sleigh into the open area near the lake, Laura was surprised to see that it was covered with a thick layer of shimmering ice. She thought it was even more appealing than it had been in the fall, and she drank in the beauty of the surrounding trees, dressed in frosty white gowns and shimmering in the morning sun like thousands of tiny diamonds.

They took a seat on a fallen log, and Eli helped Laura into his sister's skates, which were only a tad too big.

"If I ever get the chance to meet your sister, I'll have to be sure and thank her for the use of these skates."

"I'll thank her for you." Eli grinned. "You'd like Martha Rose. She's the best sister any fellow could possibly want, and we've been good friends since we were kinner." He stood and held out his hand. "Should we give those skates a try?"

"Jah, let's do."

Hand in hand, they made their way slowly around the lake. After a time, Eli set off on his own, doing fancy spins and figure eights.

Laura shielded her eyes against the glare of the sun as she watched in rapt fascination, realizing with each passing moment how much she really had come to love Eli. She tried skating by herself, but it was hard to concentrate on anything except the striking figure he made on the ice.

Her heart hammered in her chest when Eli waved and offered her a flirtatious wink. He wore a pair of black pants, a light blue shirt, and a dark gray woolen jacket. He had removed his black felt hat, and his sandy brown hair whipped against his face as he appeared to become one with the wind.

Laura decided to try and catch up to Eli, hoping she could convince him to take a break so they could talk. She needed to tell him what was in her heart.

Pushing off quickly with her right foot, she lost her balance and fell hard on the ice. Eli was at her side immediately, his blue eyes looking ever so serious. "Are you okay? You didn't break anything, I hope."

"My knee hurts, but I don't think my leg's broken."

Laura shivered as Eli pulled up her pant leg and gently probed her knee. "It looks like a bad sprain. You probably should put some ice on it."

She giggled. "I think I just did."

Eli helped Laura to her feet and put his arm around her waist as she hobbled over to the sleigh. "I'd better get you back to my place so you can rest that knee and get out of the cold."

Impulsively, Laura gripped Eli's shoulders with both hands and kissed him on the cheek.

His face flushed, and he smiled at first, but then he jerked back like he'd been stung by a bee. "Wh-why'd you do that?"

"Just my way of saying thanks for being such a good friend."

His gaze dropped to the ground, and an awkward silence followed as Eli helped her into the sleigh. She wondered if she had said or done something wrong.

"I—I think it would be best if we didn't see each other anymore," he mumbled as he picked up the reins.

"Why? Haven't you enjoyed yourself today?"

He nodded soberly. "That's the problem: I had too good of a time."

Her hand trembled as she touched his arm. "I don't see how enjoying yourself can be a problem."

"I told you once that I wanted to be your friend, but now things have changed."

"How?" Her voice rose, and her heart started to pound. "Why?"

"I can't be your friend because I've fallen in love with you, Laura." He didn't look at her, just stared straight ahead.

"Oh, Eli, I love you, too!" She buried her face in his jacket, relishing the warmth and his masculine smell.

"What we feel for each other isn't right," he mumbled.

"It feels right to me."

"It won't work for us. I think we need to end this before we both get hurt."

"Nothing could hurt worse than never seeing you again," Laura said with a catch in her voice. "We can be together if we want it badly enough."

He eased her gently away. "I don't see how."

"You could leave the Amish faith. You're not a member yet, so you won't be shunned, and when we both feel ready for marriage–"

Eli's eyebrows arched. "Marriage? Are you saying you want to marry me?"

Laura swallowed hard. Was that what she was saying? Did she really love Eli, or was he simply a prize she wanted and thought was out of her reach?

"After we've dated awhile, we might be ready for marriage," she amended.

Eli sat there several seconds, staring at the reins

in his hands. "The only reason I haven't joined the church yet is because I was waiting until I felt ready for marriage."

"Wh-what are you saying?"

"I'm saying that despite my feelings for you, I don't believe I could be happy living and working as an Englisher."

"Why not?"

"To my way of thinking, a newborn calf, freshly plowed soil, and the ripening of grain are all manifestations of God's power. Farming to many Amish men in this area isn't just a job, it's a way of life blessed by God and handed down from one generation to another. If I left the Amish faith or moved away from God, I wouldn't feel like a whole person anymore."

She grasped the collar of his jacket and gazed at his handsome face. "I'm not asking you to leave God. You can worship Him in any church. I'm only asking you to give up your Plain lifestyle so we can be together."

"Could you give up your modern way of life to become Plain?"

She shook her head. "I–I don't think so. It would be too hard for me to adjust."

"Exactly. While it is possible for outsiders to join the Amish community, it seldom happens because it would be too big of a change." Eli leaned away from her. Snapping the reins, he shouted, "Giddap there, boy. It's time to go!"

Laura's eyes stung with unshed tears. As the horse moved forward and the sleigh began to glide across the snow, she felt as though her whole world had fallen apart.

Why wouldn't Eli listen to reason? What had gone wrong with her plan?

Eli gripped the reins so hard his fingers ached. *I wish I'd never met Laura. I should have never invited her to take that first ride in my courting buggy. I was stupid for asking her to go skating with me this morning, too. It only made both of us hope for the impossible.*

As much as Eli hated to admit it, he had come to care for Laura, but he didn't think he could give up his way of life in order to marry her. At the same time, he knew it would be impossible for her to give up the only way of life she had ever known to be with him.

They rode in silence all the way back to his house, and when Eli guided the sleigh into the yard, Laura leaned close to him, sending shivers up the back of his neck. "Won't you at least think about what I said earlier? Maybe there's a reason you haven't joined the church yet. Maybe we're supposed to be together."

Eli shook his head as he swallowed around the lump in his throat. "We've let this go on too long, Laura. You and I both know that neither of us could be happy living in the other person's world. So the best thing is for us to say good-bye now, before one or both of us get hurt."

Tears filled Laura's eyes, and Eli was tempted to pull her into his arms and kiss them away. Instead, he stepped out of the sleigh and skirted around to the other side to help her down. Laura leaned down and picked up Martha Rose's skates. "Tell your sister I said thanks for giving me the opportunity to spend a few more hours with you before we had to say good-bye."

"Jah, I will."

"And you were right, Eli. It wouldn't have worked for us."

Before Eli could respond, she hopped down without his assistance and limped toward her car. Every fiber of Eli's being screamed at him to go after her, but reason won out. He turned his attention toward the horse, vowing that no matter what it took, he would forget he had ever met a fancy English woman named Laura Meade.

Chapter 13

January and February were cold. . .so cold and dreary Laura thought she would die. It wasn't just the weather making her feel that way, either. Her heart was broken because Eli had rejected her. If he really cared, he should have agreed to leave his world and join hers.

Two months had passed since their final good-bye, but Laura still longed for something she couldn't have. Visions of the happy times they had spent together danced through her mind. Losing Eli hurt so much, and she couldn't seem to do anything to ease the pain. Shopping for new clothes didn't help. Throwing herself into her studies made no difference. Even an occasional binge on hot-fudge sundaes and chocolate milkshakes did nothing to make her feel better. The barrage of e-mails and phone calls from Dean Carlson didn't soothe Laura's troubled spirit, either. She cared nothing for Dean, and she told him so.

As winter moved into spring, Laura finally began to move on with her life. At least she thought she was moving on until one of her teachers gave the class an assignment, asking each student to decorate a bedroom using something handmade by the Amish as a focal point.

Laura had her Amish quilt. . .the one she'd purchased at the farmers' market the first day she'd met Eli. However, when she and Eli broke off their relationship, she had boxed up the quilt and sent it home, unable to look at it any longer. She supposed she could call Mom and ask her to mail it back, but the assignment was due early next week, and there wasn't enough time for that. There was only one logical thing to do—go to the farmers' market and buy another quilt.

"If you can spare a few minutes, I'd like to talk to you about Laura."

Wesley halted in front of his office door and turned to face Dean. "What about her?"

Dean nodded toward the office. "Can we talk in there?"

"I guess so." Wesley stepped into the room and motioned to one of the leather chairs near his desk. "Have a seat."

Dean sat down, and Wesley took a seat in the larger chair behind the desk. "Now what did you want to say about my daughter?"

"I was wondering if you'd heard anything from her lately."

"Laura calls at least once a week, and we get e-mails nearly every day. Why do you ask?"

Dean rubbed his fingers along the edge of his chin and grimaced. "She won't answer my phone calls or any of my e-mails."

"Any idea why?"

"She turned off to me the night of the New Year's Eve party and wouldn't even let me take her home when she said she wasn't feeling well."

Wesley leaned forward with his elbows on the desk. "So you've had no contact with her since she went back to Pennsylvania?"

"Just one phone call, and she told me she didn't want to see me again."

"Then I guess you'd better take Laura at her word. She's a lot like her mother in many respects."

"How so?"

"Once my daughter makes up her mind about something, there's no changing it."

"Has she found someone else? Is that the problem?"

Wesley shrugged. "You'll have to ask her that question." He motioned to the door. "Now if you don't mind, I have work to do, and I'm sure you do, as well."

Dean stood. "The next time you talk to Laura, would you give her a message for me?"

"That all depends on what the message is."

"Tell her I'm not giving up on us, and when she finally comes to her senses, I'll be here waiting."

Before Wesley could respond, Dean sauntered out of the room.

"I'll give Laura a message all right," Wesley mumbled. "I'll tell her the best thing she ever did was drop you flat on your ear." He tapped the end of his pen against the desk a couple of times. "If you weren't such a crackerjack lawyer, I'd drop you flat, too."

As Eli headed to the farmers' market in his horse and open buggy, he kept thinking about Laura and how interested she'd seemed in his birdhouses that first day when he'd met her at the market. It had been two whole months since they'd said good-bye after their ice-skating date, and a day hadn't gone by that he hadn't thought about her.

He glanced over at his date sitting in the seat beside him. *Here I am with Pauline again. Is it fair to lead her on? Is it possible for me to learn to love her?* It wasn't a case of Pauline not being pretty. She just wasn't as pretty as Laura. It wasn't that he didn't enjoy Pauline's company. She simply wasn't as much fun to be around as Laura. But Eli had decided to give Pauline a chance, thinking it might help him forget Laura, and knowing it would please his folks if he settled down, got baptized, joined the church, and took a wife. He just wasn't sure that wife could be Pauline.

"Spring's just around the corner, jah?" Pauline said, cutting into Eli's private thoughts.

He nodded. "Many of the trees have blossoms already, and some flowers are poking their heads through the soil."

She sighed. "Won't be long and it'll be warm enough for picnics."

"Jah."

"If this warm weather holds out, maybe we

could go to the lake next Saturday."

"We'll have to see how it goes."

She reached over and touched his arm. "Guess I'll have to pray for sunshine."

He gave no reply as he guided his horse and buggy into the market parking lot.

Laura was glad Darla had agreed to go with her to the farmers' market. She didn't relish the idea of going there alone. Too many painful memories lived inside that building. Too many reminders of the day she'd met Eli.

They had taken Darla's car this morning, and as soon as it was parked, Laura hopped out and headed for the building. She knew from what Eli had told her that Saturdays were always busy at the market, and she didn't want to miss out on the best deals.

"Hey, wait for me," Darla shouted.

Laura halted. "Sorry. Guess I'm in too big a hurry to look at those beautiful quilts."

"I might just buy one myself this time."

They stepped into the building, and Laura led the way.

"I'm beginning to see why the country look fascinates you so much," Darla commented, as they browsed through a stack of colorful quilts. "The vibrant hues and various shapes in these are actually quite pretty."

Laura nodded as she fingered a monochromatic blue quilt with a Double Wedding Ring pattern.

The middle-aged Amish woman selling the quilts mentioned that it was an old patchwork design, and that as the name implied, two rings interlocked with each other.

"Some quilters use their scraps of material for the Double Wedding Ring because the pieces are quite small." She smiled and lifted one edge of the quilt. "Others plan their quilt with great care, alternating light and dark rings."

"I think I'll buy this one," Laura said. "I love the variance of colors and the interlocking rings."

"And I believe I'll keep looking awhile." Darla chuckled. "No sense picking the first one I see."

When Laura didn't answer, Darla poked her in the ribs. "Did you hear what I said?"

Laura stood frozen in her tracks. Her heart pounded like a pack of stampeding horses, and her throat felt so dry she could barely swallow.

"Laura, what's wrong? You look like you've seen a ghost."

"It's. . .it's Eli. . .and that woman." Laura's voice cracked. "I–I had no idea he would be here today. If I'd known, I wouldn't have come."

Darla craned her neck. "Where is he, and what woman are you talking about?"

"She seems really possessive and thinks she's Eli's girlfriend–and maybe she is now that I'm out of the picture. They're right over there." Laura pointed toward the root-beer stand several feet away. "I shouldn't be surprised to see them together, but it hurts, nonetheless."

Darla grabbed hold of Laura's arm. "Come on.

We've got to get you out of here right now."

Laura jerked away. "I'm not going anywhere. This is a free country, and I have as much right to be here as they do."

"I'm sure, but you don't want Eli to know you're here. Do you?"

Laura dropped her gaze to the floor and shrugged. "Maybe."

"What? The guy threw you over for someone else, and you want to grovel in the dirt in front of him?"

"He didn't throw me over, and I wasn't planning to grovel. I was just thinking I should probably say hello."

"Now that's a real brilliant idea." Darla turned back toward the stack of quilts. "You can do whatever you like, but I came here to look at handmade Amish items. That *was* our assignment, you know, not saying hello to some cute Amish guy."

Ignoring her friend's comment, Laura took a deep breath and marched straight up to the root-beer stand. "Hello, Eli. How are you?"

"Laura? What are you doing here?" Eli's eyes were wide, and his mouth hung slightly open.

"I'm looking at quilts," she answered, fixing her gaze somewhere near the center of his chest. "I–I have an assignment to do, and–"

"Come on, Eli, let's go."

Laura turned her gaze to Pauline. She stood beside Eli with one hand on his arm in a possessive gesture, and she offered Laura an icy stare.

Laura's legs felt like rubber, and tension pulled

the muscles in her neck. She had a deep sense that she had done the wrong thing when she'd asked Eli to leave his Amish faith, and she couldn't ignore it a moment longer. She took a guarded step forward. "Eli, could we talk? I need to tell you something." Her mouth went dry with trepidation as she stared into his blue eyes and recognized hesitation.

A few seconds ticked by. Then he shrugged. "I guess it would be all right." He glanced over at Pauline. "Could you wait for me at the hot dog stand? I won't be long."

Pauline scrunched up her nose. "Are you kidding me?"

He shook his head. "I'll just be a minute."

She glared at Laura, then stalked off, muttering something in Pennsylvania Dutch.

Eli turned back to Laura. "Should we go outside?"

She nodded and followed as he led the way to the nearest exit. When they stepped outside, he motioned to a wooden bench near the building.

Once they were both seated, Laura felt a bit more comfortable. At least now she could gulp in some fresh air, which she hoped might tame the brigade of bumblebees marching through her stomach.

"What did you want to talk to me about?" Eli asked.

"Us. I wanted to talk about us."

"There *is* no *us*, Laura. I thought you understood that I'm not going to leave my faith. In fact, I've decided to—"

"I do understand, and I'm sorry for asking you

to give up your way of life."

"Thank you for understanding. Someday you'll meet the right man, and–"

Laura lifted her hand and covered his mouth with her fingers. "I've already found the right man."

His eyebrows raised in obvious surprise. "You have? That's good. I wish you all the best."

She compressed her lips in frustration. Was Eli deaf, dumb, and blind? Couldn't he see how much she wanted to be with him? She grasped both of his hands and gave them a squeeze. "The man I've found is you. I want no other, and I never will."

"But, Laura–"

"I know, I know. You won't leave the Amish faith and become a fancy Englisher." She swallowed hard and drew in a deep breath. "That doesn't mean we can't be together, though."

He tipped his head and looked at Laura as if she'd lost her mind. "It doesn't?"

"No, it doesn't. Not unless you've found someone else." She leaned closer to him. "Have you, Eli? Are you in love with Pauline?"

He shook his head. "We're still just friends, but–"

"Do you still have feelings for me?"

"Jah, but you know–"

"Well, good. I can solve our problem by coming over to the other side."

A deep frown creased Eli's forehead. "I'm afraid I don't get your meaning."

"I'll join the Amish faith and become Plain."

"What?"

"I said–"

Eli held up his hand. "You don't know what you're saying, Laura. A few folks have joined our faith, but not many. It's not all cakes and pies, you know, and there would be much to learn—classes to take."

"I'm sure it wouldn't be an easy transition, but I can do it, Eli. I can do anything if I set my mind to it."

Eli couldn't believe Laura was offering to join his faith. During the time they had been seeing each other, he'd often found himself wishing for just such a turn of events, but after she'd asked him to join her world, he was certain she would never consider becoming Amish. Now she suddenly wanted to become Plain? It made no sense at all. He studied her intently. She seemed sincere, but truth be told, Laura didn't have any idea what she was suggesting.

"I do love you," he admitted, "but—"

"I'm glad to hear that." She leaned her head on his shoulder. "I was afraid you might turn me away."

Eli breathed in the strawberry scent of Laura's hair and reveled in the warmth of her touch. How could he make her understand, yet how could he say good-bye to her again?

"These last few months have been awful," Laura said with a catch in her voice. "I need to be with you."

"But you might not be happy being Amish, and then what? As I said, it would be a hard thing to change over and give up all the modern things you're used to having. You would have to learn our language and accept our religious views."

She nodded. "I know it won't be easy, but with your help, I can do it. You will help me, won't you, Eli?"

Eli filled his lungs with fresh air as he struggled to make a decision. He lifted Laura's chin with his thumb and stared into her sea-green eyes, hoping to find answers there. He wanted to be with her more than anything. Yet he didn't see how it could ever work out.

When she smiled at him the way she was now, it was hard to think. Hard to breathe. Hard to know what was right and what wasn't.

"Eli, what's your answer?"

Pushing the niggling doubts aside, he finally nodded. "You'll need time to adjust, but I'll help you in every way I can."

Chapter 14

Once Laura made her decision to become Amish, the purchase of a second quilt was completely forgotten. The first order of business was to find Darla and tell her what she planned to do. Then she would need to go back to the interior design school and withdraw. After that, she would call her parents. That was going to be the hardest part, because she was sure they wouldn't understand. Eli's job was to tell Pauline the news, and also his parents, and she was sure that wouldn't be easy, either.

Eli stood from the bench where they had been sitting. "As soon as I leave the farmers' market, I'll head over to my sister's place and see if she would be willing to let you live with her."

Laura stood, too. "Do you think she would do that?"

"Jah. Martha Rose and I are close." He chuckled. "It's always been hard for her to tell me no, and I'm sure she would be a big help in teaching you everything you'll need to know about our way of life."

Laura gripped his arm. "I'm a ball of nerves, Eli. What if Martha Rose says I can't stay there? What if your folks don't accept me? What if—"

Eli held up his hand, halting her words. "Tomorrow I'll hire a driver to pick you up at the school in Lancaster, and we'll drive over to Amon and Martha Rose's place so you can meet them."

"That's okay," she said. "I'll need to turn in the car I'm leasing, so I'll have someone from the rental company drop me off in front of the variety store in Paradise. You can pick me up there, if that's all right."

"Jah, sure." He smiled, and it gave her a sense of reassurance. "I'm sure everything will work out okay."

❧

"I still can't believe what you're planning to do," Darla said, as she and Laura drove back to their school. "Don't you realize what you'll be giving up? Don't you know how hard the transition from English to Amish will be?"

Laura nodded. "I know it won't be easy, but I can do it. I can do anything if I want it badly enough, and this is something I really want."

"You want to live the Plain life, without all the modern conveniences you've become used to?"

"Well, I—"

"Think about it, Laura. You won't be able to use your computer to send e-mails anymore. You won't be allowed to wear makeup, jeans, or any fancy clothes. You'll have to trade in your leased car for a horse and buggy."

Laura shrugged. "I'm sure it won't be easy, but I

can do it for Eli—because I love him and hope to be his wife someday."

"Can't you talk him into leaving the Amish faith? You told me once that he's not joined the church yet, so he wouldn't be shunned if he were to become English."

"I did ask him about leaving once, and it wasn't long after that he said we should go our separate ways." Laura clenched her fingers tightly together in her lap. "I was miserable those months we were apart, and I won't let Eli walk out of my life again, no matter how many sacrifices I might need to make."

Darla gave the steering wheel a couple of taps. "Suit yourself, but don't come crying to me when things don't work out."

"I won't. You can be sure of that."

As Pauline waited near the root-beer stand for Eli to return, she became increasingly anxious. What had that English woman wanted to speak with Eli about, and why had he agreed to talk to her? She hoped he hadn't given up his plans to take membership classes this summer and join the church in the fall. Surely he wasn't thinking about leaving the Amish faith and going English.

"Oh, good, I'm glad you're still here. I need to speak with you."

Pauline whirled around at the sound of Eli's voice. She felt relief to see that the English woman wasn't with him. "Is everything all right, Eli? You look kind of flushed."

He drew her away from the table and over to one corner of the room. "I need to tell you something."

"What is it?"

Eli stared at the concrete floor as he shifted his weight from one foot to the other. "I–I've tried to tell you this before, but there's really no way it could work for us to be together."

Her forehead wrinkled. "Why not? We've been courting for a couple of months now, and I thought we've been getting along fairly well."

He lifted his gaze to hers. "There's no easy way for me to say this, but I'm in love with Laura."

"The Englisher?"

"Jah."

"You're going to leave the Amish faith to be with her?"

He shook his head. "Laura wants to become Plain."

Pauline tried to let Eli's words register in her brain while fighting the tears pushing against her eyelids. This couldn't be true. It had to be some kind of horrible joke. No one just up and decided to join the church–to her knowledge very few ever had.

"You're a nice person, and I'm sorry if I've led you on or hurt you in any way." Eli touched her arm. "I thought I could forget about Laura and move on with my life, but after seeing her today, I realized that she's the one I love and want to be with."

Pauline shrugged his hand away. "It won't work, Eli. That fancy woman will never become one of us. I doubt she could last one week as an Amish woman." Pauline's heart felt like it was breaking in two, but there was no way she would admit to Eli how much he had hurt her, or that she'd hoped to become his wife someday. She lifted her chin and stared right into his blue eyes. "You're verhuddelt if you think things are going to work out for you and Laura, but if she's what you want, then don't expect any sympathy from me if things go sour." Pauline turned on her heels and stalked off.

"Where are you going? Don't you need a ride home?"

She shook her head and kept on walking. She would find her own way home, even if it meant phoning one of their English drivers for a ride.

As Eli left his sister's place and headed down the road toward home with his horse and buggy, he reflected on the conversation he'd had with Martha Rose and felt relief that she'd agreed to let Laura stay with her and Amon while she took her training to become Amish. Martha Rose had also been willing to instruct Laura in cooking, sewing, and many other things she would need to know in order to become part of the Amish community.

Eli was sure that once his sister met Laura in person and saw how nice she was and realized that she wanted to become Amish, everything would work out fine and dandy. Now all he had to do was break the news to Mom and Pop.

Mary Ellen was just putting lunch on the table

when she heard a horse and buggy come into the yard. She glanced out the kitchen window and saw that it was Eli. "I wonder what he's doing home so soon," she said to Johnny, who had just finished washing up at the sink. "I thought he and Pauline were going out to lunch after they left the market, and I figured he would be gone most of the day."

Johnny shrugged. "Guess there must have been a change of plans."

"I hope they didn't have a disagreement. Eli can be kind of headstrong sometimes."

Johnny chuckled and flicked a little water in her direction. "Wonder where he gets that trait from?"

She wrinkled her nose. "Maybe you'd best look in the mirror."

"Ha! I'd say we both tend to be a bit headstrong at times."

"I guess you're right about that." She glanced out the window again. "Eli's putting his horse away, so he'll probably be in shortly. Did Lewis and Jonas say when they were coming inside?"

Johnny dried his hands on a towel before answering. "They had a couple of things to do in the barn, but I'm sure they'll be in soon, too."

"I'll go ahead and serve up the soup. By the time they come in, it will probably be cool enough to eat."

"Makes sense to me." Johnny kissed Mary Ellen's cheek, then ambled across the room and took a seat at the table.

A few minutes later, Jonas and Lewis entered the kitchen, followed by Eli, whose face was all red and sweaty.

Mary Ellen felt immediate concern, and she placed the ladle back in the pot of soup and rushed to his side. "Is there anything wrong, son? You look kind of flushed."

"That's what Pauline said right before I told her the news." Eli flopped into a chair and let his head fall forward into his hands.

Pop reached over and touched Eli's shoulder. "What news is that? What's got you so worked up?"

Eli looked up and blew out his breath. "There's something I need to tell you."

"Are you and Pauline gettin' hitched?" The question came from Lewis, who had also pulled out a chair and sat down.

Eli shook his head. "I think it might be good if everyone took a seat. What I have to say will probably be quite a shock."

Mary Ellen's heart slammed into her chest. Was Eli going to announce that he'd decided not to join the church in the fall, after all? With a sense of dread, she took the chair closest to him.

"So, tell us what's on your mind," Johnny said, after Jonas took his seat.

"You all remember Laura Meade, right?"

"The pretty redheaded woman you brought by the house a few months back?" Lewis asked with a grin.

Eli nodded. "The thing is–I saw Laura today, and she wants to join the Amish church."

"What?" Mary Ellen could hardly believe her ears. Eli hadn't mentioned the English woman in some time, and this made no sense at all.

"I've just come from Martha Rose's place, and she's agreed to let Laura stay there."

"She'll be staying with Martha Rose and Amon?"

"Jah, Mom."

"It just doesn't seem right, her being so fancy and all," Jonas said with a shake of his head.

"Jah," Lewis agreed. "It's not gonna be easy for Laura to give up all the modern things she's been used to and start livin' as we do."

"If Laura stays with Martha Rose, she can teach her all the things she'll need to know about being Amish, and Laura and I can both take the membership classes this summer. Then by fall, we'll both be baptized and join the church."

"Whose idea was this?" Johnny asked, leaning his elbows on the table.

"The part about joining the church was Laura's idea, but I'm the one who thought of asking Martha Rose to help her." Eli scrubbed a hand down his clean-shaven face. "Laura wants it, and so do I. She knows what she's giving up, and it's her decision to do this. So won't you please give her a chance?"

"It will take a lot of gumption for her to make all the sacrifices needed to join the church," Johnny put in. "If she can do it, then I'm willing to give her a chance."

"How about the rest of you?" Eli looked around the table.

Lewis and Jonas both nodded, but Mary Ellen couldn't seem to find her voice. If Laura wanted to join the church, and Eli wanted them to take classes and be baptized together, then in all likelihood, he had plans of marrying the girl soon after that. Mary Ellen didn't like the idea, but she knew if she voiced her concerns it might drive Eli away. They had waited a long time for him to reach a decision about joining the church, and she wouldn't do anything to discourage him. She finally nodded and forced her lips into a smile. "I'll give Laura a chance, too."

As soon as Laura returned to the school, she went straight to the admissions office and told them she would be withdrawing and would try to move her things out in the morning. Then she went to her room to call her parents.

She felt relief when Dad answered the phone, because she was sure the news of her decision would be harder for Mom to handle. "Hi, Dad, it's me," she said, drawing in a quick breath for added courage.

"It's good to hear from you, Laura. How are things going with your studies?"

She shifted the phone to her other ear. "I. . . uh. . .need to tell you something."

"Oh? What's that?"

"Starting tomorrow morning, I'll be done with school."

"Done? What do you mean? You haven't even finished your first year there yet."

"I'm. . .uh. . .not planning to finish, Dad."

There was a pause, then, "Irene, you'd better pick up the phone in the kitchen. Laura's on the line."

Laura held her breath as she waited for her mother to come on. Maybe it was better this way. She could tell them both the news at the same time and be done with it.

"Hello, Laura. How are you, dear?"

"I–I'm okay."

"Our daughter has some news she wants to share with us," Dad said before Mom could add anything more.

"What news is that?"

"I've withdrawn from school, and tomorrow morning, I'll be moving in with Eli's sister so I can join the Amish church."

"What?" Mom and Dad shouted in unison.

"I'm planning to join the Amish church."

"This is not April Fool's Day, Laura," Dad said with a chuckle. "Now quit fooling around."

"I'm not kidding. I'm in love with Eli Yoder, and the only way we can be together is if I join his faith."

"Why can't he leave the Amish faith and join our world?"

"Because, Mom, his roots are deep, and he's committed to his family as well as to his religion."

"Oh, and you're not committed to your family?"

"I am, but you and Dad have your own busy lives, and you've raised me to be independent and make my own decisions." Laura paused as she groped for the right words. "This is the decision I've chosen to make."

"Laura, do you know what you're saying?" Mom's voice had risen at least an octave, and Laura had to hold the phone away from her ear. "I'm catching the next flight to Pennsylvania so I can talk some sense into you."

"You may as well save your money, because nothing you can say will make me change my mind. Besides, by the time you get here, I'll be moved out of my dorm room and into Martha Rose's house, and you don't know where that is." Laura sucked in her bottom lip. The truth was, she had no idea where Eli's sister lived, either. For that matter, she wasn't even sure Martha Rose would agree to take her in. What if the woman had said no to Eli's request? What if Laura had quit school for nothing and now had no place to go?

She shook her head, trying to clear away the troubling thoughts. It would all work out. It had to work out. Eli had said it would.

"What about Dean?" Mom asked. "I thought the two of you were–"

"It was over between me and Dean months ago. The last time we talked, I told him so, too."

"Laura, your mother and I want you to be happy," Dad said. "But is giving up the only way of life you've ever known and becoming Amish really going to make you happy?"

"Being with Eli will make me happy, and if I have to make a few sacrifices along the way in order for it to happen, then I'll learn to deal with it."

"She's got a determined spirit, this daughter of ours, and it took a lot of courage for her to make a decision such as this. I think we should give her our blessing."

Laura knew Dad was talking to Mom now, so she waited to hear what her mother's response would be.

"I don't see how you can expect me to give Laura my blessing when I know she's making the biggest mistake of her life. She won't be happy living without electricity and many other modern conveniences. She might think she's in love with this Amish man, but a few months from now, she'll change her mind; mark my words."

Laura released an exasperated sigh. "I've got to go now. I need to pack. I'll give you a call on my cell phone after I get moved so I can give you my new address. Maybe you can send me that quilt I bought at the farmers' market. It would be nice to have it in my possession again."

Mom released a couple of sobs and hung up.

"If you change your mind about this or ever need anything, don't hesitate to call," Dad said.

"Thanks, I'll remember that."

"Be happy, and please keep in touch."

"I will, Dad." Laura clicked off her cell phone and flopped onto the bed. Mom had reacted to the news pretty much the way she'd expected her to, but her father's reaction had been a complete surprise. Had he been so compliant because he wanted her to be happy, or was it possible that some part of Dad could actually identify with Laura's desire to go Plain?

Chapter 15

As Laura sat on a bench in front of the variety store in Paradise, she began to worry. She had turned in all of her books at the school, sent everything home that she didn't think she would need in her new life, and dropped off her rental car. Now she was waiting for Eli to pick her up. But what if he didn't show? What if he'd changed his mind about asking his sister to take Laura in? Maybe his folks had talked him out of his plans. Or maybe his sister had said no to his request.

She drew in a deep breath and tried to calm her nerves. The last time she'd waited on this bench for Eli and had been worried he wouldn't show, he'd only been running late. That was probably the case this time, too. At least she hoped it was.

She leaned her head against the wall behind her and tried to focus on something else. It was useless. All she could think about was Eli and how much she wanted to be with him. If he didn't show up, she would be devastated, and she'd never be able to face Darla again.

Darla had tried again this morning to get Laura to change her mind about joining the Amish faith.

She'd reminded her of how hard it was going to be and said that Laura needed to give it more thought.

Ever since the day Laura had met Eli, he'd never been far from her thoughts. She dreamed about him at night, compared him to Dean during the day, and imagined what it would be like to be Mrs. Eli Yoder.

The *clip-clop* of horse's hooves drew Laura's attention to the parking lot, and a feeling of relief flooded her soul. Eli was here. He had come for her just like he'd promised. Everything would be okay now.

As Eli led Laura up the steps to his sister's home, her insides quivered with anticipation. She'd been relieved when Eli had told her that Martha Rose had agreed to let her stay, but that was only half the battle. Laura still had lots to learn, and she worried about whether she would be accepted among Eli's friends and family.

"Don't be nervous now," Eli whispered as he opened the back door. "You'll like it here, I promise."

Laura forced a smile. "I–I hope so."

When they entered the kitchen, they were greeted by a tall, large-boned woman with a flawless complexion, hair the color of chestnuts, and dark brown eyes. She offered a warm, friendly smile. "You must be Laura."

Laura's only reply was a quick nod.

"I'm Eli's sister, Martha Rose."

Laura extended her hand. "It's nice to meet

you, and I appreciate your letting me stay here."

Martha Rose glanced over at Eli and smiled. "I'd do most anything for my little brother."

Eli chuckled. "Should I bring in Laura's things while you show her around?"

"Jah, sure." Martha Rose motioned toward the door leading to a hallway. "Why don't we start with the upstairs, since that's where Laura's bedroom will be?"

Eli disappeared out the back door, and Laura followed Martha Rose up the stairs.

"This will be yours," Martha Rose said, opening the door to the second room on the left. "It's right across the hall from the bathroom."

Laura breathed a sigh of relief. At least this Amish farm had indoor plumbing, and for that she felt grateful. Darla had told her that most Amish in the area used diesel or propane-operated generators, so they had indoor bathrooms with hot and cold running water, but a few homes still used outhouses.

As Laura stepped into the bedroom where she would soon take up residence, a shockwave spiraled through her. It was even smaller than her dorm room at the school had been. Plain. . .so very plain. There was a double bed, a chest of drawers with a washbowl and pitcher sitting on top, and a small cedar chest at the foot of the bed. Dark shades hung at the two windows, and except for a small, braided throw rug, the hardwood floor was bare. Instead of a closet, a row of wooden pegs was connected to a narrow strip of wood lining one wall.

"Here are a few dresses you can wear." Martha Rose handed Laura two long, cotton frocks. One was navy blue, the other a dark shade of green. "You're a bit shorter than me, so they might be kind of long." She grinned. "Better too long than too short."

Laura was too dumbfounded to even speak. In her excitement to join the Amish faith and win Eli's heart, she had almost forgotten that she would be expected to wear such plain, simple clothing.

"I have a white head covering for you. And you'll need a dark bonnet to wear over it when you go out at certain times."

Laura nodded mutely as she was given the rest of her new wardrobe. *What have I gotten myself into? Can I really exchange my jeans and T-shirts for long, plain dresses?* She inhaled deeply, reminding herself that she could do this and that it was for a good cause. Her determination and love for Eli would see her through.

"We'll go to the boot and harness shop tomorrow and buy you some black leather shoes for church and other special occasions," Martha Rose said. "If you already own a pair of sneakers, you can wear them for everyday." She looked down at her bare feet and smiled. "Of course, most of us just go barefoot around home, especially during the warmer weather. It saves our shoes, and it's much cooler."

Laura shifted from one foot to the other. Barefoot? Sneakers and black leather shoes? Were those her only choices? "Don't your feet get dirty and sore, running around barefoot?"

"Jah, but they toughen up, and I always wash my feet before going to bed."

Laura shrugged. What could she really say? She'd gotten herself into this predicament, and it was of her own choosing that she had decided to go Plain. She would simply draw from her inner strength and do whatever was necessary in order to convince Eli and his family she was worthy of being part of their clan.

The next few weeks were busy. . .busier than Laura ever imagined. She had so much to learn about cooking, sewing, baking, and doing laundry and other household chores, not to mention the outside jobs. Gathering eggs, slopping the hogs, and cultivating the garden were all things she had never done before. It was dirty, backbreaking work, and she made so many foolish mistakes at first.

One morning after breakfast, as Laura was in her room getting ready for a date with Eli, she glanced at herself in the hand mirror she'd found in the drawer and dug underneath her underwear for the satchel of makeup she had stashed away. She knew Amish women didn't wear makeup, but she wasn't ready to part with those things, so she hadn't mailed them home with all her clothes.

Today was Saturday, and Eli would be coming soon to take her for a buggy ride. They planned to go into Paradise and do some shopping, then stop for a picnic on the way home.

Laura stared longingly at the tube of lipstick

she held in her hand. *What would it hurt to apply a little color to my pale lips so Eli will find me attractive? I wouldn't want him to lose interest in me and go back to Pauline.*

Laura blended the coral lipstick with the tips of her fingers, then reached inside the makeup case for some blush. A little dab blended on each cheek made her look less pale. She added a coat of mascara to her eyelashes and filled in her brows with a soft cinnamon pencil.

"There now," she whispered to her reflection. "I almost look like my old self—not nearly so plain." She glanced down at her plain green dress and scowled. "What I wouldn't give to put on a pair of jeans and a T-shirt." She slipped her head covering on and sighed. "Guess I'd better get used to this if I'm ever going to fit in here."

Downstairs in the kitchen, Laura found Eli's sister and his mother sitting at the table, drinking a cup of tea and eating shoofly pie. Just the smell of the molasses-filled pastry made Laura's stomach churn. She didn't think she would ever acquire a taste for this particular dessert.

"*Guder mariye*," Martha Rose said cheerfully when Laura joined them.

"Good morning," she responded with a slight nod. Learning Pennsylvania Dutch was another challenge for Laura, along with studying the Bible and learning the church rules, which the Amish called the *Ordnung*. She glanced over at Eli's mother. "I didn't realize you were here, Mary Ellen."

"Came to help Martha Rose do some baking."

Mary Ellen studied Laura intently, making her feel like a bug under a microscope. "What's that you've got on your face?"

Laura shrugged and reached for an apple from the ceramic bowl sitting in the center of the table. "Just a little color to make me look less pale," she mumbled as she bit into the succulent fruit.

"Makeup's not allowed. Surely you must know that."

Laura blinked a couple of times as she stared at Mary Ellen. "What harm is there in trying to make myself a bit more attractive?"

" 'Favour is deceitful, and beauty is vain: but a woman that feareth the Lord, she shall be praised,' " Mary Ellen quoted.

Laura squinted her eyes. "Where'd you hear that?"

"It's in the book of Proverbs," Martha Rose answered, before her mother had a chance to respond.

Mary Ellen looked right at Laura. "Face powder may catch some men, but it takes baking powder to hold them."

Martha Rose giggled, and her mother chuckled behind her hand, but Laura sat stony-faced. She didn't see what was so funny. Besides, she had the distinct impression these two Plain women were laughing at her, not at the joke Eli's mother had just shared.

Laura felt foolish for doing something she knew was wrong, but it irritated her that Mary Ellen had made a joke at her expense. She was sure the woman didn't like her. With a sigh of frustration, she pushed her chair away from the table and stood. "Sorry about the mistake. I'll go wash the makeup off my face now."

Eli whistled as he hitched his horse to the open buggy. He was looking forward to his date with Laura, but he still couldn't believe she had actually agreed to become Plain. She was beautiful, talented, and smart. He was sure she could have any man she wanted, yet it was him and his way of life she had chosen. It almost seemed too good to be true.

"I'll make her happy," he said aloud. The horse whinnied and nuzzled the back of Eli's arm.

"At least *you* aren't givin' me a hard time. If Mom and Pop had their way, I'd be married to Pauline by now, not courting Laura."

Eli knew his parents had his best interests at heart, but they didn't understand how much he loved Laura. Even though his folks had agreed to try and make her feel welcome, he was sure it was only to please him. Deep in his heart, Eli felt they were just waiting for Laura to give up and leave so they could say, "I told you so."

He was glad Martha Rose seemed to be on his side and had agreed to let Laura stay there. It was a comfort to know his sister was willing to mentor his fancy English woman who wanted to become Plain. Mom and Pop were another matter. They were no more thrilled about the idea of Laura joining the Amish faith than they had been about Eli seeing her when she was still English. It was hard to understand how Mom, who normally was so pleasant and easygoing, had seemed almost rude to Laura when she'd first visited their home. Even now, as Laura prepared to become Amish, there was a coolness in the way his mother spoke to Laura. He hoped things would change once Laura took her training and was baptized into the faith.

Eli climbed into the driver's seat and gathered up the reins. He knew Mom had gone over to Martha Rose's this morning so she would see Laura before he did.

He clucked to the horse, and it moved forward. "Let's hope things went well between Laura and Mom, for if they didn't, I'm likely to have a cross woman on my hands for the rest of the day."

When Laura greeted Eli at the back door, he thought she looked like she'd lost her best friend. "What's wrong? Aren't you happy to see me this morning? Do you still want to go to Paradise and then on a picnic?"

"Of course I want to go."

"Would you like to come in and have a piece of shoofly pie?" Mom asked.

Eli glanced at his mother, who sat at the kitchen table with Martha Rose. "Jah, sure."

"I think we should be on our way," Laura said, stepping between Eli and the table.

He frowned. "What's your hurry?"

"I've got quite a bit of shopping to do, and we

don't want to get to the lake too late." She rushed past him, pulled a dark blue sweater from the wall peg by the back door, and grabbed the wicker picnic basket sitting on the cupboard.

Eli looked at Laura standing by the door, tapping her foot. He glanced back at the table, and his mouth watered just thinking about how good a hunk of that pie would taste.

As though sensing his dilemma, Martha Rose said, "Why don't you take a few pieces along? You and Laura can have it with the picnic lunch she made."

Eli shrugged. "I guess I can wait that long to sample some of your good cooking, sister."

He reached for the pie, but Martha Rose was too quick for him. She had already begun slicing it by the time he got to the table. "If you really want to help, get some waxed paper from the pantry," she instructed.

He did as he was told, not caring in the least that his big sister was bossing him around. He'd grown used to it over the years. Besides, she really didn't mean to sound so pushy. Martha Rose had always been a take-charge kind of person. She was pleasant and kind, so he could tolerate a little ordering about now and then.

"You two have a good day," Martha Rose said as Eli and Laura started out the back door.

"Jah, and be sure to be home in time for chores and supper," Mom called.

"I will," Eli said, closing the door behind them.

Laura stopped at the bottom of the stairs, and

Eli nearly ran into her. "What'd you stop for? I could have knocked you to the ground."

She scowled at him. "You're henpecked. Do you know that?"

His eyebrows furrowed. "You don't know what you're saying, Laura."

Her nose twitched as she blinked rapidly. "Those two women have you eating out of the palms of their hands."

Eli started walking toward his open buggy. "They do not. I just happen to like pleasing them, that's all. I love Mom and Martha Rose, and they're both mighty good to me."

"Well, they're not so good to me."

Eli whirled around to face Laura. She looked madder than one of his father's mules when a big old horsefly had taken a bite out of its ear. "How can you say they're not good to you? Martha Rose took you in, didn't she?"

Laura opened her mouth, but before she could respond, Eli rushed on. "She gave you some of her dresses to wear, took you shopping for shoes and the like, and both she and Mom have taken time out of their busy days to teach you about housekeeping, cooking, Bible reading, and so many other things you'll need to know before joining the church."

Laura's lip protruded as she handed Eli the picnic basket. "I should have known you wouldn't understand. You're one of them."

"What's that supposed to mean?" Eli asked as he climbed into his rig and took up the reins.

Laura stood on the other side of the buggy with

her arms folded. "It means you're Amish and I'm not. I'm still considered an outsider, and I don't think anyone in your family will ever accept me as anything else."

"Of course they will." He glanced at her out of the corner of his eye. "Are you getting in or not?"

"Aren't you going to help me?"

He groaned. "I might have, if you hadn't been naggin' at me. Besides, if you're going to be Amish, then you'll need to learn how to get in and out of our buggies without any help when you're going someplace on your own."

Laura was so angry she was visibly shaking. If she hadn't been sure she would be expected to help with the baking, she would have turned around and marched right back to the house. It would serve Eli right if she broke this date!

"Time's a-wasting," Eli announced.

She sighed deeply, lifted her skirt, and practically fell into the buggy.

Eli chuckled, then snapped the reins. The horse jerked forward, and Laura was thrown against her seat. "Be careful! Are you trying to throw my back out?"

Eli's only response was another deep guffaw, which only angered her further.

Laura smoothed her skirt, reached up to be sure her head covering was still in place, then folded her arms across her chest. "I'm glad you think everything's so funny. You can't imagine what I've been through these past few weeks."

"Has something bad happened?" Eli looked over at her with obvious concern.

She moaned. "I'll say."

"What was it? Did you get hurt? How come I didn't hear about it?"

She shook her head. "No, no, I wasn't hurt. At least not in the physical sense."

"What then?"

"I've nearly been worked to death every day since I moved to your sister's house. It seems as though I just get to sleep and it's time to get up again." She frowned. "And that noisy rooster crowing at the top of his lungs every morning sure doesn't help things, either."

"Pop says the rooster is nature's alarm clock," Eli said with a grin.

How can he sit there looking so smug? Laura fumed. *Doesn't he care how hard I work? Doesn't he realize I'm doing all this for him?*

"In time, you'll get used to the long days. I bet someday you'll find pleasure in that old rooster's crow."

"I doubt that." She held up her hands. "Do you realize that every single one of my nails is broken? Not to mention embedded with dirt I'll probably never be able to scrub clean. Why, the other morning, Martha Rose had me out in the garden, pulling weeds and spading with an old hoe. I thought my back was going to break in two."

"You *will* get used to it, Laura."

She scrunched up her nose. "Maybe. If I live to tell about it."

Chapter 16

Laura's days at the Zook farm flew by despite her frustrations. As spring turned quickly into summer, each day became longer, hotter, and filled with more work. Instead of "becoming used to it," Laura found herself disliking each new day. How did these people exist without air-conditioning, ceiling fans, and swimming pools? How did the women deal with wearing long dresses all summer instead of shorts?

Laura and Martha Rose had gone wading in the creek near their house a few times, while Amon taught little Ben how to swim. The chilly water helped Laura cool down some, but she missed her parents' swimming pool and air-conditioned home.

Another area of Amish life Laura hadn't become used to was the three-hour church service held every other Sunday in a different member's home. She had gone to church only a few times in her adult life—mostly on Easter and Christmas—but she'd never had to sit on backless, wooden benches or been segregated from the men. The Amish culture still seemed strange to her and very confusing. She couldn't visit with Eli until the service was over, lunch had been served, and everything had been cleaned up. If Laura had ever thought life as an Amish woman was going to be easy, she'd been sorely mistaken. She couldn't even keep her cell phone charged because Amon's farm had no electricity. On days like today when she was hot and tired, she wondered if she had made a mistake by asking to join the Amish church.

"It's not too late to back out," she muttered as she set a basket of freshly laundered clothes on the grass underneath the clothesline that extended from the porch into the yard. "I can go back to the school in Lancaster or home to Mom and Dad in Minneapolis. At least they don't expect me to work so hard."

A pathetic *mooo* drew Laura's attention to the fence separating the Zooks' yard from the pasture. Three black-and-white cows stood on the other side, swishing their tails and looking at her.

"Just what I need—a cheering section. Go away, cows! Get back to the field, grab a hunk of grass, start chewing your cuds, then go take a nice, long nap." She bent down, grabbed one of Amon's shirts, gave it a good shake, then clipped it to the clothesline. "At least you bovine critters are allowed the privilege of a nap now and then. That's more than I can say for any of the humans who live on this farm."

"*Kuh,*" a small voice said.

Laura looked down. There stood little Ben, gazing up at her with all the seriousness of a three-year-old. He'd said something in Pennsylvania Dutch, but she wasn't sure what he was talking about. She'd been studying the Amish dialect for a few months, but she still encountered many unfamiliar words.

"Kuh," the child repeated. This time he pointed toward the cows, still gawking at Laura like she was free entertainment.

"Ah, the cows. You're talking about the cows, aren't you?" She dropped to her knees beside the little boy and gave him a hug.

Ben looked up at her and grinned. He really was a cute little thing, with his blond, Dutch-bobbed hair, big blue eyes, and two deep dimples framing his smile. He studied the basket of clothes a few seconds as his smile turned to a frown.

"*Loch,*" he said, grabbing one of Amon's shirts.

Laura smiled when she realized the child was telling her about his father's shirt with a hole. She patted the top of Ben's head. "No doubt that shirt will end up in my pile of mending."

Ben made no comment, but then, she knew he didn't understand what she'd said. He would be taught English when he started school. With an impish grin, the boy climbed into the basket of wet clothes.

Laura was about to scold him, but Ben picked up one of his mother's dark bonnets and plunked it on top of his head. She sank to her knees and laughed so hard that tears ran down her face. The cows on the other side of the fence mooed, and the little boy giggled.

Maybe life on this humble Amish farm wasn't so bad after all.

Pauline sat on the front porch, staring at the flowers blooming in her mother's garden but not really seeing them. She'd been miserable ever since Eli had told her they had no future together and had begun dating that fancy English woman. Not that Laura looked so fancy anymore. She wore the same plain clothes as the other Amish women in their community, but there was something about the way she walked, talked, and held her body so prim and proper that made her seem out of place among the other women in their district.

Every time Pauline saw Laura at church or some other community event, it made her feel sick to the pit of her stomach. She didn't know if she would ever get over the bitterness she felt over losing Eli to someone outside their faith.

She won't be outside the faith once she's baptized and joins the church, Pauline reminded herself. *She'll be one of us, and I'll have to accept her as such, no matter how much it hurts.*

"What are you doing sitting out here by yourself?" Pauline's mother asked as she seated herself on the step beside Pauline. "I figured you'd be anxious to get some baking done before it gets too hot."

"I don't feel much like baking today. Can't it wait for another day?"

"I suppose, but we're almost out of bread, and you know how much your daed likes those ginger cookies you make so well."

Pauline made no comment; she just sat there breathing in and out, feeling as though she couldn't get enough air.

"Are you okay? You look kind of peaked this morning."

"I'm fine. Just tired is all."

Mom laid a gentle hand on Pauline's arm. "Still not sleeping well?"

"Not since. . ." Pauline couldn't finish the sentence. It pained her to think about Eli, much less speak his name.

"You've got to put your broken relationship with Eli Yoder behind you, daughter. You can't go through the rest of your life pining for something that's not meant to be."

Pauline released a shuddering sob. "It was meant to be, until *she* came along and ruined things. Eli and I were getting closer, and I was sure he would ask me to marry him after he finished his membership classes at the end of summer." Tears slipped from her eyes and rolled down her cheeks. "It's not fair, Mom. It's just not fair."

"Many things in life aren't fair, but we must learn to accept them as God's will and move on."

"I'm not sure I can do that. Not when I have to see Eli and that woman together all the time."

"Maybe you should go away for a while."

Pauline wiped her eyes with the backs of her hands and turned to face her mother. "Go away? Where would I go?"

"Maybe you could stay with your daed's sister, Irma, in Kidron, Ohio."

"I'll have to think about it."

Mom patted Pauline's hand. "You do that. Think and pray about the matter."

Laura sat at the kitchen table, reading the Bible Martha Rose had given her. Why did it seem so confusing? She had been to Sunday school and Bible school a few times when she was a girl. She'd even managed to memorize some Bible passages in order to win a prize. Why couldn't she stay focused now?

"You've been at it quite awhile. Would you like to take a break and have a glass of iced tea with me?" Martha Rose asked, pulling out a chair and taking a seat beside Laura.

Laura looked up and smiled. She really did need a break. "Thanks, I'd like that."

Martha Rose poured two glasses of iced tea and piled a plate high with peanut butter cookies.

"Are you trying to fatten me up?" Laura asked when the goodies were set on the table.

Martha Rose chuckled. "As a matter of fact, you are pretty thin. I figured a few months of living here, and you'd have gained at least ten pounds."

"Your cooking is wonderful, but I'm trying to watch my weight."

"You need to eat hearty in order to keep up your strength." Martha Rose pushed the cookie plate in front of Laura. "Please, have a few."

Laura shrugged. "I guess two cookies wouldn't hurt."

"How are your studies coming along? Has little

Ben been staying out of your way?"

"He's never been a problem. Your little boy is a real sweetheart."

"Jah, well, he can also be a pill at times." Martha Rose shook her head. "This morning I found him playing in the toilet, of all things. Said he was goin' fishing, like he and his daed did last week."

Laura laughed. "Where's the little guy now?"

"Down for a nap. I'm hoping he stays asleep awhile, because I've got a bunch of ripe tomatoes waiting to be picked. Not to mention fixing lunch and getting a bit more cleaning done. Church will be here this Sunday, you know."

"I'd almost forgotten. Guess that means we'll have to do more cooking than usual." Laura reached around to rub a tight muscle in her back, probably caused from standing long hours at the stove.

"Not really. I'm just planning to fix a pot of bean soup and some sandwiches."

"Isn't the weather kind of hot to be having soup?"

"We enjoy soup most any time of the year, and my daed always says, 'A little heat on the inside makes the outside heat seem cool.' " Martha Rose chuckled. "Dad has lots of sayings like that, and plenty of jokes to tell, too."

Laura bit into a cookie and washed it down with a sip of cold tea. She hadn't really seen a humorous side to Eli's father and wondered if he held back because of her. She had a feeling Mary Ellen wasn't the only one in Eli's family who didn't care for her, and she had to wonder if she would ever truly feel a part of them.

"How's the Pennsylvania Dutch coming along?" Martha Rose asked. "Do you feel like you're understanding the words better yet?"

"I can figure out what many words mean, but I'm still having trouble speaking them."

"Practice makes perfect. I think it might help if we spoke less English to you."

Laura nearly choked on the second bite of cookie she had taken. "You're kidding, right?"

Martha Rose shook her head. "I think you need to hear more Deitsch and less English. It will force you to try saying more words yourself."

Laura groaned. Wasn't it enough that she had to wear plain, simple clothes, labor all day on jobs she'd rather not do, conform to all kinds of rules she didn't understand, and get along without modern conveniences? Must she now be forced to speak and hear a foreign language most of the time?

As if she could read her thoughts, Martha Rose reached over and patted Laura's hand. "You do want to become one of us, don't you?"

Tears gathered in Laura's eyes, obscuring her vision. "I love Eli, and I'd do anything for him, but I–I didn't think giving up my way of life would be so hard."

"You say you love my brother, but what about your love for God? It's Him you should be trying most to please, not Eli."

Laura swallowed hard. How could she tell Martha Rose that, while she did believe in God, she'd never really had a personal relationship with Him? She wasn't even sure she wanted one. After all, what had God ever done for her? If He were on her side, then wouldn't Eli have been willing to leave his religion and become English? They could have worshiped God in any church.

"Laura?" Martha Rose prompted.

She nodded. "I do want to please God. I just hope He knows how hard I'm trying and rewards me for all my efforts."

Martha Rose's forehead wrinkled as she frowned. "We should never have to be rewarded for our good deeds or service to God. We're taught to be humble servants, never prideful or seeking after the things of this world. There's joy in loving and serving the Lord, as well as in ministering to others."

Laura thought about that. The Amish people she was living among did seem to emanate a certain kind of peaceful, joyful spirit. She couldn't figure out why, since they did without so many things.

Martha Rose pushed away from the table. "I think we should end this discussion and get busy picking in the garden, don't you?"

Laura eased out of her chair. While she had no desire to spend the next few hours in the hot sun bent over a bunch of itchy tomato plants, at least she wouldn't have to listen to any more sermons about God and what He expected of people.

A short time later, as Laura crouched in front of a clump of rosy, ripe tomatoes, she thought about home and how she'd never had a fresh out-of-the-garden tomato until she'd come here. Yesterday, she'd gone over to the Petersons, who were Martha Rose's closest English neighbors, to call her parents.

Dad had been gone on a fishing trip, which was a surprise since he rarely did anything just for fun; and Mom had mentioned that she would be hosting a garden party this weekend and was having it catered.

Probably won't have anything this fresh or tasty to eat, Laura thought as she plucked a plump tomato off the vine.

Her thoughts went to Eli. Martha Rose had told Laura that Eli liked homemade tomato ketchup, which Laura hadn't learned to make yet. There were so many things she still didn't know, and even though she disliked many of the chores she was expected to do and still hadn't gotten used to wearing a dress all the time, she never got tired of spending time with Eli. The more they were together, the more she was convinced she had done the right thing when she'd decided to become Amish. Despite the fact that Eli could get under her skin at times, he treated her with respect—nothing like Dean had done when they were dating.

Laura wasn't looking forward to another long church service this Sunday, but the promise of attending a singing that night gave her some measure of joy. It would be held in the Beachys' barn, and Eli had promised to take her. Since he would be coming to Amon and Martha Rose's for the preaching service, he would probably stick around all day, then later escort Laura to the singing. If things went as planned, she should be baptized into the Amish church by early fall, and she hoped she and Eli could get married sometime in November. Of course, he needed to propose to her first.

Eli felt a mounting sense of excitement over his date with Laura, and even though he'd told her awhile back that she should learn to get into the buggy herself, he helped her in this time, not wishing to cause another rift between them. Truth be told, Eli worried that Laura might not like the Amish way of life well enough to stay, and he didn't think he could deal with it if she decided to return to her old life.

"I've been looking forward to tonight," Laura murmured as she settled against the buggy seat.

"Jah, me, too." Eli glanced over at her and smiled. "You're sure pretty, you know that?"

Laura lifted her hand and touched her head covering. "You really think so?"

He nodded. "I do."

"But my hair's not long and beautiful anymore."

"Your hair's still long. You're just wearing it up in the back now."

"I know, but it looks so plain this way."

He reached over to gently touch her arm. "You may become one of the Plain People, but you'll never be plain to me."

When they arrived at the Beachy farm a short time later, the barn was already filled with young people. The huge doors were swung open wide, allowing the evening breeze to circulate and help cool the barn.

Soon the singing began, and the song leader led the group in several slow hymns, followed by a few faster tunes. There were no musical instruments, but the young people's a cappella voices permeated the air with a pleasant symphony of its own kind. Laura got caught up in the happy mood and was pleasantly surprised to realize she could actually follow along without too much difficulty.

When the singing ended, the young people paired off, and the games began. Laura was breathless by the time she and Eli finished playing several rounds of six-handed reel, which to her way of thinking was similar to square dancing.

"Would you like a glass of lemonade and some cookies?" Eli asked as he led Laura over to one of the wooden benches along the wall.

She nodded. "That sounds wunderbaar."

Eli disappeared into the crowd around the refreshment table, and Laura leaned her head against the wooden plank behind her. She caught a glimpse of Pauline Hostetler sitting across the room with her arms folded. She appeared to be watching her, and not with a joyful expression.

It was obvious to Laura that Pauline wasn't fond of her. In the months since Laura had been part of the Amish community, Pauline hadn't spoken one word to her. *I'm sure she's jealous because Eli chose me and not her, and I guess I can't really blame her.*

"Here you go." Eli handed Laura a glass of cold lemonade. "I was going to get us some cookies, but the plate was empty. I didn't want to wait around 'til one of the Beachy girls went to get more."

"That's okay. I ate a few too many of your sister's peanut butter cookies earlier this week, and I don't want to gain any weight."

Eli frowned. "I think you could use a few extra pounds."

Do you want me to end up looking like your slightly plump mother? Laura didn't vocalize her thoughts. Instead, she quietly sipped her lemonade. They would be going home soon, and she didn't want to say anything that might irritate Eli or provoke another argument.

Chapter 17

If you're ready to go home now, I'll get the horse and buggy," Eli told Laura after they had finished their refreshments.

She smiled up at him. "I'm more than ready."

"I won't be long. Come outside when you see my horse pull up in front of the barn. There's no point in us both getting bit up by all the swarming insects tonight." He strolled out the door, leaving Laura alone by the refreshment table. She caught sight of Pauline, who had exited the barn only moments after Eli.

"I hope she's not going after him," Laura muttered under her breath.

"What was that?"

Laura whirled around and was greeted with a friendly smile from a young woman about her age, whom she'd seen before but had never personally met.

"I was talking to myself," Laura admitted, feeling the heat of a blush creep up the back of her neck.

The other woman nodded. "I do that sometimes." Her smile widened. "My name's Anna Beachy, and you're Laura, right?"

Laura nodded. "I'm staying with Martha Rose Zook and her family."

"I know. Martha Rose and I are friends. Have been since we were kinner, but I don't see her so much now that she's married and raising a family." Anna's green eyes gleamed in the light of the gas lamps hanging from the barn rafters. "Our moms were friends when they were growing up, too."

Laura kept on nodding, although it was a mechanical gesture. While this was interesting trivia, and Anna seemed like a nice person, she was most anxious to get outside and see if Eli had the buggy ready. What was taking him so long, anyway?

"Our families have been linked together for quite a spell," Anna continued. "Martha Rose's mamm, Mary Ellen, is the stepdaughter of Miriam Hilty. The dear woman's gone to heaven now, but Miriam, who everyone called 'Mim,' was a good friend of Sarah Stoltzfus, Rebekah Beachy's mamm. Rebekah's my mamm, and she's partially paralyzed. She either uses a wheelchair or metal leg braces in order to get around. Has since she was a young girl, I'm told." Anna paused a moment, but before Laura could comment, she rushed on. "Now, Grandma Sarah is living with my aunt Nadine, and–"

Laura tapped her foot impatiently, wondering how she could politely excuse herself. "I see," she said in the brief seconds Anna came up for air. "It does sound like you have a close-knit family." She cleared her throat a few times. "It's been nice chatting with you, Anna, but Eli's outside getting his horse and buggy ready to take me home. I'd better not keep him waiting."

"Jah, okay. Tell Eli I said hello, and let him know he should inform his big sister that she owes me a visit real soon."

"Since I'm staying with Martha Rose, I'll be sure she gets the message." Laura hurried away before Anna could say anything more.

Once outside, she headed for the long line of buggies parked alongside the Beachys' barn. She stopped short when she saw Eli talking to Pauline.

When Pauline reached out and touched Eli's arm, he took a step back, bumping against his buggy. What was going on here? This didn't set well with him. Didn't Pauline know he was courting Laura?

"That English woman will never make you happy," Pauline murmured. "Take me home tonight, and let her find another way."

Eli brushed Pauline's hand aside. "I can't do that. I brought Laura to the singing, and I'll see that she gets home." He sniffed. "Besides, I love her, and as soon as she and I join the church, I'm planning to ask her to be my wife."

Pauline's pinched lips made her face look like a dried-up prune. "You're not thinking straight, Eli. You haven't been right in the head since that fancy woman came sashaying into your life."

"You have no right to say anything about Laura," Eli defended. "You don't even know her."

"I know her well enough to know she's not right for you."

Eli glanced toward the barn and spotted Laura heading out the door. "I need to go. Laura's waiting for me to give her a ride home."

Tears pooled in Pauline's eyes, and her chin trembled. "I–I thought there was something special between us. I thought–" She choked on a sob and fell into his arms.

Eli just stood there, not knowing what to do, but before he could think of anything, Laura showed up, and he knew right away that she was hopping mad.

"What's going on here?"

Pauline pivoted toward Laura. "What's it look like? Eli was hugging me."

Eli's face heated up. "Pauline, that isn't so, and you know it." He could see Laura's face in the moonlight, and it was nearly as red as his felt. How could he make her understand what had really happened? He knew she was a bit insecure in their relationship, and he was sure that seeing Pauline with her arms around him hadn't helped any.

"I should have known you were chasing after Eli when I saw you leave the barn." Laura's voice shook as she stood toe-to-toe with Pauline.

Pauline didn't flinch, nor did she back down. "All I did was say a few words to Eli, and it's not my fault he decided to give me a hug."

Eli touched Pauline's arm, and she whirled back around to face him. "I know you're not happy about me and Laura, but lying isn't going to help."

Pauline shrugged his hand away. "You'll be sorry you chose her and not me. Just wait and see if you're not." She wrinkled her nose and stalked off.

Laura was fit to be tied. Did Eli really make the first move, or had Pauline deliberately hugged him just to stir up trouble? Even if it broke her heart, she needed to know what had transpired. She had to know the truth.

"Are you ready to go home?" Eli gave her a sheepish look.

"I was ready half an hour ago. And don't go thinking you can soft-soap me with that cute, little-boy look of yours, either."

"You remind me of *en wiedicher hund*," Eli said with a chuckle. "You've got quite a temper, but seeing how you acted when you saw me and Pauline together lets me know how much you really love me."

Laura folded her arms and scowled at him. "I'm beginning to know a lot more of your Pennsylvania Dutch language, and I'll have you know, Eli Yoder, I do not look like a mad dog."

He tickled her under the chin. "You do love me though, right?"

"You know I do. That's why it always makes me angry whenever I see that woman with you." She leaned a bit closer to him. "Tell me the truth, Eli. Did she hug you, or was it the other way around?"

Eli pursed his lips. "She hugged me. Honest."

"Did you encourage her in any way?"

He shook his head. "She knows I love you, Laura, and she's jealous, so she wants to make you think there's something going on with us." He helped Laura into the buggy. "Think about it. Who's the woman

I've been courtin' all summer?"

"As far as I know, only me."

Eli went around and took his own seat, then picked up the reins and got the horse moving. "Let's stop by the lake on the way home."

Laura gazed up at the night sky. It was a beautiful evening, and the grass was lit by hundreds of twinkling fireflies. The buggy ride should have been magical for both of them. Instead, Pauline had thrown a damper on things.

Laura knew she was probably being paranoid where Pauline was concerned, but she couldn't seem to help herself. "I'm not much in the mood for love or romance right now, so I think it would be good if we just head straight to your sister's house."

Eli moaned. "Maybe our next date will go better."

"Jah, let's hope so."

Laura felt closer to Eli's sister than she did the rest of his family. Martha Rose had patiently taught her to use the treadle sewing machine; bake shoofly pies; and given her lessons in milking, gathering eggs, and slopping pigs. It was none of those things that made Martha Rose seem special, however. It was her friendly attitude and the way she had accepted a complete stranger into her home. Laura wasn't sure if it was Martha Rose's hospitable nature or if she was only doing it to please her brother, but living with this young woman and her family for the past few months had helped Laura understand the true meaning of friendship.

Having been raised as an only child in a home where she lacked nothing, Laura knew she was spoiled. The Amish lived such a simple life, yet they seemed happy and content. It was a mystery she couldn't explain. Even more surprising was the fact that on days like today, she almost felt one with the Plain People. Their slow-paced, quiet lifestyle held a certain measure of appeal. Although Laura still missed some modern conveniences and the freedom to dress as she pleased, she also enjoyed many things about being Amish.

Little Ben was one of the things she enjoyed most. He often followed her around, asking questions and pointing out things she had never noticed before. He was doing it now, out in his mother's herb garden.

"*Guck emol datt!*" the child said, pointing to a clump of mint.

Laura nodded, knowing Ben had said, "Just look at that." She plucked off a leaf and rubbed it between her fingers, the way she'd seen Martha Rose do on several occasions.

Ben sniffed deeply and grinned. "*Appeditlich!*"

"Jah, delicious," Laura said with a chuckle. She was amazed at the little boy's appreciation for herbs, flowers, and all the simple things found on the farm. Most of the English children she knew needed TV, video games, and electronic toys to keep them entertained.

In spite of Laura's fascination with little Ben, she had no desire to have any children of her own. If she ever were to get pregnant, she would lose her shapely figure and might never regain it. If she had children, she might not be a good mother.

The baptismal ceremony and introduction of new members was scheduled for early September. Laura kept reminding herself that she needed to be ready by then, since most Amish weddings in this area were held in late November or early December after the harvest was done. If she wasn't able to join the church before then, it would probably be another year before she and Eli could be married. Of course, he hadn't actually proposed yet, but she was hopeful it would be soon.

For that matter, Eli still hadn't kissed her. She worried he might have lost interest in her. Maybe he was in love with Pauline and just wouldn't admit it. If only she could be sure.

Laura saw more of Eli's sister than she did him these days. His job at the furniture store kept him busy enough, but now he was also helping his father and brothers in the fields. Over the last month, she'd only seen him twice, and that was on bi-weekly church days.

"So much for courting," Laura complained as she trudged wearily toward the chicken coop. "If I weren't so afraid of losing Eli to Pauline, I'd put my foot down and give Eli an ultimatum. I'd tell him either he'd better come see me at least once a week, or I'm going home to Minnesota."

There was just one problem. Laura didn't want to go home. She loved Eli and wanted to be with him, no matter what hardships she had to face.

❧

The day finally arrived for Laura and Eli, as well as several other young people, to be baptized and join the church.

Laura was as nervous as a cat about to have kittens. She paced back and forth across the kitchen floor, waiting for Amon to pull the buggy out front.

Little Ben jerked on his mother's apron while she stood at the sink, finishing with the dishes. "*Boppli,*" he said, pointing to her stomach.

Laura stopped pacing and whirled around to face Martha Rose. "Boppli? Are you pregnant, Martha Rose?"

Martha Rose nodded. "I found out for sure a few days ago."

"How is it that Ben knew and I didn't?"

"He was there when I told Amon. I planned to tell you soon."

"Oh," was all Laura could manage. Maybe she wasn't as much a part of this family as she had believed.

Amon stuck his head through the open doorway and grinned at them. A thatch of blond hair hung across his forehead, and his brown eyes seemed so sincere. "All set?"

"Jah." Martha Rose smiled at Laura. "Let's be off then, for we sure wouldn't want to be late for Laura's and Eli's baptisms."

❧

Eli paced nervously across the front porch of their farmhouse. Today's preaching service would be held at their home, and he could hardly wait. This was the day Laura would become one of them. This was the day they would both be baptized and join the church. He was sure that, even before he'd met Laura, she was the reason he'd held off joining the church, because they were meant to be together.

The sight of Amon Zook's buggy pulling into the yard halted Eli's thoughts. He skirted around a wooden bench and leaped off the porch, skipping over all four steps.

Laura offered him a tentative-looking smile as she stepped down from the buggy. He took her hand and gave it a squeeze. "This is the day we've both been waiting for, Laura."

She nodded, and he noticed there were tears in her eyes.

"What's wrong? You aren't having second thoughts, I hope."

"No, I'm just a bit nervous. What if I don't say or do the right things today? What if–"

He hushed her words by placing two fingers against her lips. "You went through the six weeks of biweekly instructions just fine. Today's only a formality. Say and do whatever the bishop asks. Everything will be okay; you'll see."

"I hope so," she whispered.

The service started a few minutes after Eli and Laura entered the house. He took his seat on the men's side, and she sat with the women.

The song leader led the congregation in several hymns, all sung in the usual singsong fashion, and the baptismal rite followed two sermons.

When Bishop Wagler called the candidates for baptism to step forward, Laura's legs shook so hard she feared she might not be able to walk. The deacons provided a small pail of water and a cup, and the bishop told the twenty young people to get on their knees. He then asked them a question. "Are you willing, by the help and grace of God, to renounce the world, the devil, your own flesh and blood, and be obedient only to God and His church?"

Laura cringed. If she were to answer that question truthfully, she would have to say that she wasn't sure. But she couldn't let anyone know how weak her faith was or that she had no real understanding of God's grace, so along with the others, she answered, "Jah."

"Are you willing to walk with Christ and His church, and to remain faithful through life and until death?"

"Jah."

"Can you confess that Jesus Christ is the Son of God?"

Numbly, as though her lips had a mind of their own, Laura repeated along with the others, "I confess that Jesus Christ is the Son of God."

The congregation then stood for prayer, while Laura and the others remained on their knees. Bishop Wagler placed his hands on the first applicant's head, while Deacon Shemly poured water into the bishop's cupped hands and dripped it onto the candidate's head.

Laura awaited her turn, apprehensive because she wasn't sure she believed the things she had said, and trembling with joy at the prospect of hopefully receiving a marriage proposal from Eli soon. As water from the bishop's hands trickled onto Laura's head and down her forehead, she nearly broke down in tears. She would have plenty of time to think about her relationship with God. Right now, all she wanted was to be with Eli. Her love for him was all that mattered.

Chapter 18

When the service was over, Laura felt relief as she stepped outside into the crisp fall air. It was official. She was no longer a fancy English woman. For as long as she chose to remain Amish, she would be Plain.

Most of the women were busy getting the noon meal set out, but Laura didn't care about helping. All she wanted to do was find Eli. It didn't take her long to spot him, talking with Deacon Shemly over near the barn.

Are they talking about me? Is Eli asking the deacon if he thinks I'm sincere? Laura grabbed the porch railing and gripped it until her knuckles turned white. *What if one of the deacons or Bishop Wagler suspects that I'm not a true believer? What if he's counseling Eli to break up with me?*

"We could use another pair of hands in the kitchen," Martha Rose said as she stepped up behind Laura. "The menfolk are waiting to eat."

Laura spun around to face her. "Why don't the menfolk fix the meal and wait on us women once in a while?"

Martha Rose poked Laura's arm. "You're such a

kidder. Everyone knows it's a woman's duty to serve the men."

Laura opened her mouth, fully intending to argue the point, but she stopped herself in time. She had just joined the Amish church. It wouldn't be good to say or do anything that might get her in trouble. Especially not with Eli out there talking to Deacon Shemly. She might be reprimanded if she messed up now.

"What do you need help with?" Laura asked, stepping into the house and offering Martha Rose a smile.

"Why don't you pour coffee?" Martha Rose motioned to a table nearby. "The pitchers are over there."

Laura shrugged and started across the room. "Jah, okay."

As Pauline began to serve the men their meal, she tried to keep her mind focused on what she was doing and not on the terrible pain chipping away at her heart. She didn't know how she had made it through the baptismal service. It was so hard to see the joyful look on Laura's face when she was greeted with a holy kiss and welcomed into the church by Alma, the bishop's wife.

Pauline knew full well that the ritual of baptism placed Laura into full fellowship, with the rights and responsibilities of adult church membership. From this day on, she would have the right to partake of the elements during the Communion services held twice a year. She would be free to marry Eli, too, and Pauline was fairly certain he would propose to Laura as soon as possible now that they were both part of the Amish church.

She glanced across the room and spotted Laura serving the table where Eli sat. She could barely stand to see the happy expression on Eli's face, not to mention Laura's smug look. She knew it was wrong to harbor such bitterness, and it had been wrong to lie about Eli hugging her after the singing, but she couldn't seem to help herself. *Why can't Eli love me? Why can't he see how much better I would be for him than Laura?*

She squeezed her eyes shut. *Oh, God, please help me learn to deal with this.*

Lunch was finally over, and everyone had eaten until they were full. Laura was just finishing with the cleanup when she saw Eli heading her way.

"Come with me for a walk," he whispered, taking Laura's hand and leading her away from the house.

"Where are we going?"

"You'll see."

A few minutes later, they stood under a huge weeping willow tree out behind the house, away from curious stares. Eli's fingers touched Laura's chin, tipping her head back until they were staring into each other's eyes. "You're truly one of us now," he murmured.

She nodded, feeling as though her head might explode from the anticipation of what she felt certain was coming. "We're both officially Amish."

Eli bent his head, and his lips touched hers in a light, feathery kiss. She moaned softly as the kiss deepened.

When Eli pulled away, she leaned against him for support, feeling as if her breath had been snatched away. It seemed as though she had waited all her life to be kissed like that. Not a kiss of passion, the way Dean had done, but a kiss with deep emotion. Eli loved her with all his heart; she was sure of it now.

"I can finally speak the words that have been in my heart all these months," Eli said, gazing deeply into her eyes. "I love you, Laura, and I want you to be my wife."

Tears welled in her eyes and spilled over onto her cheeks. "Oh, Eli, I love you, too." She hugged him tightly. "Jah. . .I will marry you."

"I just spoke with Deacon Shemly," Eli said. "If it's all right with you, we can be married on the third Thursday in November."

"It's more than all right." Laura blinked away another set of tears. "I can't wait to call my parents and give them the news."

Eli thought his heart would burst from the sheer joy of knowing Laura would soon be Mrs. Eli Yoder. She loved him; he was sure of it. Why else would she have given up her old life and agreed to become Plain? He wanted to shout to the world that he was the luckiest man alive and had found a most special woman to share the rest of his life with.

While he wasn't able to shout it to the world, Eli knew he could share his news with the family. Grabbing Laura by the hand, he started to run.

"Where are we going?"

"To tell my folks our good news."

Laura skidded to a halt. "Do you think that's such a good idea? I mean, can't you wait and tell them later. . .after you go home?"

Eli grimaced. "Now why would I want to wait that long? The family deserves to hear our news now, when we're together."

"They may not want you marrying a foreigner," Laura argued. "Your mother doesn't like me, and–"

Eli held up his hand to stop her words. "You're not a foreigner anymore, and I'm sure Mom likes you just fine."

Laura drew in a deep breath and released it with a moan. "Okay. Let's get this over with then."

Eli spotted his folks sitting in chairs on the porch, visiting with Martha Rose and Amon. Little Ben played at their feet, dragging a piece of yarn in front of an orange-colored barn cat's nose.

Eli led Laura up the steps and motioned her to take a seat in one of the empty chairs. He pulled out another one for himself and sat beside her.

"Today's baptism was good." Mom smiled at Eli. "We're glad you finally decided to join the church."

He grinned. "And Laura, too. She's a baptized member now, same as me."

Mom nodded and looked over at Laura. "We welcome you into our church."

"Jah, you're one of us now," Pop agreed.

"Danki." Laura offered them a smile, but it appeared to be forced.

In an attempt to reassure her, Eli took her hand. "Laura's agreed to become my wife. We'd like to be married the third Thursday of November."

Mom and Pop exchanged glances, and Eli was afraid they might say something negative about his plans. Much to his relief, Mom gave a nod in Laura's direction. "We hope you'll be happy being Amish, Laura, and we hope you will make our son happy, as well."

"Eli's a fine man with much love to give," Pop put in. "He'll make a good husband and father; just you wait and see."

Martha Rose left her seat and bent down to give Laura a hug. "Congratulations. Soon we'll be like sisters."

Amon thumped Eli on the back and then added his well wishes.

Eli grinned. "I think Laura was a bit naerfich about telling you, but I knew you would all share in our joy."

Laura shot him an exasperated look, and he wondered if he'd said too much. Maybe he shouldn't have mentioned that she felt nervous.

He was trying to think up something to say that might make her feel better, when Pop spoke again. "Say, Eli, if you're gonna marry this little gal, then don't ya think you should try to fatten her up some?"

Eli looked at Laura, then back at his father, but before he could open his mouth to reply, she said,

"Why would Eli want to fatten me up?"

"I've seen you at some of our meals, and you don't hardly eat a thing. Why, you'll waste away to nothing if you don't start eatin' more."

Laura stood so quickly, she nearly knocked over her chair. "I have no intention of becoming fat, Mr. Yoder!"

Pop tipped his head back and howled. "She's a feisty one, now, isn't she, Eli?" When he finally quit laughing, he looked at Laura and said, "If you're gonna marry my son, then don't ya think you should start callin' me Johnny? Mr. Yoder makes me feel like an old man." He glanced over at Mom and gave her knee a few pats. "I'm not old yet, am I, Mary Ellen?"

Mary Ellen grunted as she pushed his hand aside. "Go on with you, now, Johnny. You've always been a silly boy, and I guess you always will be."

Mom and Pop both laughed, and soon Martha Rose and Amon were chuckling pretty good, too.

Laura tapped her foot against the porch floor, and Eli figured it was time to end it all before she said or did something that might embarrass them both.

He stood and grabbed her hand. "I think Laura and I should take a walk down to the creek. She needs to get cooled off, and I need to figure out how I ended up with such a laughable family."

Two weeks before the wedding, Laura's and Eli's names were officially published at the close of the preaching service, which was held in the Zook home.

Laura's heart bubbled with joy as she helped her future sister-in-law and several other women get lunch served after church had let out. Everyone had a job to do, even Anna Beachy's mother, Rebekah, who sat at the table in her wheelchair, buttering a stack of bread.

Martha Rose handed Laura a jar of pickled beets. "Would you mind opening these?"

Laura glanced at the other four women, but they all seemed focused on their job of making ham-and-cheese sandwiches. She shrugged and took the jar over to the cupboard, wondering why no one had said anything about her upcoming marriage. Were they displeased with Eli's choice for a wife? Would they have rather heard Pauline's name published with Eli's?

She held her breath as she forked out the beet slices and placed them in a bowl. She disliked the smell of pickled beets. If she lived to be a hundred, she would never figure out what anyone saw in those disgusting, pungent things. She had just finished putting the last one in the bowl, when Pauline entered the kitchen.

"The tables are set up in the barn." Pauline glanced over at Martha Rose. "Do you have anything ready for me to carry out there?"

"You can take this plate of sandwiches." Mary Ellen held up a tray, and Pauline took it from her, never once looking Laura's way or acknowledging her presence.

Pauline was almost to the door when Martha Rose spoke. "Laura, why don't you go with Pauline? You can take the beets, then stay to help pour beverages."

Laura drew in a deep breath and let it out in a rush. The last thing she needed was another close encounter with her rival. She didn't wish to make a scene, however, so she followed Pauline out of the room without a word of protest.

They had no more than stepped onto the porch when Pauline whirled around and faced Laura. "You think you've won Eli's heart, don't you? Well, you're not married yet, so there's still some hope for me. You may have fooled Eli, but I can see right through you."

Laura took a few steps back, wanting to get away from Pauline, and wondering if the young woman really did know she wasn't being completely honest with Eli. Sure, she loved him and wanted to get married. She had become Amish, too. But deep down inside, she didn't think she needed God and was sure she could do everything in her own strength.

"I'm sure Eli will come to his senses soon," Pauline continued to rant. "He's blinded by romantic notions right now, but one of these days he'll realize you're not really one of us and can't be trusted." She gazed into Laura's eyes, making her feel like a child who had done something wrong.

Laura's mind whirled as she tried to figure out some kind of appropriate comeback. All she could think to do was run–far away from Pauline's piercing gaze. She practically flew into the barn, dropped the bowl of beets onto the nearest table, and sprinted off toward the creek.

When Eli looked up from the table where he sat with his brothers and saw Laura dash out of the barn, he knew something wasn't right. He was about to go after her, but Pauline stepped between him and the barn door. "Let her go, Eli. I'm sure she just needs to be alone."

Eli's forehead wrinkled. "What's going on, Pauline? Did you and Laura have words?"

Pauline placed the plate of sandwiches on one of the tables and motioned him to follow her out of the barn. When they were out of earshot and away from scrutinizing eyes, she stopped and placed both hands on Eli's shoulders.

He shrugged them away. "What's this all about?"

"That English woman will never make you happy. She's an outsider and always will be. She doesn't belong here, so you'd better think twice about marrying her."

Eli's face heated up. "I love Laura, and she's not an outsider. She's a member of our church now and has agreed to abide by our Ordnung."

Pauline squinted. "You're blinded by her beautiful face and smooth-talking words, but I know what's in her heart."

"What gives you the right to try and read someone else's mind?"

"I didn't say *mind*, Eli. I said *heart*. I have a sixth

sense about things, and my senses are telling me—"

"I don't care what your senses are telling you." Eli drew in a deep breath to steady his nerves and tried to offer her a smile. "Look, Pauline, I'm sorry things didn't work out between us, but if you'll search your own heart instead of trying to see what's in other people's hearts, I'm sure you'll realize that we could never have been anything more than friends."

Pauline's blue eyes flashed angrily. "We could have been more than friends if she hadn't come along and filled your head with all sorts of fancy English ideas."

Eli was trying hard to be civil, but he'd had as much of Pauline's meddling as he could stand. He had to get away from her. He needed to be with Laura.

"I never meant to hurt you," he said sincerely, "but I love Laura, and she loves me. She gave up being English so we could be together, and nothing you say is going to change my mind about her."

Pauline's eyes filled with tears, making Eli feel like a heel. He was sorry for hurting her, but it didn't change anything. He didn't love her now and never had. Even when they'd been courting, he'd only seen her as a friend.

Eli gently touched her arm. "I pray you'll find someone else to love." He walked away quickly, hoping she wouldn't follow. His life was with Laura, and she needed him now.

Laura sank to the ground and leaned heavily against the trunk of a tree as she gazed at the bubbling creek. *Maybe I made a mistake thinking I could become part of a world so plain and simple. Maybe Eli should have chosen Pauline.*

She sucked in her bottom lip, and a fresh set of tears coursed down her cheeks. Could Pauline really see through her? Did the accusing young woman know Laura was only pretending to be a follower of God?

But how could she know? No one knew what was in Laura's heart or mind. She'd taken her biblical training classes, studied the Amish language, and learned how to cook, sew, and keep house. She wore plain clothes and no makeup and had learned to live without electricity or many other modern conveniences. What more was there? Why would Pauline think she couldn't be trusted?

"Because you can't," a voice in her head seemed to taunt. *"You're lying to Eli, and you're lying to yourself."*

Laura dropped to the ground and sobbed. She knew what she wanted out of life–Eli Yoder. She wanted him more than anything. If she had to pretend to have a relationship with God in order to join the Amish faith so she and Eli could be married, what harm had been done?

Laura jerked her head when someone touched her shoulder. She looked up and saw the face of the man she loved staring down at her.

"What's wrong? Why are you crying?" he asked, helping Laura to her feet.

"I–I had an encounter with your ex-girlfriend." She sniffed and reached up to wipe the tears from her face. "Pauline doesn't like me, and she's trying to come between us."

"No, she's not. I just spoke with Pauline, and I put her in her place but good."

"You did?"

He pulled her into his arms. "I told Pauline it's you I love, and nothing she says will ever change my mind."

"You mean it?"

"Jah, I do. Pauline and I have never been anything more than friends, and she knows it. I don't understand why she's bent on making trouble, but don't worry, because I'll never stop loving you, Laura." Eli bent to kiss her, and Laura felt like she was drowning in his love. Everything would be all right now. It had to be.

Chapter 19

Laura was excited about the wedding and pleased that her parents would be coming soon. She was anxious for them to meet Eli. Her friend Shannon wouldn't be coming, because she had gone to California to visit her grandmother who was dying of cancer. Darla wouldn't be coming, either, because she had to work. But that was all right with Laura. She knew Darla didn't approve of her becoming Amish. The last letter she'd received from Darla had said that she'd finished school and was working in Philadelphia, designing windows for one of the big department stores.

Laura had asked Anna Beachy and Nancy Frey, the schoolteacher, to be her attendants, and the ceremony would be held at Amon and Martha Rose's house, since Laura lived with them.

"When are your parents arriving?" Martha Rose asked as she and Laura sat at the table, putting the finishing touches on Laura's wedding dress.

Laura snipped a piece of thread and smiled. "Their plane was supposed to get into Harrisburg late last night, and they were going to rent a car and drive out here as soon as they'd had some breakfast this morning, so I expect they should be showing up soon."

"They're more than welcome to stay with us. We have plenty of room."

"I know you do, and it's a kind offer, but Mom and Dad are hotel kind of people. I don't think they would last five minutes without TV or a microwave."

Martha Rose pursed her lips. "You're managing."

"Jah." Laura smiled. "I'm anxious for them to get to know all of you before the wedding on Thursday."

"It will be nice to meet them, as well."

"Since tomorrow will be such a busy day for us, what with getting things ready for the wedding and all, I figured it would be best if they weren't in the way."

Martha Rose's eyebrows lifted in question. "Why would they be in the way? If they'd like to help, I'm sure we can find plenty for them to do."

"The Amish lifestyle is quite different from what they're used to, and Mom's idea of work is a full day of shopping or traipsing around town trying to drum up donations for one of her many charity functions." Laura sighed. "I just hope they don't try to talk me out of marrying Eli."

"Why would they do that? I'm sure you've told them how much you love my brother."

"Oh, yes, and Dad said if I was happy, then he was, too. I think it gives him pleasure to see me get what I want."

"Having one's way is not always of the Lord," Martha Rose admonished. "We're taught to be selfless, not self-centered. Surely you learned that from your religious training prior to baptism."

"Certainly. I just meant when I was younger and didn't know much about religious things, I was rather spoiled." She shrugged. "Dad still thinks of me as his little girl, but I know he and Mom both want my happiness."

"So, you're happy being Amish?"

"Of course. Why wouldn't I be?"

Martha Rose opened her mouth as if to answer, but their conversation was interrupted when a car came up the graveled driveway, causing their two farm dogs to carry on.

Laura jumped up and darted to the back door. "It's them! My folks are here!" She jerked the door open and ran down the steps.

Her father was the first to step from their car, and the bundle of fur in his hands brought a squeal of delight from Laura's lips. "Foosie!" Her arms went around Dad's waist, and she gave him a hug.

"Your mother and I thought you might like to have your cat, now that you're about to be married and will soon have your own home."

Mom stepped out of the car and embraced Laura. "It's good to see you." She frowned and took a few steps back. "Oh, dear, you've changed, and you look so tired. What happened to our beautiful, vibrant daughter, and why are you dressed in such plain clothes?"

Laura had expected some reservations on her parents' part, but her mother's comment took her by surprise. If she wasn't beautiful anymore, did that mean she was ugly?

"Laura is still beautiful. . .in a plain sort of way, and you should know enough about the Amish to understand why she's dressed that way." Dad raised his eyebrows at Mom, then handed the cat over to Laura. "Here you go, sweetie."

Laura rubbed her nose against Foosie's soft fur and sniffed deeply. "I–I don't think I can keep her."

"Why not?" Mom asked.

"Eli and I will be living with his parents until our own house is complete." Laura stroked Foosie's head. "Since it will be several months before it's done, Eli's folks might not appreciate having an inside cat invade their home."

"But I thought Amish people liked animals." Dad gazed around the farmyard and pointed to the cows in the field. "See, there's a bunch of animals."

"Don't forget about those dreadful dogs that barked at us when we pulled in," Mom added.

Laura shook her head. "Those are farm animals. They're not pampered pets."

"Be that as it may, I would think your husband would want you to be happy," Mom said as she fluffed the sides of her windblown hair.

Before Laura could respond, Martha Rose was at her side, offering Laura's parents a wide smile. "I'm Martha Rose Zook. And you must be Laura's folks."

Mom nodded, and Dad extended his hand. "I'm Wesley Meade. This is my wife, Irene."

"I'm glad to meet you," Martha Rose said, shaking his hand.

"This is a nice place you've got here. I've always

had a fondness for the country life," Dad said in a wistful tone.

Martha Rose motioned toward the house. "Won't you please come inside? It's kind of nippy out here in the wind, and I've got some hot coffee and freshly baked brownies waiting."

"Sounds good to me." Dad's wide grin brought a smile to Laura's lips. He looked like an enthusiastic child on Christmas morning.

Everyone followed Martha Rose to the house. When they stepped onto the back porch, Laura halted. "Uh, what would you like me to do with my cat?"

Martha Rose blinked. "Ach! I didn't realize you were holding a cat. Where'd it come from?"

"We brought it from Minnesota," Dad answered. "Foosie is Laura's house pet."

Laura rocked back and forth on her heels. What if Martha Rose made her put Foosie out in the barn? She knew the cat would never get along with the farm cats. Besides, she might get fleas.

"Bring the cat inside," Martha Rose said, opening the door. "I'm sure Ben would love to play with her awhile."

Once Laura's parents were seated at the kitchen table, Laura placed Foosie on the floor beside Ben. He squealed with delight and hugged the cat around the neck.

"Now don't *dricke* too hard," Martha Rose admonished her son. She quickly poured mugs of steaming coffee, and Laura passed around the plate of brownies.

"What's a dricke?" Mom asked.

"It means 'squeeze,' " Laura explained.

"Schee bussli," Ben said, as Foosie licked his nose.

"Ben thinks Foosie is a nice kitten," Laura said, before either of her parents could raise the question.

Martha Rose handed Laura's father a mug. "Laura says you plan on staying at a hotel in Paradise while you're here."

He nodded. "That's right. We made our reservations as soon as Laura phoned and told us about the wedding, and that's where we stayed last night when we got in."

"You're more than welcome to stay here. We have plenty of room."

Dad's eyes brightened. "Really? You wouldn't mind?"

Mom shook her head while smiling sweetly. "That's kind of you, Martha Rose, but I think it would be less hectic if we stay at the hotel."

Dad shrugged, but Laura didn't miss the look of disappointment on his face. "Whatever you think best, dear," he mumbled.

"I made my own wedding dress." Laura held up the pale blue dress she'd been hemming earlier.

Mom's mouth dropped open. "Oh, my! It doesn't look anything like a traditional wedding gown."

"It's a traditional Amish dress," Martha Rose stated.

"I see."

Laura could see by the pinched look on her mother's face that she was anything but happy about this Plain wedding. For that matter, she was probably upset about Laura marrying an Amish man. Mom most likely thought her only daughter had lost her mind.

Laura turned to look at her dad. He was grinning like a Cheshire cat and obviously enjoying the homemade brownies, for he'd already eaten three.

"Eli and his parents are coming over for supper," Laura said, changing the subject. "I'm anxious for you to meet him."

Martha Rose nodded. "Eli's excited about meeting your folks, too."

Eli opened the Zooks' back door and stepped inside, along with his folks and two brothers. Laura, who had been standing near the kitchen sink, rushed to his side. "My parents are here, and I'm so glad you came!"

Eli grinned and squeezed her hand. "I'm glad, too."

Introductions were soon made, and Eli knew right away that he was going to like Laura's father. He wasn't so sure about her mother, though. Irene seemed to be scrutinizing everything in the room, and she had said very little to either Eli or his family.

Soon everyone took their seats at the table. Laura and Martha Rose had made a scrumptious-looking supper of ham, bread stuffing, mashed potatoes, green beans, coleslaw, and homemade bread.

All heads bowed in silent prayer, and Eli noticed that Laura looked relieved when her parents followed suit.

"Laura tells me you work in a law office," Eli

said as he passed Laura's dad the platter of ham.

"Sure do. In fact, I have several other lawyers working for me." Wesley grinned and forked two huge pieces of meat onto his plate. "Umm. . .this sure looks tasty."

"Pop raises some hogs," Lewis spoke up. "He's always got plenty of meat to share with Martha Rose and Amon."

Eli's father nodded and spooned himself a sizable helping of bread stuffing. "I'm not braggin' now, but I think I've got some of the finest hogs in Lancaster County."

Mom reached over and patted Pop's stomach. "Jah, and some pretty good milking cows, too."

Laura moved the fork slowly around her plate, and Eli noticed that she hadn't taken more than a few bites of food since they'd sat down.

Pop glanced over at Laura's father and frowned. "Say, I'm wonderin' just how much influence you have on that daughter of yours."

Wesley gulped down some milk before he answered. "I'm not altogether sure. Why do you ask?"

Pop pointed a finger at Laura's plate. "She eats like a bird. Just look at her plate. Hardly a thing on it!"

Laura's face blanched, then turned red as a cherry. "I eat enough to sustain myself. I just don't think one needs to become chubby in order to prove one's worth."

The room became deathly quiet, and Eli could almost feel her embarrassment. It wasn't like Laura to blurt something out like that, and he had to wonder what had gotten into her. Was she nervous because her fancy English parents were here? Did she feel embarrassed for them to be sitting at the same table with a bunch of Plain folks?

"I. . .um. . .meant to say, I prefer to watch my weight," Laura quickly amended. "If others choose to overeat, that's their right."

"Laura, what are you saying?" Eli whispered. "Are you trying to make some kind of trouble here tonight?"

She shook her head. "I–I'm sorry. I don't know what came over me."

"I think our daughter might be a bit nervous." Irene offered a pleasant smile as she patted Laura's arm. "It isn't every day she introduces her father and me to her future husband and in-laws."

Martha Rose nodded. "Laura's been jittery as a dragonfly all day. Haven't you, Laura?"

Laura's only reply was a quick shrug.

"In fact, Laura did most of the work today, just to keep her hands busy," Martha Rose added.

"I did work pretty hard, but that's because I wanted Martha Rose to rest." Laura glanced over at her mother. "Martha Rose is in a family way."

Irene's eyebrows furrowed. "Family way?"

"She's pregnant, hon." Wesley chuckled. "I haven't heard that expression since I was a boy growing up on the farm, but I sure can remember what 'being in a family way' means."

"Your folks were farmers?" The question came from Pop, who leaned his elbows on the table as he scrutinized Laura's father.

Wesley nodded. "My parents farmed a huge

spread out in Montana, but my father sold the farm several years ago since none of us boys wanted to follow in his footsteps." His forehead wrinkled. "Sometimes I wonder if I made the wrong choice, becoming a fancy city lawyer instead of an old cowhand."

Little Ben, who up until this moment had been busy playing with the bread stuffing on his plate, spoke up for the first time. "*Maus!*" He pointed to the floor, disrupting the conversation.

"Maus? Where is it?" Martha Rose was immediately on her feet.

"*Schpringe*, bussli!" Ben bounced up and down in his chair.

"What on earth is going on?" Irene's high-pitched voice held a note of concern.

"Aw, it's just a little mouse, and Ben's tellin' the kitty to run," Jonas said with a chuckle. "I'll bet that fluffy white cat will take 'em in a hurry."

"Fluffy white cat?" Mom's eyes were wide. "When did you get an indoor cat, Martha Rose?"

Martha Rose gave no reply, just held a broom in her hand and ran around the kitchen, swinging it this way and that. It was a comical sight, and Eli laughed, right along with the rest of the men.

Foosie dodged the broom and leaped into the air, as the tiny, gray field mouse scooted across the floor at lightning speed. By now, everyone at the table was either laughing or shouting orders at Martha Rose.

"Open the door!" Amon hollered. "Maybe it'll run outside."

Laura jumped up and raced for the door. "No, don't open that door! Foosie might get out, and I'd never be able to catch her once the dogs discovered she was on the loose."

Foosie was almost on top of the mouse, but just as her paw came down, the critter darted for a hole under the cupboard, leaving a very confused-looking cat sitting in front of the hole, meowing for all it was worth.

Laura's father was laughing so hard that tears rolled down his cheeks. "Well, if that doesn't beat all. In all the years we've had that cat, I don't believe I've ever seen her move so fast." He wiped his eyes with a napkin and started howling again.

Laura planted both hands on her hips. "I don't see what's so funny, Dad. Poor Foosie has never seen a mouse before. She could have had a heart attack, tearing around the kitchen like that."

Another round of laughter filled the room. Even Martha Rose, who moments ago had been chasing the mouse with her broom, was back in her seat, holding her sides and chuckling as hard as everyone else.

Eli stood and moved to Laura's side. "I think you were nervous for nothing. The cat and mouse game got everyone in a happy mood."

"So what did you think of Eli and his family?" Wesley asked his wife as they drove back to their hotel in Paradise later that evening.

She shrugged, a small sigh escaping her lips.

"They seemed like nice enough people, but I don't understand how our daughter thinks she can ever fit in with them."

He drummed his fingers along the edge of the steering wheel. "She's already one of them, Irene. Laura has joined the Amish church and is about to marry an Amish man."

"I know that, Wesley, but Laura is used to nice things—modern conveniences, pretty clothes, makeup, and pampering. It doesn't seem right to see her dressed so plainly or watch her washing dishes over a sink full of hot water the way she did tonight after we ate dinner."

"Have you heard her complain?"

"Not in so many words, but you saw how tired she looked, and I sensed her unhappiness." She paused and released another sigh. "And what of that comment she made tonight about not wanting to get fat?"

"She was feeling nervous about us meeting Eli and his folks. You mentioned that yourself."

"Maybe so, but I've got a feeling our daughter will be making a mistake by marrying Eli, and I'm afraid she won't realize it until it's too late." She glanced over at him and shook her head. "The Amish don't believe in divorce, you know. Laura mentioned that in one of her letters."

He shrugged. "I think you worry too much. It was obvious to me by the way Laura and Eli looked at each other that they're very much in love. If our daughter loves a man so much that she can give up her fancy way of life and become Plain, then I say more power to her."

She clicked her tongue noisily. "If I didn't know better, I would think *you* had a desire to join the Amish faith."

Wesley shook his head. "You needn't worry about that. I like my favorite TV shows too much." He grinned over at her. "It would be nice to live our lives at a little slower pace, though, don't you think?"

Irene leaned her head against the seat and closed her eyes. "Dream on, dear. Dream on."

Chapter 20

Today's the big day," Martha Rose said when Laura entered the kitchen bright and early Thursday morning. "Did you sleep well last night?"

Laura yawned, reached into the cupboard for a mug, and poured herself some coffee from the pot sitting at the back of the stove. "Actually, I hardly slept a wink. I was too nervous about today."

Martha Rose pulled out a chair and motioned for Laura to take a seat. "I understand how you feel. I was a ball of nerves on my wedding day, too."

"Really? Except for that incident with the mouse the other night, I've never seen you act nervous or upset about anything."

"I wasn't really nervous about the mouse. Just wanted to get it out of my kitchen." Martha Rose got another chair and seated herself beside Laura. "I think all brides feel a bit anxious when they're about to get married."

Laura took a long, slow drink from her cup. "I hope I can make Eli happy."

"You love him, don't you?"

"Of course I do."

"Then just do your best to please him. Always

trust God to help you, and your marriage will go fine; you'll see."

Laura nodded, but she wasn't sure it would be as easy as Martha Rose made it seem. Especially since she didn't have any idea how she was going to put her trust in God.

When Pauline heard a knock on her bedroom door, she pulled the pillow over her head. A few seconds later, the door opened, and her mother called, "What are you still doing in bed? We'll be late for Eli and Laura's wedding if we don't get a move on."

"I'm not going."

"Not going?"

Pauline pushed the pillow aside and groaned. "I'm not feeling so well."

Mom took a seat on the edge of the bed and placed her hand on Pauline's forehead. "You don't have a fever."

"Maybe not, but my head is sure pounding. It feels like it's going to split wide open."

"Maybe once you've had some breakfast you'll feel better."

"I'm feeling kind of *iwwel*, too. In fact, I'm so nauseated I doubt I could keep anything down."

"Are you sure you're not just looking for an excuse to stay home from the wedding because you don't want to see Eli marry someone else?"

Unbidden tears rolled down Pauline's cheeks, and she swiped at them with the back of her hand.

"I can't go to that wedding, Mom. I just can't deal with it."

Mom offered Pauline a look of understanding as she patted her arm. "Jah, all right then. You stay here and rest in bed." She slipped quietly from the room.

Pauline rolled over so she was facing the wall and let the tears flow. She knew she had to find the strength to deal with this somehow, but if she stayed in Lancaster County, where she would see Eli and Laura so often, she didn't think her broken heart would ever mend. Maybe she would consider going to visit Aunt Irma in Ohio for a while. She might even stay there indefinitely.

The wedding began at eight thirty, with the bride and groom and their wedding party already sitting in the front row. The ministers then took their places, followed by the parents of the bride and groom, the groom's grandparents, other relatives, and friends. The men and women sat in separate sections, just as they did at regular church services.

When everyone was seated, Eli's brother-in-law, Amon, announced a hymn from the *Ausbund*. On the third line of the song, all the ministers in attendance rose to their feet and made their way up the stairs to the room that had been prepared for them on the second floor. Eli and Laura followed them to the council room.

Laura drew in a deep breath as she glanced down at her light blue wedding dress, which was covered with a white organdy apron. *Am I really doing the right thing? Will Eli and I always be as happy as we are right now? I've given up so many things to become Amish, but can I be content to do without worldly things for the rest of my life?*

She glanced over at her groom standing straight and tall and looking as happy as a child with a new toy. He was so handsome, dressed in a pair of black trousers, a matching vest, and a collarless, dark jacket. Accentuating Eli's white cotton shirt was a black bow tie, making him look every bit as distinguished as any of the lawyers who worked at her father's law firm.

Once they had entered the council room upstairs, Laura and Eli were instructed to be seated in two straight-backed chairs, where they received encouragement and words of advice from the ministers. Then Bishop Wagler asked if Eli and Laura had remained pure. With a solemn expression, Laura was glad she could answer affirmatively, along with Eli.

The bride and groom were then dismissed, while the ministers remained for council among themselves. This would be the time when they would decide who would take the different parts of the wedding ceremony.

Eli and Laura were met at the bottom of the stairs by their attendants. When they returned to the main room with the young men leading the women, the congregation sang the third verse of "*Lob Lied*," the second hymn sung at most Amish church services. The wedding party came to the six chairs reserved for them and sat in unison, the three women facing the three men.

As the congregation finished "Lob Lied," the ministers reentered the room and took their respective seats. Deacon Shemly delivered a sermon, alluding to several Bible verses related to marriage. When the sermon was over, they offered a silent prayer. All those present turned and knelt, facing the bench on which they had been sitting. Laura was relieved to see that her parents did the same.

When the prayer was over, the congregation stood, and the deacon read a passage of scripture from Matthew 19, verses 1–12. When he was done, everyone returned to their seats.

Next, Bishop Wagler stepped forward and delivered the main sermon, which included several more biblical references to marriage. Then, looking at the congregation, he said, "If any here has objection to this marriage, he now has the opportunity to declare it."

There was a long pause, and Laura glanced around the room, half expecting Pauline to jump up and announce that she was in love with Eli and would make him a better wife than Laura ever could. However, there was no sign of Pauline, and for that, Laura felt hugely relieved. Maybe Pauline had stayed home today, unable to deal with seeing Eli marry someone other than herself. Laura couldn't blame the woman. She would feel the same way if she were in Pauline's place.

"You may now come forth in the name of the Lord," the bishop said, motioning for Eli and Laura to join him at the front of the room. Laura felt the touch of Eli's arm against hers, and it gave her added courage. This was it. This was the moment she had been waiting for all these months.

There was no exchange of rings, but when the bishop asked Eli if he would accept Laura as his wife and not leave her until death separated them, Laura felt as if the tie that bound them together was just as strong as if they had exchanged circular gold bands. As Laura answered a similar question from the bishop, she couldn't help but notice that her groom's eyes were brimming with tears, and the smile he wore stretched from ear to ear. She knew without question that he really did love her, and she hoped they would be this happy for years to come.

When the wedding ceremony was over, Eli and Laura moved outside to the front lawn, while the benches were moved aside and tables were set up for the meal. Even though there was a chill in the air, the sun shone brightly, and the sky looked as clear and blue as the small pond behind his parents' home. It was a perfect day for their wedding, and Eli was content in the knowledge that Laura was now his wife.

Many who had stepped outside came over to offer Eli and Laura their congratulations, including Laura's parents. When Wesley and Irene hugged their daughter, Eli noticed the tears in their eyes, and he felt a pang of guilt. He knew he was the cause of Laura leaving her fancy life and becoming one of the Plain People. Because of her love for him, she wouldn't see her own family so much, and he wondered if she had any regrets about giving up all the modern things her wealthy father could offer and Eli couldn't.

When Wesley shook Eli's hand, Eli smiled and said, "I'll take good care of your daughter. I hope you know that."

Wesley nodded. "I believe you're an honest man, and I can see how much you love Laura."

"Jah, I do."

"Please, let her keep Foosie," Irene put in. "Our daughter needs a touch from home."

Eli grinned. "I'll speak to Mom and Pop about the cat. I'm sure they won't mind having a pet inside as long as it's housebroke."

"Oh, she is." Laura reached for Eli's hand. "Foosie's never made a mess in the house. Not even when she was a kitten."

Eli's sister stepped up to them, along with Amon and little Ben. Martha Rose hugged Eli and Laura, then excused herself to go help in the kitchen. Laura bent down and scooped Ben into her arms, and he kissed her on the cheek. It was obvious that the child was enamored with her, and she seemed to like him equally well.

She'll make a good mudder, Eli mused. *Lord willing, maybe we'll have a whole house full of kinner.*

The wedding meal was a veritable feast. Wesley had never seen so much food in one place. Long tables had been set up in the living room and adjoining room, and the benches that had been used during the ceremony were placed at the tables. Eli's parents invited Wesley and Irene to sit at a table with them, while Laura and Eli took their place at a corner table Laura had referred to as the *eck*. They were served roasted chicken, mashed potatoes, bread filling, creamed celery, coleslaw, applesauce, fruit salad, bread, butter, jelly, and coffee. Then there were the cakes–three large ones in all.

"After eating so much food, I probably won't sleep a wink tonight," Wesley said, nudging his wife with his elbow.

She grimaced. "Can't you restrain yourself and practice moderation?"

Johnny reached for another piece of chicken and snickered. "No man can practice moderation when there's food involved."

"Our two children do look happy, don't they?" Irene said, leaning close to Eli's mother, who sat on her left.

Mary Ellen nodded. "For a while, I wasn't sure things would work out between the two of them, but now that Laura's joined the church and has proven herself, I've come to believe things will turn out okay."

Johnny thumped Wesley on the back. "I'll bet in another year or so, you two will be makin' a trip back here to see your first grandchild."

As Laura and Eli sat at their corner table, eating and visiting with their guests, Eli eyed Laura's plate and noticed that she hadn't eaten much at all.

"Eat hearty, *fraa*." Eli needled her in the ribs with his elbow. "Today's our wedding day, and this is no time to diet."

She turned to face him. "If I eat too much today, I might have to go without food for the rest of the week."

He snickered. "Jah, right."

Laura glanced across the room and nodded at her parents, sitting at a table with Eli's folks. "Mom and Dad seem to be having a good time, despite the fact they hardly know anyone."

Eli nodded. "Want to sneak away with me for a bit?"

"Sneak away? As in leave this place?"

"Jah. I think it's time for us to get a little fresh air."

They pushed away from the table and slipped out the back door.

"I'll race you to the creek," Eli said, once they were on the porch.

"You're on!"

Laura was panting for air by the time they reached the water, and so was Eli. She collapsed on the grass, ignoring the chill, and Eli dropped down beside her, laughing and tickling Laura until she finally called a truce.

"So, it's peace you're wanting, huh?" Eli teased. "All right, but you'll have to pay a price for it."

Laura squirmed beneath his hands. "Oh, yeah? What kind of payment must I offer the likes of you, Eli Yoder?"

"This," he murmured against her ear. "And

this." He nuzzled her neck with his cold nose. "Also this." His lips trailed a brigade of soft kisses along her chin, up her cheek, and finally came to rest on her lips. As the kiss deepened, Laura snuggled closer to Eli.

When he finally pulled away, she gazed deeply into his dazzling blue eyes. "I love you, Eli, and I always will."

"And I love you, my *seelich*, blessed gift."

Laura and Eli spent their first night as husband and wife at Martha Rose and Amon's house so they could help with the cleanup the following morning. Then they would live with Eli's parents until their own place was finished, hopefully by spring. The thought of living with her in-laws caused Laura some concern. Would Mary Ellen scrutinize her every move? Would Laura be expected to do even more work than she had while living with the Zooks?

Forcing her anxiety aside, Laura stepped into Martha Rose's kitchen. Eli had kissed her good-bye some time ago and left with his brothers to take the benches that had been used yesterday back over to the Hiltys' place, where church would be held next week. Laura knew her folks would be here soon to say their good-byes, and she hoped Eli would be here in time.

Martha Rose was busy baking bread, but she looked up and smiled when Laura entered the room. "Did you sleep well?"

Laura shuffled across the kitchen, still feeling

the effects of sleep. She nodded and yawned. "I'm sorry I overslept. After Eli left to take the benches back, I must have dozed off again."

"Guess you needed the rest. Yesterday was a pretty big day."

"Yes, it was." Laura reached for the pot of coffee on the stove.

"There are still some scrambled eggs left." Martha Rose gestured with her head toward the frying pan at the back of the stove. "Help yourself."

Laura moaned. "After all I ate yesterday, I don't think I need any breakfast."

"Breakfast is the most important meal of the day, and now that you're a married woman, you'll need to keep up your strength."

Laura dropped into a chair at the table. "What's that supposed to mean?"

"Just that you'll soon be busy setting up your own house."

"Not really. Eli and I will be living with your folks, remember?"

Martha Rose nodded. "Jah, but not for long. If I know my brother, he'll be working long hours on your future home." She winked at Laura. "He's a man in love, and I think he'd like to have you all to himself."

Laura felt the heat of a blush stain her face. "I–I'd like that, too."

"So, dish up plenty of eggs now."

Laura opened her mouth to offer a rebuttal, but the sound of a car pulling into the yard drew her to the window. "It's my parents. They've come to say good-bye." She jerked open the door and ran down the stairs. If she was going to get all teary-eyed, she'd rather not do it in front of Eli's sister.

As soon as Mom and Dad stepped from the car, the three of them shared a group hug.

"I'll miss you," Laura said tearfully.

"Be happy," her mother whispered.

"If you ever need anything—anything at all—please don't hesitate to call." Dad grinned at her. "I know you Amish don't have phones in your houses, but you can always call from a payphone or from one of your English neighbors' like you did before."

Laura nodded as a lump formed in her throat. She didn't know why saying good-bye to her folks was so hard; she'd been away from them for some time already. Maybe it was the reality that she was a married woman now—an Amish woman, to be exact. There could be no quick plane trips home whenever she felt the need, and it wasn't likely that Mom and Dad would come here to visit that often, either.

"We should really go inside and say good-bye to your new sister-in-law," Mom said as she started for the house.

"Where's Eli?" Dad asked. "We do get to tell our son-in-law good-bye, I hope."

"Eli went with his brothers to return the benches we used at the wedding," Laura explained. "He's not back yet."

Mom's mouth dropped open. "The day after your wedding?"

Laura nodded.

Dad glanced at his watch. "We should leave

soon if we're going to make our plane."

"I'm sure Eli will be here shortly, but if you can't wait, I'll tell him–" Laura's words were halted by a piercing scream. At least she thought it was a scream. She turned toward the sound coming from the front porch and saw Foosie clinging to one of the support beams, hissing and screeching, with Amon's two dogs yapping and jumping after her.

"Foosie must have slipped out the doorway behind me." Laura turned back to face her parents. "I'd better go rescue her, and you two had better get to the airport. You don't want to miss your flight."

Mom gave Laura a quick peck on the cheek, then climbed into their rental car. Dad embraced Laura one final time, and just before he took his seat on the driver's side, he said, "Don't forget to call if you need us."

Laura nodded and blinked back tears. She offered one final wave, then raced toward the house.

Chapter 21

Laura had visited Eli's parents' home several times, but she'd never had occasion to use the restroom. It wasn't until she and Eli moved her things to his house and were settled into their room that Laura was hit with a sickening reality. Despite the fact that most Amish homes in the area had indoor bathrooms, the Yoders still used an outhouse.

"I'll never be able to use that smelly facility," she complained to Eli as they prepared for bed that night.

He flopped onto the bed with a groan. "I can't do anything about it tonight, but I promise as soon as our own home is done, it will have a bathroom."

"That will be fine for when the time comes that we get to move, but what about now? I'll need a *real* bathroom here, too, Eli."

"I'll see about turning one of the upstairs closets into a bathroom when I can find the time."

"Why can't your father or brothers build the bathroom?"

"They're busy with other things, too, and to tell you the truth, I don't think having an inside bathroom is all that important to any of 'em."

Laura paced back and forth in front of their

bedroom window. "So while I'm waiting for you to find the time, how am I supposed to bathe?"

"We have a large galvanized tub in the washroom for that. You'll heat water on the stove, and—"

"What?" Laura whirled around to face him. "I can hardly believe you would expect me to live under such primitive conditions!"

Eli looked at her as if she'd taken leave of her senses. "Calm down. You'll wake up the whole house, shouting that way." He left the bed and joined her at the window. "You've gotten used to living without other modern things, so I would think you could manage this little inconvenience. After all, it's really not such a *baremlich* thing."

She squinted. "It's a terrible thing to me. And this is not a 'little' inconvenience. It's a catastrophe!"

"Such resentment I see on your face." He brushed her cheek with the back of his thumb. "You've done well adjusting to being Amish, and I'm proud of you."

How could she stay mad with him looking at her that way? His enchanting blue eyes shone like the moonlight, and his chin dimple looked even more pronounced with his charming smile.

Laura leaned against Eli's chest and sighed. "Promise me you'll build us a decent bathroom as soon as you can."

"I promise."

The next few weeks flew by as Laura settled into her in-laws' home. There wasn't as much privacy as

Laura would have liked, but she knew the situation would only be temporary.

One evening as she and Eli were in their room looking at some of the wedding gifts they had received, Laura commented that her favorite gift was the oval braided rug in rich autumn hues that Martha Rose had made. With a smile of satisfaction, she placed it on the wooden floor at the foot of their bed. "Look how well it goes with the quilt I purchased at the farmers' market that first day we met." She motioned toward the lovely covering on their bed. "These two items can be the focal points in our room."

Eli raised his eyebrows. "I don't know anything about focal points, but the rug does looks good." He pulled Laura to his chest and rubbed his face against her cheek. "Almost as good as my beautiful wife."

"Eli, you're hurting me. Your face is so scratchy!"

He stepped back, holding her at arm's length. "It'll be better once my beard grows in fully."

She stared up at him. "I know Amish men are expected to grow a beard once they're married, but I'm going to miss that little chin dimple of yours."

Eli grinned. "It'll still be there; you'll just have to hunt for it."

Laura giggled. "You're such a tease."

He tickled her under the chin. "And that's why you love me so much, jah?"

She nodded and gave him a hug. "I surely do."

Eli knew Laura wasn't happy living with his folks,

and the absence of an indoor bathroom was only part of the problem. Almost every day when he came home from work, she greeted him with some complaint about his mother. He wasn't sure if the problem was Mom's fault or Laura's, but he hoped it would work itself out.

One Saturday, Eli decided to take Laura out for lunch at the Bird-in-Hand Family Restaurant, which had always been one of his favorite places to eat.

"This is such a nice surprise," Laura said, as the two of them were seated at a table inside the restaurant. "It's been so long since we did anything fun, I'd forgotten what it was like."

Eli snickered. "I think you're exaggerating some, but I'm glad you're enjoying yourself."

Laura glanced at the buffet counter behind them. "I might not be enjoying myself so much after I count up the calories I'll be consuming here today."

Eli's forehead wrinkled. "You worry way too much about your weight, Laura. What are you gonna do when you're in a family way?"

Laura opened her mouth as if to respond, but Selma and Elmer Hostetler stepped up to their table just then.

"Did I hear that someone's expecting a boppli?" Selma asked with a curious expression.

Laura's face turned red, and Eli shook his head. "Not us, but my sister is."

"So I heard." Selma smiled. "How many kinner are you two hoping to have?"

"Oh, as many as the good Lord allows," Eli replied.

Laura's mouth dropped open like a broken window hinge. "Huh?"

Elmer nudged his wife on the arm. "What kind of question is that for you to be askin' these newlyweds? You're worse than our outspoken daughter, and now you've embarrassed Laura."

Selma's face had reddened, too, and Eli felt the need to change the subject. "Speaking of Pauline. . . is she here with you today?"

"Nope. She moved to Kidron, Ohio, last week."

"Kidron? What's she doing there?"

"Went to be with her aunt."

Selma shifted her weight from one foot to the other as she cleared her throat. "I. . .uh. . .think she needed a change of scenery in order to get over her breakup with you. I'm sure she'll be back when she feels ready."

Eli couldn't help but feel a little guilty for being the cause of Pauline leaving her family, but what should he have done–married the girl just to make her happy?

"We ought to get ourselves some food and get back to our seats, don't ya think?" Elmer nudged Selma again.

"Jah, sure. Enjoy your meal," she said, nodding at Eli and then Laura.

When the Hostetlers moved away, Eli stood. "Guess we'd better get some food now, too."

Laura made no reply; just pushed away from the table and moved over to the buffet counter with a disgruntled expression. When they returned to the table a short time later, Eli felt a sense of concern seeing how little food she had put on her plate.

"Aren't you hungry?"

"I was until Pauline's folks showed up."

"Why would them stopping by our table make you lose your appetite?"

Laura took a drink from her glass of iced tea before she spoke. "Well, let me see now... First, Selma embarrassed me by asking if I was pregnant; then she asked how many children we planned to have. As if that wasn't enough, she made sure you knew why Pauline has moved to Ohio." She grimaced. "Didn't that make you feel uncomfortable, Eli?"

"Jah, a bit, but Selma's right about Pauline needing a change of scenery, and I'm sure it is my fault that she decided to go."

"How can it be your fault? You told me there was nothing but friendship between you and Pauline. I never understood why she thought there was more."

Eli shrugged. "I guess she wanted there to be, and when I started seeing her again after you and I decided it would be best if we went our separate ways—"

Laura held up her hand. "Just a minute. It was you who decided that, not me."

He nodded. "You're right, but that was before you'd made the decision to become Amish."

She leaned forward, staring hard at him. "So if I hadn't made that decision, would you have married Pauline?"

Eli took a sip of his water, hoping it would help cool him down. What he'd wanted to be a pleasant afternoon for the two of them was turning into a most uncomfortable situation, and if he didn't do something soon, they might end up in an argument.

"Well, Eli. . .are you going to answer my question or not?"

He set his glass on the table. "I can't rightly say, but I don't think I would have married her."

"You don't *think* so? If you never loved her, then marrying her shouldn't have been an option." Laura's voice had risen so high, Eli feared those sitting nearby would hear. "I'll bet you would have married her if I hadn't agreed to become Amish, wouldn't you?"

He put a finger to his lips. "Let's talk about something else, okay?"

"Let's just eat our food and forget about conversation."

"That suits me fine." Eli bowed his head for silent prayer, and when he lifted it, he noticed that Laura had already begun to eat. He didn't know if she had joined him in prayer or not, but he decided it was best not to ask. They could finish this discussion later.

On the buggy ride home, Laura kept her eyes shut, hoping Eli would think she was asleep and wouldn't try to make conversation. The last thing she wanted was another argument, and she was pretty sure they would quarrel if she told him all the things that were going on in her mind.

When Laura felt the buggy turn sharply and heard the wheels crunch through some gravel, she figured they had pulled into the Yoders' driveway, so she opened her eyes.

Before they got to the yard, Eli pulled back on the reins and guided the horse and buggy to the edge of the driveway.

"What are you doing? Why are we stopping?"

"So we can talk."

"There's nothing to talk about."

"I think there is."

She drew in a deep breath and released it with a weary sigh. "What do you think we need to talk about?"

"This business with you thinking I would have married Pauline, for one thing. If I've told you once, I've told you a hundred times, Pauline and I were never more than friends."

"She wanted it to be more." Laura balled her hands into fists. "I think your mother did, too."

"Mom? What's Mom got to do with this?"

Laura pursed her lips as she squinted. "Oh, Eli, don't look so wide-eyed and innocent. We've been living with your folks several weeks now. Surely you can feel the tension between me and your mother."

He merely shrugged in response.

"She's mentioned Pauline a few times, too. I think she believes Pauline would have made you a better wife."

A vein on the side of Eli's neck began to bulge, and Laura wondered if she had hit a nerve.

"Your mom is always criticizing me," she continued. "I can never do anything right where she's concerned."

"I don't believe that."

"Are you calling me a liar?"

"No, but I think I know Mom pretty well."

"You don't know her as well as you think. She scrutinizes my work, and she—"

"Enough! I don't want to hear another word against my mamm!"

As the days moved on, Laura became more frustrated. Nothing seemed to be going right. Their house still wasn't done; Eli wasn't nearly so cheerful and fun-loving anymore; Foosie was an irritant to Eli's mother; Laura dreaded the extra chores she was expected to do; and worst of all, she couldn't stand that smelly outhouse! She was on her way there now and none too happy about it.

On previous trips to the privy, she'd encountered several disgusting spiders, a yellow jackets' nest, and a couple of field mice. She was a city girl and hated bugs. She shouldn't have to be subjected to this kind of torture.

Laura opened the wooden door and held it with one hand as she lifted her kerosene lantern and peered cautiously inside. Nothing lurking on the floor. She held the lamp higher and was about to step inside when the shaft of light fell on something dark and furry. It was sitting over the hole.

Laura let out a piercing scream and slammed the door. She sprinted toward the house and ran straight into Eli, coming from the barn.

"Laura, what's wrong? I heard you hollering and

thought one of Pop's pigs had gotten loose again."

Laura clung to Eli's jacket. "It's the outhouse. . . there's some kind of monstrous animal in there!"

Eli grinned at her. "*Kumme*–come now. It was probably just a little old maus."

"It was not a mouse. It was dark and furry. . .and huge!"

Eli slipped his hand in the crook of her arm. "Let's go have a look-see."

"I'm not going in there."

He chuckled. "You don't have to. I'll do the checking."

Laura held her breath as Eli entered the outhouse. "Be careful."

She heard a thud, followed by a loud *whoop*. Suddenly, the door flew open and Eli bolted out of the privy, chased by the hairy creature Laura had seen a few moments ago. It was a comical sight, but she was almost too frightened to see the full humor in it.

"What was that?" she asked Eli, as the two of them stood watching the critter dash into the field.

"I think it was a hedgehog," Eli said breathlessly. "The crazy thing tried to attack me, but I kicked him with the toe of my boot, right before I walked out of the outhouse."

Laura giggled as her fear dissipated. "Don't you mean, '*ran* out of the outhouse'?"

Eli's face turned pink, and he chuckled. "Guess I was movin' pretty fast."

The two of them stood for a few seconds, gazing into each other's eyes. Then they both started laughing. They laughed so hard, tears streamed down their faces, and Laura had to set the lantern on the ground for fear it would fall out of her hand. It felt good to laugh. It was something neither of them did much anymore.

When they finally got control of their emotions, Eli reached for her hand. "I'll see about indoor plumbing as soon as spring comes; I promise."

Chapter 22

Wesley sat on the couch, staring at the Christmas tree. The little white lights blinked off and on, and the red bows hung from the evergreen branches in perfect order—but this Christmas would be anything but perfect.

He glanced at the unlit fireplace. A garland of fake holly had been strung across the mantel, but there was no Foosie lying on the rug by the hearth.

The Christmas cards they had received were stacked neatly in a red basket on the coffee table, but the only card that mattered to him was the one they'd gotten from Laura and Eli. It had included an invitation to come there for Christmas, and Laura had even suggested they stay there with them. Wesley had wanted to go, and he'd even been willing to adjust his work schedule so they could, but Irene wouldn't hear of it. She had insisted that she couldn't leave town during the holidays because she had too many commitments.

"Yeah, right," he mumbled. "She just doesn't want to give up all the modern conveniences she's convinced she can't do without."

"Who are you talking to, Wesley?"

He glanced at the doorway and was surprised to

see Irene standing there holding a large poinsettia plant in her hands.

"I didn't hear you come in. Did you just get home?"

She nodded and placed the plant on the end table near the couch. "I've been out shopping."

"That figures."

"What was that?"

"Nothing."

Irene slipped off her coat and laid it neatly on one end of the couch. Then she took a seat in her recliner and picked up the remote. "How come you're not watching television? Isn't it about time for your favorite show?"

"I get tired of watching TV."

"Since when?"

"Since I came to the conclusion that there are better things I can do with my time."

"You mean like sitting here staring at the tree?"

"Christmas is just a few days away. It seemed like the thing to do."

She wrinkled her nose. "Are you being sarcastic?"

"I wouldn't dream of it."

"Wesley, are you still pouting because we can't go to Pennsylvania for Christmas?"

"What do you mean, 'We can't go to Pennsylvania'?" He stood and began to pace. "We could have gone if you weren't so busy with *things*."

"Those *things* are important, and I—"

He stopped pacing and whirled around to face her. "Don't you miss our daughter? Wouldn't you rather spend Christmas with her than go to some silly ball?"

"Of course I'd like to be with Laura, but I've been planning this gala affair for several months." She released a sigh. "How would it look if the person in charge of the Christmas ball wasn't there to see that everything went according to plan?"

He grunted and started across the room.

"Where are you going?"

"Upstairs to bed. I'll need to get my beauty rest if I'm going to escort Princess Irene to the ball on Christmas Eve."

Laura stood in front of the living-room window, staring out at the blanket of pristine snow covering the ground and every tree in the Yoders' yard. It looked like a picture postcard, and despite the fact that Laura missed her parents, she felt happier today than she had in weeks.

She moved away from the window and took a seat in the wooden rocker by the fireplace. Even though there was no Christmas tree inside the house or colored lights decorating the outside of the house, a few candles were spaced around the room, along with several Christmas cards from family and friends. *Guess I did end up with an Early-American look after all. It's just a little plainer than I had expected it to be.*

Laura spotted the Christmas card they had received from her parents, along with a substantial check, and her heart clenched. *I do miss Mom and Dad, and I wish Eli and I could have gone there for Christmas or that they would have come here. But*

Mom was involved with a Christmas ball she'd planned at the country club, and even though Dad sounded like he wanted to come, he never seems to get his way where Mom's concerned. Maybe he should take lessons from Eli and his father. They don't have much trouble making a decision, even if it goes against what their wives might want.

Eli had been looking forward to Christmas. He'd made Laura a special gift, and this afternoon, his sister and her family would be joining them for Mom's traditional holiday feast.

"Life couldn't be any better," he said to the horse he was grooming. "Maybe later we'll hitch you up to the sleigh, and I'll take my beautiful wife for a ride."

The horse whinnied as if in response, and Eli chuckled. "You kind of like that idea, don't you, old boy?"

Eli entered the house a short time later, holding Laura's gift under his jacket. "Where's my fraa?" he asked Mom, who was scurrying around the kitchen.

She nodded toward the living room. "Your wife's in there. I guess she thinks I don't need any help getting dinner on."

Eli merely shrugged and left the kitchen. No point getting Mom more riled than she already seemed to be. He found Laura sitting in the rocking chair, gazing at the fireplace. "*En hallicher Grischtdaag!*"

She looked up and smiled. "A merry Christmas to you, too."

Eli bent down and kissed the top of her head. "I have something for you."

"You do? What is it?"

Eli held his jacket shut. "Guess."

She wrinkled her nose. "I have no idea. Tell me. . . please."

He chuckled and withdrew an ornate birdhouse, painted blue with white trim.

"Oh, Eli, it's just like the one you showed me at the farmers' market the day we first met."

He smiled. "And now you will have a place for it, come spring."

She accepted the gift, and tears welled in her eyes. "Thank you so much. It's beautiful."

"Does my pretty fraa have anything for her hardworking husband?" Eli asked in a teasing tone.

"I do, but I'm afraid it's not finished."

"You made me something?"

She nodded. "I've been sewing you a new shirt, but your mom's kept me so busy, I haven't had time to get it hemmed and wrapped."

Eli took the birdhouse from Laura and placed it on the small table by her chair. He pulled her toward him in a tender embrace. "It's okay. You'll get the shirt finished soon, and I'll appreciate it every bit as much then as I would if you'd given it to me now."

Laura rested her head against his shoulder. "I love you, Eli. Thanks for being so understanding."

Silent prayer had been said, and everyone sat around the table with expectant, hungry looks on their faces. Mary Ellen had outdone herself. Huge platters were laden with succulent roast beef and mouthwatering ham. Bowls were filled with buttery mashed potatoes, candied yams, canned green beans, and coleslaw. Sweet cucumber pickles, black olives, dilled green beans, and red-beet eggs were also included in the feast, as well as buttermilk biscuits and cornmeal muffins.

Everyone ate heartily. Everyone except for Laura and little Ben. Their plates were still half full when Mary Ellen brought out three pies—two pumpkin and one mincemeat—along with a tray of chocolate doughnuts.

Ben squealed with delight. "*Fettkuche!*"

"No doughnuts until you eat everything on your plate," Martha Rose scolded.

Ben's lower lip began to quiver, and his eyes filled with tears.

"Being a crybaby won't help you get your way," Amon admonished.

"He's only a child." Laura pulled one of the pumpkin pies close and helped herself to a piece. "Surely he can have one little doughnut."

All eyes seemed to be focused on Laura, and Ben, who had moments ago been fighting tears, let loose with a howl that sent Laura's cat flying into the air.

"Now look what you've done." Amon shook his finger at Ben. "You've scared that poor bussli half to death."

Foosie ran around the table, meowing and swishing her tail. Laura bent down and scooped her up, but the pinched expression on Mary Ellen's face was enough to let her know that in this house, cats didn't belong at the table. Laura mumbled an apology and deposited Foosie back on the floor.

"You're not settin' a very good example for the boy, Laura." This reprimand came from Eli's father. "If you're not gonna eat all your food, then I don't think you should take any pie." Johnny looked pointedly at Eli. "What do you think, son? Should your fraa be allowed to pick like a bird, then eat pie in front of Ben, who's just been told he can't have any fettkuche 'til he cleans his plate?"

Laura squirmed uneasily as she waited to see how Eli would respond. She felt his hand under the table, and her fingers squeezed his in response.

"Don't you think maybe you should eat everything else first, then have some pie?" Eli's voice was tight, and the muscle in his jaw quivered. Was he upset with her or only trying to please his father?

"I'm watching my weight, and the only way I can keep within my calorie count is to leave some food on my plate."

"You could pass up the pie," Mary Ellen suggested.

Laura grimaced. Why was everything she did always under scrutiny? Why did she have to make excuses for her behavior all the time? She pushed away from the table. "I'm not really hungry enough for pie, anyway." She gave Eli a quick glance, then rushed out of the room.

Chapter 23

Spring came early, and the building of Eli and Laura's home resumed as soon as the snow had melted. It couldn't be finished soon enough as far as Mary Ellen was concerned. Ever since Eli had married Laura, she had tried to be a good mother-in-law, but it wasn't easy when Laura seemed so distant and often touchy. Here of late, she'd been acting moodier than ever, and Mary Ellen wondered if *she* might be the cause of Laura's discontent.

"Why don't the two of us do some baking today?" she suggested to Laura one morning after breakfast. "We can make a couple of brown sugar sponge rolls. How's that sound?"

Laura groaned. "Do we have to? I'm really tired this morning, and I thought it would be nice to sit out on the back porch and watch the men work on my house."

Mary Ellen's forehead wrinkled. "Are you feeling poorly?"

"I'm fine. Just tired."

"Maybe a good spring tonic is what you need." She opened the cupboard near Laura and plucked out a box of cream of tartar, some sulfur, and a container of Epsom salts. "All you have to do is mix a little of each of these in a jar of water. Then take two or three swallows each morning for a few days, and you'll feel like your old self in no time at all."

Laura's face paled, and she coughed like she was about to gag. "I'm fine, really. Just didn't sleep well last night. A few cups of coffee, and I'll be good to go."

Mary Ellen shrugged and stepped aside. "Suit yourself, but remember the spring tonic in case you're still not up to par come morning."

"Danki. I'll keep it in mind."

As they rode home from church one Sunday afternoon, Eli worried. Laura had seemed so pensive lately. Had someone said or done something to upset her? He offered her a smile. "Sure was a good day, wasn't it?"

"Uh-huh."

"Is there something troubling you? You seem kind of down in the dumps today."

She shrugged. "I'm just getting tired of going to other people's houses and seeing that they have indoor plumbing, while we still have none."

"I said I'd build one in our new home, and I'm still planning to put one in Mom and Pop's house as soon as I find the time."

"You've been saying that for months, Eli, and it's taking a lot longer than I thought it would." She grunted. "I can't stand that smelly outhouse!"

Eli glanced over at her and squinted. "I'm

working every free moment I have, and so are Pop and my brothers. Can't you learn to be patient?"

Laura sat staring straight ahead with her lips pursed and said nothing.

"The Bible says, 'The trying of your faith worketh patience.' It's in the book of James."

"My faith in things getting better has definitely been tried, and so has my patience," she mumbled.

Eli blinked. Was there no pleasing this woman? He'd said he would install indoor plumbing in their new home. That ought to be good enough.

"Eli, could I ask you a question?"

He blew out his breath. "Not if it's about indoor plumbing."

"It's not."

"Okay, ask the question then."

She reached across the seat and touched his arm. "Do you think Pauline Hostetler would have made you a better wife?"

Eli lifted one eyebrow and glanced over at Laura. "Pauline? What's she got to do with anything?"

"I just want to know if you think–"

"I can't believe you would bring that up again, Laura. You should know by now how much I love you."

Her eyes filled with tears and she sniffed.

"What's wrong? Why are you crying?"

"Your mother and I were doing some baking the other day, and she brought up the subject of Pauline."

"Oh? What'd she say?"

"Just that Pauline is a good cook and likes to

bake." Laura's voice rose a notch. "I'm sure she thinks Pauline would have made you a better wife than me."

Eli pulled sharply on the reins, steered the buggy to the side of the road, and gathered her into his arms. "I love you, Laura. Only you."

"I'm glad to hear that." Laura snuggled against his jacket. "But that doesn't take care of things with your mother. Do you have any idea what I can say or do to make her realize that I'm a better wife for you than Pauline could ever have been?"

Eli touched her chin lightly with his thumb. "You'd best leave that up to me."

When Eli and Laura entered the house a short time later, Laura went up to their room, saying she was tired and needed a nap.

Eli found his mother sitting in the living room on the sofa, reading a book. Apparently his folks had gotten home from church quite a bit ahead of them. He decided this might be a good time to speak with her about the conversation she'd had with Laura the other day. "Mom, can I talk to you for a minute?"

She looked up and smiled. "Jah, sure. What's on your mind?"

He took a seat in the rocking chair across from her. "It's about Laura."

"Is she feeling all right? The other day she mentioned that she was really tired, and I suggested she take a spring tonic."

Eli winced at the remembrance of drinking his mother's sour-tasting tonics when he was a boy. "I don't think a spring tonic will take care of what ails my fraa."

"Is she still fretting over your house not being done? She's mentioned several times that she can't wait until it's finished." Mom's forehead wrinkled. "I think she's anxious to have her own place to run, and to tell you the truth, I'm looking forward to having my space, too."

"Jah, it will be good for both of you when the house is done." Eli sat there a few minutes, trying to formulate the right words to say what was on his mind.

"You're looking kind of pensive, son. Is there something more you wanted to say?"

He nodded. "Laura thinks you would have been happier if I'd married Pauline instead of her. When you mentioned how well Pauline can cook the other day, it really hurt Laura's feelings."

"I think Laura's too sensitive for her own good." Mom clicked her tongue. "I meant nothing by what I said."

"Are you sure about that?"

Mom stared at the book she held in her hands. "I–I suppose I was kind of hoping you would choose Pauline, but once your decision was made, I accepted it."

"Then why did you bring Pauline up to Laura, and why does Laura feel as if you don't approve of her?"

"As I said before. . .she tends to be rather sensitive."

Eli nodded. Laura was touchy about some of the things he said, too—especially in recent weeks.

"I'll apologize to her and try to be more careful with what I say," Mom promised.

"Danki. I appreciate that."

"I'm not feeling well. I think I'll stay home from church today," Laura mumbled when Eli tried to coax her out of bed two Sundays later.

"You were feeling all right last night."

"That was then. This is now."

"You should get up and help Mom with breakfast," Eli murmured against her ear.

She groaned. "I don't feel like helping today."

Eli touched her forehead. "You're not running a fever."

"I'm not sick. . .just terribly tired."

"Maybe you should consider taking Mom's spring tonic. It does put a spring in your step; I promise."

"I'm not taking any tonic. I would feel fine if I could get a little more rest."

Eli pulled back the covers, hopped out of bed, and stepped into his trousers. He walked across the room to where the water pitcher and bowl sat on top of the dresser. After splashing a handful of water on his face and drying it with a towel, he grabbed his shirt off the wall peg and started for the door. "See you downstairs in five minutes."

When the door clicked shut, Laura grabbed her pillow and threw it across the room. "Maybe I should go home to my parents for a while. I wonder how you'd like that, Eli Yoder!"

Laura was quiet on the buggy ride to preaching, and during the service she didn't sing. Not only was she still tired, but she felt irritation with Eli for not having any understanding and insisting that she get up and help his mother with breakfast this morning. He should have had a little sympathy and agreed that she could stay home and rest.

Laura's attention was drawn to the front of the room as Bishop Wagler began his sermon, using Mark 11:25 as his text. "In Jesus' own words, we are told: 'And when ye stand praying, forgive, if ye have ought against any: that your Father also which is in heaven may forgive you your trespasses.' "

Laura frowned. *That verse doesn't make any sense to me. How can I forgive Mary Ellen for her comments about Pauline the other day when she didn't even say she was sorry? And Eli never said he was sorry for the way he talked to me this morning, either.*

She glanced over at Martha Rose, who sat on the bench beside her. She wore a smile on her face and looked almost angelic. But then, Eli's sister always seemed to be happy, even when she had a bout of morning sickness or things weren't going so well. *Maybe it's because she doesn't have to share her home with her mother-in-law!*

"I thought Bishop Wagler's sermon was good,

didn't you?" Eli asked as he glanced over at Laura on their trip home from church later that day.

She merely shrugged in response.

"If we don't forgive others, we can't expect God to forgive us."

Still no reply.

"I forgive you for throwing that pillow at me this morning."

Her mouth dropped open. "You knew?"

He nodded. "Heard it hit the door."

"I wasn't really throwing it at you," she said, as a smile tugged at the corners of her mouth. "Just venting was all."

"Because I asked you to get out of bed and help my mamm?"

"Jah."

Holding the reins with one hand, he reached his free hand over and took hold of Laura's hand. "Didn't mean to sound so bossy. Will you forgive me?"

She nodded and slid closer to him. "Of course I forgive you."

His eyebrows raised. "Is that all you've got to say?"

She sat silently for several seconds; then a light seemed to dawn. "I'm sorry, too."

He grinned and gave her fingers a gentle squeeze. "You're forgiven."

Laura leaned her head on his shoulder and sighed. "I'm glad we got that cleared up. Now if I could just get your mother to apologize for what she said to me about Pauline."

Eli's eyebrows raised. "She hasn't apologized yet? She said she was going to."

Laura shook her head.

"She probably got busy and forgot. Want me to have another talk with her?"

"No, just forget it. We'll move into our house soon; then things should be better."

Chapter 24

Eli and Laura's house was finally ready, and Eli had included a small bathroom, just as he'd promised. He and his father had also put one in their house, so Laura knew she would have that convenience handy whenever they visited his folks. Eli and Laura's new home had five bedrooms, a roomy kitchen, a nice-sized living room, and of course, the small bathroom.

Mary Ellen had given Eli and Laura some furniture, and Laura was glad to finally have a home she could call her own. It would be a welcome relief not to have Eli's mother analyzing everything she said and did. As far as Laura was concerned, the completion of her house was the best thing that had happened since she'd moved onto the Yoders' farm.

On the first morning in her new home, Laura got up late. When she entered the kitchen, she realized Eli was already outside doing his chores. She hurried to start breakfast and was just setting the table when he came inside.

"Your cereal is almost ready," she said with a smile.

He nodded. "Is my lunch packed? I have to leave

for work in five minutes."

"Oh, I forgot. I'm running late this morning. Usually your mother gets breakfast going while I make your lunch."

"It's okay. I'll just take a few pieces of fruit and some cookies." Eli opened his lunch pail and placed two apples, an orange, a handful of peanut butter cookies, and a thermos of milk inside. He took a seat at the table, bowed his head for silent prayer, and dug into the hot oatmeal Laura handed him.

"Can you stop by the store and pick up a loaf of bread on your way home tonight?" Laura asked, taking the seat beside him.

Eli gave her a questioning look.

"I won't have time to do any baking today. I have clothes to wash, and I want to spend most of the day organizing the house and setting out some of our wedding gifts."

Eli gulped down the last of his milk and stood. "Jah, okay. I know it's important for you to set things up the way you want them." He leaned over and kissed her cheek.

"Ouch! You're prickly!"

"Sorry." Eli grabbed his lunch pail and headed for the door.

"Wait! Can't you visit with me awhile this morning? You've been working such long hours lately, and it seems like we never get to talk anymore."

"We'll talk later. I've got to go now, or I'll be late for work."

Laura waved at his retreating form. When she shut the door, she sighed deeply and surveyed her kitchen. "This house is so big. Where should I begin?"

❧

As Laura stood at the kitchen sink doing the breakfast dishes, she began to fret. Eli had changed since their marriage. He not only looked different, what with his scratchy beard, but he never seemed to have time for her anymore.

"Work, work, work, that's all he ever thinks about," she muttered. "If Eli cared about me the way he does his job, I'd be a lot happier. Whatever happened to romance and long buggy rides to the lake?"

A single tear rolled down her cheek, and she wiped it away with a soapy hand. "Life is so unfair. I gave up a lot to become Eli's wife, and now he won't even listen to me." Laura glanced down at Foosie, who lay curled at her feet. "Too bad Mom and Dad can't come for a visit." She sniffed deeply. "No. . . they're too busy, just like Eli. Dad has his law practice, and Mom runs around like a chicken hunting bugs, trying to meet all of her social obligations."

The cat purred contentedly, seemingly unaware of her frustrations.

"You've got life made, you know that?"

A knock at the back door drew Laura's attention away from Foosie. *Oh, no. I hope that's not Mary Ellen.*

She dried her hands on her apron and dabbed the corners of her eyes with a handkerchief, then went to answer the door.

To her surprise, Martha Rose and little Ben stood

on the porch, each holding a basket. Martha Rose's basket held freshly baked apple muffins, and Ben's was full of ginger cookies.

Laura smiled. She was always glad to see her sister-in-law and that adorable little boy. "Come in. Would you like a cup of tea?"

Martha Rose, her stomach now bulging, lowered herself into a chair. "That sounds good. We can have some of the muffins I brought, too."

Ben spotted Foosie, and he darted over to play with her.

"What brings you by so early?" Laura asked as she pulled out a chair for herself.

"We're on our way to town to do some shopping, but we wanted to stop and see you first," Martha Rose answered. "We have an invitation for you and Eli."

Laura's interest was piqued. "What kind of invitation?"

"Since tomorrow's Saturday and the weather's so nice, Amon and I have decided to take Ben to the lake for a picnic supper. We were wondering if you and Eli would like to come along."

Laura dropped a couple of tea bags into the pot she'd taken from the stove before she sat down. "Would we ever! At least, I would. If Eli can tear himself away from work long enough, I'm sure he'd have a good time, too."

Martha Rose nodded. "We'll meet you there around four o'clock. That'll give everyone time enough to do all their chores." She waved her hand. "Speaking of chores–you look awfully tired. Are you working too hard?"

Laura pushed a stray hair under her head covering and sighed. "I have been feeling a little drained lately. I'll be fine once I get this house organized."

Martha Rose opened her mouth to say something, but Laura cut her off. "What should I bring to the picnic?"

"I thought I'd fix fried chicken, two different salads, and maybe some pickled-beet eggs. Why don't you bring the dessert and some kind of beverage?"

"That sounds fine," Laura answered, feeling suddenly lighthearted. They were going on a picnic, and she could hardly wait.

"How was your day?" Eli asked, as he stepped into the kitchen that evening and found Laura sitting at the table, tearing lettuce leaves into a bowl.

"It was okay. How about yours?"

"Busy. We got several new orders at the store today, and my boss said we might have to put in more overtime in order to get them done."

She groaned. "I hope not. You work too much as it is."

He placed his lunch pail on the counter and joined her at the table. He was too tired to argue, and it seemed like he never won an argument with Laura anyway, so what was the use?

"Your sister and little Ben came by today." Laura looked over at him and smiled. "She invited us to join their family on a picnic at the lake tomorrow."

"What time?"

"She said for supper, and that they'd be there by four."

"That might be okay. I'll need to work in my shop awhile, and I promised Pop I'd help him do a couple of chores, too."

"What time will you be done?"

"Probably by four, I would imagine."

"Then we can go on the picnic?" Laura's expression was so hopeful, there was no way Eli could say no.

He leaned over and kissed her cheek. "Jah, tomorrow we'll join my sister and her family for a picnic."

❧

The lake was beautiful, and Laura drank in the peacefulness until she felt as if her heart would burst.

Martha Rose was busy setting out her picnic foods, and the men were playing ball with little Ben. Laura brought out the brownies and iced mint tea she had made, and soon the plywood table they'd brought from home was brimming with food.

Everyone gathered for silent prayer, and then the men heaped their plates full. Laura was the last to dish up, but she only took small helpings of everything. When she came to the tray of pickled-beet eggs, a surge of nausea rolled through her stomach like angry ocean waves. Pickled eggs were sickening—little purple land mines, waiting to destroy her insides.

Laura dropped her plate of food and dashed for the woods. Eli ran after her, but he waited until she had emptied her stomach before saying anything.

"You okay?" he asked with obvious concern.

Laura stood on wobbly legs. "I'm fine. It was the sight of those pickled eggs. They're disgusting! How can anyone eat those awful things?"

Eli slipped his arm around her waist. "Maybe you've got the flu."

She shook her head. "It was just the eggs. Let's go back to the picnic. I'm fine now, honest."

The rest of the day went well enough, and Laura felt a bit better after drinking some of her cold mint tea. She even joined a friendly game of tag, but she did notice the looks of concern Eli and his sister exchanged. At least nobody had said anything about her getting sick, and for that, she was glad.

A few days later while Laura was outside gathering eggs from the henhouse, she had another attack of nausea. She hadn't eaten any breakfast, so she figured that was the reason. Besides, the acrid odor of chicken manure was enough to make anyone sick.

On her way back to the house, she spotted Eli's mother hanging laundry on the line. Mary Ellen waved and called to Laura, but Laura only nodded in return and hurried on. She was in no mood for a confrontation with her mother-in-law this morning, and she certainly didn't want to get sick in front of her.

"I'm almost finished here," Mary Ellen called. "Come have a cup of coffee."

Laura's stomach lurched at the mention of coffee, and she wondered how she could graciously get out of the invitation.

Mary Ellen called to her again. "I know you're busy, but surely you can take a few minutes for a little chat."

Laura inhaled deeply and released a sigh. "All right. I'll set this basket of eggs inside, then be right over." *May as well give in, or Mary Ellen will probably report to Eli that his wife is unsociable.*

Laura entered the house and deposited the eggs in the refrigerator. Then she took a glass from the cupboard and went to the sink for a cool drink of water. She drank it slowly and took several deep breaths, which seemed to help settle her stomach some.

She opened the back door. "Well, here goes nothing."

When she stepped into the Yoders' kitchen a few minutes later, she found Mary Ellen seated at the table. Two cups were sitting there, and the strong aroma of coffee permeated the air.

Laura's stomach did a little flip-flop as she took a seat. "Uh, would you mind if I had mint tea instead of coffee?"

Mary Ellen pushed her chair aside and stood. "If that's what you prefer." She went to the cupboard and retrieved a box of tea bags, then poured boiling water from the teapot on the stove into a clean mug and added one bag. "You're looking kind of peaked this morning." she said, handing Laura the tea.

"I think I might have a touch of the flu."

"You could be in a family way. Have you thought about that?"

Laura shook her head. "It's the flu. Nothing to worry about."

"Would you like some shoofly pie or a buttermilk biscuit?"

"I might try a biscuit."

Mary Ellen passed Laura a basket of warm biscuits. "So, tell me, how long has this flu thing been going on?"

"Just a few days."

"If it continues, maybe you'd better see the doctor."

There she goes again, telling me what to do. Laura reached for the small pitcher on the table and poured some milk into the tea, stirring it vigorously. With a splash, some of the hot liquid splattered onto her hand, and she grimaced. "I'll see the doctor if I don't feel better soon."

Mary Ellen moved her chair a little closer to Laura's. "I. . .uh. . .have been meaning to apologize for bringing Pauline up to you a few weeks ago. I shouldn't have said anything about the woman's cooking skills."

"Apology accepted." Laura took a sip of tea. "Have you heard anything about Pauline since she moved to Ohio?"

"Just that she got there safely and seems to like it well enough."

"Any idea how long she'll be staying?"

Mary Ellen shrugged. "Guess it all depends."

Laura drummed her fingernails along the edge of the tablecloth. "On how soon she gets over Eli? Is that what you mean?"

"Jah."

"Eli has told me several times that he and Pauline were never more than friends, but I guess she was hoping for more."

Mary Ellen wasn't sure how to respond, because the truth was she'd been hoping for more, too. She had always liked Pauline and had thought she would have made Eli a good wife. *Maybe if Eli hadn't played around during his rumpschpringe years so long and had settled down and joined the church sooner, he would have married Pauline. Probably wouldn't have met Laura, either.*

"Are you about finished with your tea? Would you like another cup?" she asked, hoping the change of subject might clear the air between them.

"I am almost done, but I'm feeling kind of tired all of a sudden, so I think I'll head home and rest awhile."

Mary Ellen studied Laura. Dark circles showed under her eyes, and her face looked pale and drawn. Either she'd been working too hard setting up her new household, or there was something physically wrong. She figured it would be best not to make an issue of it, though. No point in setting herself up to say something wrong and then need to apologize again. So she merely smiled and said, "Guess I'd better get busy making some pickled-beet eggs I promised Johnny he could have. Have a good rest of the day, Laura."

Laura nodded, pushed her chair aside, and dashed from the room.

Mary Ellen shook her head. "Something tells me there's a lot more going on with Eli's wife than she's willing to admit."

Chapter 25

Laura's nausea and fatigue continued all that week, but she did her best to hide it from Eli. She didn't want him pressuring her to see the doctor, or worse yet, asking a bunch of questions the way his mother had.

One morning, Laura decided to go into town for some supplies. She asked Eli to hitch the horse to the buggy before he left for work, as she still didn't feel comfortable doing that on her own. As soon as her morning chores were done, she set her dark bonnet in place over her white *kapp* and climbed into the waiting buggy.

When Laura arrived in town, her first stop was the pharmacy. She scanned the shelves until she found exactly what she was looking for. She brought the item to the checkout counter and waited for the middle-aged clerk to ring it up. He gave her a strange look as he placed the small box inside a paper sack. Laura wondered if she was the first Amish woman who had ever purchased a home pregnancy kit.

The test couldn't be taken until early the next morning, so when she got home later in the day, Laura found a safe place to hide it. The last thing she needed was for Eli to discover it and jump to the wrong conclusions. He would surely think she was pregnant, and she was equally sure she wasn't. She couldn't be. Of course, she had missed her monthly, but that wasn't too uncommon for her. Then what about the fatigue and nausea? Those were definite signs of pregnancy; even she knew that much.

Laura waited until Eli left for work the following morning before going to her sewing basket, retrieving the test kit, and rushing to the bathroom.

Moments later, Laura's hands trembled as she held the strip up for examination. It was bright pink. The blood drained from her face, and she sank to the floor, steadying herself against the unyielding wall. "Oh, no! This just can't be!"

She studied it longer, just to be sure she hadn't read it wrong. It was still pink. "I can't be pregnant. What will it do to my figure?"

Some time later when Laura emerged from the bathroom, her eyes felt sore and swollen from crying. She went straight to the kitchen sink and splashed cold water on her face.

I can't tell Eli or even my folks about this yet. I need time to adjust to the idea first.

"How long can I keep a secret like this?" she moaned. After some quick calculations, she figured she must be about eight weeks along. In another four to six weeks, she might be starting to show. Besides, if she kept getting sick every day, Eli would either suspect she was pregnant or decide she was definitely sick and take her to the doctor.

"What am I going to do?" she wailed, looking

down at Foosie, asleep at her feet.

No response. Just some gentle purring from the contented-looking cat.

Laura glanced out the window and saw the mail truck pull up to the box by the road. "Guess I'll walk out and get the mail while I think about this situation some more."

Laura found a stack of letters in the box and was surprised to see one from Darla. She hadn't heard anything from her friend from school in several months, and she'd figured Darla had probably forgotten her by now.

Back in the kitchen, Laura took a seat at the table and opened Darla's letter. It didn't say much except that she had a few days off from her job in Philadelphia and wondered if Laura would like to meet her for lunch at a restaurant near Strasburg on Friday of next week.

Laura figured there was plenty of time to get a letter sent back to Darla before Friday, so she moved over to the desk on the other side of the room and took out a piece of paper and a pen. Having lunch with Darla wouldn't solve her immediate problem, but at least it would be a nice outing and was something to look forward to.

Before Laura left the house the following Friday, she wrote Eli a note telling him where she was going and that she would try to be back in time to get supper going before he got home. Then she hitched one of their most docile mares to the buggy and headed out.

When Laura pulled into the restaurant parking lot some time later, she was pleased to see Darla's little sports car parked there. She climbed down from the buggy, secured the horse to the hitching rail, and headed into the restaurant.

She spotted Darla sitting at a table near the window and hurried over to her. "Hey, it's good to see you," she said, taking a seat on the other side of the table. "Thanks for inviting me to join you."

Darla smiled at first, but then her forehead wrinkled as she frowned. "I barely recognized you in those Amish clothes. You sure have changed."

Laura nodded and held out her hands. "Just look at my nails."

Darla shook her head and grunted. "Every one of them is broken." She stared at Laura, making her feel suddenly uncomfortable. "You look tired. What do you do, work all day and never sleep?"

Laura reached for the glass of water the young waitress had just brought and took a sip. "I do work hard, but my fatigue doesn't come from just that."

"What then? Did you jog all the way here or something?"

Laura would have laughed if she hadn't felt so crummy. She wished there were some soda crackers on the table, because she needed something to help calm her nausea.

"You're looking kind of pasty there, kiddo. Are you feeling sick?"

Laura nodded, and tears welled in her eyes. "I—I'm pregnant."

Darla's eyebrows lifted high on her forehead.

"I knew marrying that Amish guy would bring you nothing but trouble."

"I don't need any lectures," Laura snapped. "Besides, I could have gotten pregnant no matter who I'd married."

"So what are you going to do about it?"

"Do?"

"Yeah. It's obvious to me by the look on your face that you're anything but happy about being pregnant."

Laura sighed. "I enjoy being around Eli's nephew, and I would like to have a baby of my own sometime. I just hadn't expected it would be this soon or that I would feel so rotten." She looked down at her still-flat stomach. "I wonder how long it will be before I lose my shape."

"Probably won't take too long at all. How far along are you?"

"A little over eight weeks, according to my calculations."

"Good. Then it's not too late to have an abortion."

"A what?" Laura nearly choked on the water she'd put in her mouth.

"You don't want to be pregnant; am I right?"

"Well, no, but–"

"There's a clinic in Philly, and I can make the appointment for you if you'd like." Darla leaned across the table. "No one but you and me would ever have to know, and I'm sure you would feel better once this was all behind you."

Laura shook her head. "Oh, no, I couldn't. . ."

"If money's a problem, I could float you a loan."

"This is not about money." Laura's voice rose to a high pitch, and her hands trembled so badly, she had to set her glass down to keep from spilling the water.

"If you've got enough money, then what's the problem?"

"The problem's with the abortion, Darla. I could never do anything like that."

"Why not?"

"It–it's against the Amish beliefs to take the life of an unborn baby." The tears Laura had been fighting to keep at bay spilled over and dripped onto her cheeks. "And I would never dream of doing such a thing." She placed her hand against her stomach. "This baby is part of me and Eli, and even though I'm not looking forward to being fat and unattractive, I want to make him happy. I want to do what's right."

Darla's gaze went to the ceiling. "Not only have you changed in appearance, but I can see that you've gotten all self-righteous and sappy now, too."

Laura gripped the handles of her black purse and pushed away from the table. "This was a mistake," she said through clenched teeth. "I should never have agreed to meet you for lunch."

"Where are you going?"

"Home. To tell Eli I'm going to have his baby."

Laura lifted the teakettle from the back of the stove and poured herself a cup of raspberry tea. This afternoon she felt better than she had in many days, and the reason was because she had put Darla in her place and decided to come home and wait for Eli so she could give him the news of her pregnancy.

She thought about little Ben—always playful and curious, so full of love, all cute and cuddly. Laura had never cared much for children until she met Ben. She loved that little boy and was sure she would love her own child even more.

If Laura had listened to Darla, it not only would have ended her baby's life but it would also have ruined things between her and Eli. She was sure she would have been excommunicated from the Amish church, too.

Did Darla really think Laura could take the life of her unborn child and go on as though nothing had ever happened? While Laura might not understand all the biblical implications of the Amish beliefs, she did want to be a good wife to her husband, and she was sure that having Eli's child would only strengthen their marriage. She would just have to work twice as hard at counting calories once the baby came so she could get her figure back as quickly as possible.

The screen door creaked open, pulling Laura out of her musings. Eli hung his straw hat on a wall peg and went to wash up at the sink. "I hope supper's about ready, because I'm hungry as a mule!"

"There's a chicken in the oven, and it should be done soon." Laura turned to him and smiled. "I was wondering if we could talk before we eat, though."

He shrugged. "Sure, what's up?"

She motioned him to sit down, then poured him a cup of tea. "How do you really feel about children,

Eli?" she asked, keeping her eyes focused on the cup.

"I've told you before, someday I hope to fill our house with kinner."

"Would November be soon enough to start?"

His forehead wrinkled.

"I'm pregnant, Eli. You're going to be a father soon."

Eli stared at her with a look of disbelief. "A boppli?"

She nodded.

He jumped up, circled the table, pulled Laura to her feet, and kissed her so soundly, it took her breath away. "The Lord has answered my prayers!" He grinned and pulled away, then started for the back door.

"Where are you going?"

"Over to my folks'. I've got to share this good news with them. Have you told your parents yet?"

She shook her head. "I wanted to tell you first."

"Guess you should go over to the neighbors' after supper and use their phone. I'm sure your folks will be as happy about this news as I know mine will be."

Laura swallowed around the lump in her throat. She hoped they would all be happy.

Laura hung the last towel on the line and wiped her damp forehead with her apron. It was a hot, humid June morning, and she was four months pregnant. She placed one hand on her slightly swollen belly and smiled. A tiny flutter caused her to tremble. "There really is a boppli in there," she murmured.

She bent down to pick up her empty basket, but an approaching buggy caught her attention. It was coming up the driveway at an unusually fast speed. When it stopped in front of the house, Amon jumped out, his face all red and sweaty, his eyes huge as saucers. "Where's Eli's mamm?" he panted.

Laura pointed to Mary Ellen's house. "Is something wrong?"

"It's Martha Rose. Her labor's begun, and she wants her mamm to deliver this baby, just like she did Ben."

Laura followed as Amon ran toward the Yoders'. They found Mary Ellen in the kitchen, kneading bread dough. She looked up and smiled. "Ah, so the smell of bread in the making drew the two of you inside."

Amon shook his head. "Martha Rose's time has come, and she sent me to get you."

Mary Ellen calmly set the dough aside and wiped her hands on a towel. "Laura, would you please finish this bread?"

"I thought I'd go along. Martha Rose is my friend, and–"

"There's no point wasting good bread dough," Mary Ellen said, as though the matter was settled.

Amon stood by the back door, shifting his weight from one foot to the other. Laura could see he was anxious to get home. "Oh, all right," she finally agreed. "I'll do the bread, but I'm coming over as soon as it's out of the oven."

When Laura arrived at the Zooks' some time

later, she found Amon pacing back and forth in the kitchen. Ben was at the table, coloring a picture. "Boppli," he said, grinning up at her.

Laura nodded. "Jah, soon it will come." She glanced over at Amon. "It's not born yet, is it?"

He shook his head. "Don't know what's takin' so long. She was real fast with Ben."

"How come you're not up there with her?"

Amon shrugged. "Mary Ellen said it would be best if I waited down here with the boy."

"Want me to go check?"

"I'd be obliged."

Laura hurried up the stairs. The door to Martha Rose and Amon's room was open a crack, so she walked right in.

Mary Ellen looked up from her position near the foot of the bed. "It's getting close. I can see the head now. Push, Martha Rose. . .push!"

Laura's heart began to pound, and her legs felt like two sticks of rubber. She leaned against the dresser to steady herself.

A few minutes later, the lusty cry of a newborn babe filled the room. Tears stung the backs of Laura's eyes. This was the miracle of birth. She had never imagined it could be so beautiful.

"Daughter, you've got yourself a mighty fine girl," Mary Ellen announced. "Let me clean her up a bit; then I'll hand her right over."

Martha Rose started to cry, but Laura knew they were tears of joy. She slipped quietly from the room, leaving mother, daughter, and grandmother alone to share the moment of pleasure.

Laura had seen Dr. Wilson several times, and other than a bit of anemia, she was pronounced to be in good condition. The doctor prescribed iron tablets to take with her prenatal vitamins, but she still tired easily, and Eli felt concern.

"I'm gonna ask Mom to come over and help out today," he said as he prepared to leave for work one morning.

Laura shuffled across the kitchen floor toward him. "Please don't. Your mom's got her hands full helping Martha Rose with the new baby. She doesn't need one more thing to worry about."

Eli shrugged. "Suit yourself, but if you need anything, don't think twice about calling on her, you hear?"

She nodded and lifted her face for his good-bye kiss. "Have a good day."

Eli left the house and headed straight for his folks' house. Laura might think she didn't need Mom's help, but he could see how tired she was. Dark circles under her eyes and swollen feet at the end of the day were telltale signs that she needed more rest.

He found Mom in the kitchen, doing the breakfast dishes. "Shouldn't you be heading for work?" she asked.

He nodded. "I wanted to talk with you first."

"Anything wrong?"

He shrugged and ran his fingers through the back of his hair. "Laura's been working too hard, and I think she could use some help."

"Want me to see to it, or are you thinking of hiring a *maad*?"

"I'd rather it be you, instead of a maid, if you can find the time."

She smiled. "I think I can manage."

"Danki." Eli grasped the doorknob, but when another thought popped into his head, he pivoted back around. "Do you think Laura's happy, Mom?"

She lifted an eyebrow in question. "Why wouldn't she be? She's married to you, after all."

He shrugged. "I ain't no prize." His eyebrows drew together. "Do you think she's really content being Amish?"

Mom dried her hands on a towel and moved toward him. "Laura chose to become Amish. You didn't force her, remember?"

"I know, but sometimes she looks so sad."

"Ah, it's just being in a family way. Many women get kind of melancholy during that time. She'll be fine once the boppli comes."

Eli gave her a hug. "You're probably right. I'm most likely worried for nothing."

Chapter 26

A few days before Eli and Laura's first anniversary, Eli arrived home from work one afternoon and found Laura lying on the sofa, holding her stomach and writhing in pain.

Alarm rose in his chest as he rushed to her side. "What is it, Laura?"

"I–I think the baby's coming."

He knelt in front of the sofa and grasped her hand. "When did the pains start?"

"Around noon."

"What does my mamm have to say?"

"She doesn't know."

"What?" Eli couldn't believe Laura hadn't called his mother. She'd delivered many babies and would know if it was time.

"I wasn't sure it was labor at first," Laura said tearfully. "But then my water broke, and–"

Eli jumped up and dashed across the room.

"Wh-where are you going?"

"To get Mom!"

Laura leaned her head against the sofa pillow and stiffened when another contraction came. "Oh,

God, please help me!" It was the first real prayer Laura had ever uttered, and now she wasn't even sure God was listening. Why would He care about her when she'd never really cared about Him? She had only been pretending to be a Christian. Was this her punishment for lying to Eli, his family, and even herself?

Moments later, Eli bounded into the room, followed by his mother.

"How far apart are the pains?" Mary Ellen asked as she approached the couch.

"I–I don't know for sure. About two or three minutes, I think," Laura answered tearfully. "Oh, it hurts so much! I think Eli should take me to the hospital."

Mary Ellen did a quick examination, and when she was done, she shook her head. "You waited too long for that. The boppli's coming now."

Eli started for the kitchen. "I'll get some towels and warm water."

"Don't leave me, Eli!"

"Calm down," Mary Ellen chided. "He'll be right back. In the meantime, I want you to do exactly as I say."

Laura's first reaction was to fight the pain, but Mary Ellen was a good coach, and soon Laura began to cooperate. Eli stood nearby, holding her hand and offering soothing words.

"One final push and the boppli should be here," Mary Ellen finally said.

Laura did as she was instructed, and moments later, the babe's first cry filled the room.

"It's a boy! You have a son," Mary Ellen announced.

Laura lifted her head from the pillow. "Let me see him. I want to make sure he has ten fingers and ten toes."

"In a minute. Let Eli clean him up a bit," Mary Ellen instructed. "I need to finish up with you."

"Mom, could you come over here?" Eli called from across the room. His voice sounded strained, and a wave of fear washed over Laura like a drenching rain.

"What is it? Is something wrong with our son?"

"Just a minute, Laura. I want Mom to take a look at him first."

Laura rolled onto her side, trying to see what was happening. Eli and Mary Ellen were bent over the small bundle wrapped in a towel, lying on top of an end table. She heard whispering but couldn't make out their words.

"What's going on? Tell me now, or I'll come see for myself."

Eli rushed to her side. "Stay put. You might start bleeding real heavy if you get up too soon."

Laura drew in a deep breath and grabbed hold of Eli's shirtsleeve. "What's wrong?"

"The child's breathing seems a bit irregular," Mary Ellen said. "I think we should take him to the hospital."

"I'd like Laura to be seen, too," Eli said with a nod.

Laura had only gotten a glimpse of her son before they rushed him into the hospital nursery, but what she'd seen concerned her greatly. The baby wasn't breathing right. He looked kind of funny, too. He had a good crop of auburn hair, just like Laura's, but there was something else. . .something she couldn't put her finger on.

"Relax and try to rest," Eli said as he took a seat in the chair next to Laura's hospital bed. "The doctor's looking at little David right now, and—"

"David?" Laura repeated. "You named our son without asking me?"

Eli's face flamed. "I. . .uh. . .thought we'd talked about naming the baby David if it was a boy."

She nodded slowly. "I guess we did. I just thought—"

Laura's words were interrupted when Dr. Wilson and another man entered the room. The second man's expression told her all she needed to know. Something was wrong.

"This is Dr. Hayes," Dr. Wilson said. "He's a pediatrician and has just finished examining your son."

Eli jumped to his feet. "Tell us. . .is there something wrong with David?"

Dr. Hayes put a hand on Eli's shoulder. "Please sit down."

Eli complied, but Laura could see the strain on his face. She felt equally uncomfortable.

"We still need to run a few more tests," the doctor said, "but we're fairly sure your boy has Down syndrome."

"Are you saying he's going to be handicapped?" Eli's voice squeaked, and his face blanched.

"Quite possibly. The baby has an accumulation

of fluid in his lungs. It's fairly common with Down syndrome. We can clear it out, but he will no doubt be prone to bronchial infections—especially while he's young."

Laura was too stunned to say anything at first. This had to be a dream—a terrible nightmare. This couldn't be happening to her and Eli.

"Once we get the lungs cleared and he's breathing well on his own, you should be able to take the baby home," Dr. Hayes continued.

"Take him home?" Laura pulled herself to a sitting position. "Did you say, 'Take him home'?"

The doctor nodded, and Eli reached for her hand. "Laura, we can get through this. We—"

She jerked her hand away. "We've just been told that our son probably has Down syndrome, and you're saying, 'We can get through this'?" She shook her head slowly. "The baby isn't normal, Eli. He doesn't belong with us."

Eli studied Laura a few seconds. "Who does he belong with?"

"If he's handicapped, he belongs in a home for handicapped children."

Eli looked at her as if she had lost her mind. "That's not our way, Laura. We take care of our own—even the handicapped children."

"But I don't know how."

"You'll learn, same as other parents with handicapped children have done."

Laura turned her head toward the wall. "Leave me alone, Eli. I need to sleep."

He bent to kiss her forehead. "I'll be back

tomorrow, and we can talk about this then."

As soon as Eli left the room, Laura reached for the phone by the side of her bed. It was time to call Mom and Dad.

❧

"Meade Residence, this is Wesley speaking."

"Dad, it's me."

"Laura, it's good to hear your voice. Your mother and I were just talking about you. We were wondering how you're doing and–"

"Is Mom there?"

"Yes, she's out in the kitchen."

"You'd better put her on the phone. I have something important to tell both of you." Laura's voice trembled, and he felt immediate concern.

"Irene, pick up the phone in there," Wesley hollered. "Laura's on the line."

A few seconds later, his wife came on the phone. "Hello, Laura. How are you, dear?"

Laura sniffed and sucked in her breath, like she was choking on a sob. "N-not so good, Mom. The baby's here, and–"

"You've had the baby? Oh, that's wonderful. What did you have?"

Wesley shifted the phone to his other ear while he waited for Laura's response. If she was only calling to tell them that the baby had been born, would she sound so upset?

"The doctors have some more tests to run, but they think David–our son–might have Down syndrome."

Wesley winced as he heard his wife's sharp intake of breath. "Laura, could you repeat that?"

"The baby was born this evening, and his breathing is irregular. He's got auburn hair like mine, but he doesn't look right, Dad." There was a pause. "The doctors told us awhile ago that they suspect Down syndrome, and Eli expects–" Laura's voice broke on a sob.

"Eli expects what, Laura?" Wesley prompted.

"He expects me to take care of the baby, even if he is handicapped."

"What? He's got to be kidding!" Irene's voice came through the line so shrill that Wesley had to hold the phone away from his ear. "Laura, if the baby is handicapped, he should be put in a home."

"That's what I said, too, but Eli said it's not the thing to do, and–" Laura coughed and sniffed. "I know nothing about caring for a disabled child, Mom. I'm not even sure I can take care of a *normal* baby."

Wesley's forehead beaded with sweat, and he reached up to wipe it away. "Do you want us to come there, Laura? I can see about getting some plane tickets right away."

"Oh, but Wesley, I have a hectic schedule with that benefit dinner I'm planning for the hospital guild this week. It would be hard for me to find someone to fill in for me at this late date."

He gritted his teeth. How could Irene think of a benefit dinner at a time like this? Didn't she realize how much Laura needed them right now? "If your mother's too busy, I'll fly out there myself."

Laura drew in a shuddering sigh. "Could you wait a few days–until we get the test results back on David, and Eli and I have had time to figure out what we're going to do?"

"Sure, I can do that. Maybe by then your mother will be free to come with me."

No comment from Irene. What was that woman thinking, anyhow?

"I'd better go," Laura said. "A nurse just came into the room to check my vitals."

"Okay, honey. Call us as soon as you have some news."

"I will. Bye."

As soon as Wesley hung up the phone, he headed straight for the kitchen. If nothing else got resolved tonight, he was going to give his wife a piece of his mind!

Chapter 27

The baby was brought to Laura the following day, and she could barely look at him. The nurse held David up and showed her that he had ten fingers and ten toes.

Fingers that are short and stubby, Laura thought bitterly. She noticed the infant's forehead. It sloped slightly, and his skull looked broad and short. The distinguishing marks of Down syndrome were definitely there. The doctor had been in earlier and explained that David might also be likely to have heart problems, hearing loss, or poor vision. He'd said that Down syndrome was a genetic disorder, resulting from extra chromosomes.

How could this have happened? Laura screamed inwardly as tears rolled down her cheeks. She looked away and told the nurse to take the baby back to the nursery.

Laura was still crying when Eli entered the room, carrying a potted plant. "I got you an African violet from the Beachys' greenhouse, and–" He dropped it onto the nightstand and moved quickly to the bed. "What's wrong? Is it something about David?"

She hiccupped loudly and pulled herself to a

sitting position. "I just saw the baby and was told earlier that he does have Down syndrome."

Eli sank to the chair beside her bed and groaned. "I was afraid of that."

"I called my parents last night."

"What'd they say?"

"Mom said David should be put in a home."

"No."

"I think she's right, Eli. A disabled child would take a lot of work."

He nodded. "Jah, I know, but David has just as much right to live a normal life as any other child."

"But he's not normal, and I–I don't know how to care for him."

"Mom will be there to help whenever you need her."

Laura shook her head as another set of tears streamed down her cheeks. "I can't do this, Eli. Please don't ask it of me."

Eli rubbed his thumb gently back and forth across her knuckles. "God gave us David so He must have had a reason for choosing us as his parents. Now we'll love him. . .cherish him. . .protect him. . ."

Laura's eyes widened. "God was cruel to allow such a thing!"

"God knows what's best for each of us. The book of Romans tells us that all things work together for good to them that love God," Eli said softly. He pointed to the African violet. "Just like this plant needs to be nourished, so does our son. God will give us the strength and love we need to raise him."

Laura closed her eyes and turned her head away

from Eli. Was she somehow responsible for this horrible nightmare?

Laura went home from the hospital the following morning, but the baby would have to stay a few more days. The doctors said he might be ready to take home next week, so this gave Laura a short reprieve. She needed some time to decide what to do about the problem.

Eli had taken time off from work to hire a driver and pick her up at the hospital, but soon after the driver dropped them off at home and Eli had seen that Laura was settled in, he left for work. It was better that way. She wanted to be alone, and if he'd stayed home with her, they would have argued about Eli expecting her to care for David.

Laura poured herself a cup of chamomile tea and curled up on the living-room couch. Reliving her dialogue with Eli at the hospital, her heart sank to the pit of her stomach.

She closed her eyes and tried to shut out the voice in her head. *God is punishing me for pretending to be religious. I tricked Eli into marrying me by making him think I had accepted his beliefs and his way of life.*

Laura's eyes snapped open when she heard a distant clap of thunder. She stared out the window. Dark clouds hung in the sky like a shroud encircling the entire house.

"The sky looks like I feel," she moaned. "My life is such a mess. I wish I had never met Eli Yoder. We should never have gotten married. I should not have gotten pregnant."

The realization of what she'd said hit Laura with such intensity, she thought she had been struck with a lightning bolt. "Oh, no! Dear Lord, no!" she sobbed. "You're punishing me for not wanting to be pregnant, not just for lying to Eli about my religious convictions." She clenched her fists so tightly that her nails bit into her skin as she grappled with the reality of the moment. "That's why David was born with Down syndrome–because God is punishing me." Laura fell back on the sofa pillows and sobbed until no more tears would come.

When the wave of grief finally subsided, she sat up, dried her eyes, and stood. She knew what she had to do. She scrawled a quick note to Eli, placed it on the kitchen table, and went upstairs.

"Laura, I'm home!" Eli set his lunch pail on the cupboard. No sign of Laura in the kitchen. He moved through the rest of the downstairs, calling her name. She wasn't in any of the rooms.

She must be upstairs resting. She's been through a lot this week, so I'd better let her sleep awhile.

Eli went back to the kitchen. He would fix himself a little snack, then go outside and get started on the evening chores.

There was an apple-crumb pie in the refrigerator, which Mom had brought over last night. He grabbed a piece, along with a jug of milk, and placed them on the table. Not until he took a seat did Eli see the note lying on the table. He picked it up and read it:

Dear Eli,

It pains me to write this letter, even more than the physical pain I endured in childbirth. I know you don't understand this, but I can't take care of David. I just don't have what it takes to raise a handicapped child.

I have a confession to make. I'm not who you think I am–I'm not really a believer. I only pretended to be one so you would marry me. I tried to be a good wife, but I could never seem to measure up.

Pauline was right when she said she would be better for you. It would have saved us all a lot of heartache if you had married her instead of me.

I hope you'll forgive me for leaving you in the lurch, but I've decided to go home to my parents. I know I'm not deserving of your forgiveness, but please know that I do love you. I've always loved you.

Always,
Laura

The words on the paper blurred. Eli couldn't react. Couldn't think. Could hardly breathe. He let the note slip from his fingers as a deep sense of loss gnawed at his insides. *Laura wouldn't pack up and leave without speaking with me first, without trying to work things out.*

When the reality of the situation fully registered, he propped his elbows on the table and cradled his head in his hands. "Oh, Laura. . .I just didn't know."

During her first few days at home, Laura slept late, picked at her food, and tried to get used to all the modern conveniences she had previously taken for granted. Nothing seemed to satisfy her. She was exhausted, crabby, and more depressed than she'd ever been in her life. Things had changed at home. Maybe it was she who had changed, for she now felt like a misfit.

Today was her and Eli's first anniversary, and she was miserable. As she sat at the kitchen table, toying with the scrambled eggs on her plate, Laura thought about their wedding day. She could still hear Bishop Wagler quoting scriptures about marriage. She could almost feel the warmth of Eli's hand as they repeated their vows. She had promised to be loyal to Eli, to care for him and live with him until death separated them, but she'd failed miserably. A painful lump lodged in her throat. She deserved whatever punishment God handed down.

Mom entered the kitchen just then, interrupting Laura's thoughts. "This came in the mail," she said, handing Laura a letter. "It's postmarked 'Lancaster, Pennsylvania.' "

Laura's fingers shook as she tore open the envelope, then began to read:

Dear Laura,

I knew you were upset about the baby, and I'm trying to understand. What I don't get is how you could up and leave like that without even talking to me first. Don't you realize how much David and I need you? Don't you know how much I miss you?

David's breathing better now, and the doctors let him come home. Mom watches him when I'm at work, but it's you he's needing. Won't you please come home?

Love,
Eli

Tears welled in Laura's eyes and spilled onto the front of her blouse. Eli didn't seem angry. In fact, he wanted her to come home. He hadn't even mentioned her lies. Had he forgiven her? Did Eli really love her in spite of all she'd done?

Maybe he doesn't believe me. He might think I made everything up because I couldn't deal with our baby being born handicapped. He might want me back just so I can care for his child.

Laura swallowed hard and nearly choked on a sob. No matter how much she loved Eli and wanted to be with him, she knew she couldn't go back. She was a disgrace to the Amish faith, and she had ruined Eli's life.

The days dragged by, and Laura thought she would die of boredom. The weather was dreary and cold, and even though Mom tried to encourage her to get out and socialize, Laura stayed to herself most of the time. She thought modern conveniences would bring happiness, but they hadn't. Instead of watching TV or playing computer games, she preferred to sit in front of the fire and knit or read a book. There was something about the Amish way of life she couldn't quite explain. At times when she'd been living with Eli, she had felt a sense of peace and tranquillity that had calmed her soul like nothing else she'd ever known.

It was strange, but Laura missed the familiar farm smells—fresh-mown hay stacked neatly in the barn, the horses' warm breath on a cold winter day, and even the wiggly, grunting piglets always squealing for more food. Laura was reminded of something Eli had once said, for much to her surprise, she even missed the predictable wake-up call of the rooster each morning. She missed her plain clothes, too, and felt out of place wearing blue jeans again.

By the middle of December, Laura felt stronger physically, but emotionally she was still a mess. Would she ever be able to pick up the pieces of her life and go on without Eli? Could she forgive herself for bringing such misery into their lives?

If God was punishing her, why did Eli have to suffer, as well? He was a kind, Christian man who deserved a normal, healthy baby. He had done nothing to warrant this kind of pain. How could the Amish refer to God as "a God of love"?

Laura sat on the sofa in the living room, staring at the Christmas tree, yet not really seeing it. *What's Eli doing right now? Does he miss me, like he said in his letter? No doubt he and the baby will be spending the holidays with his parents. If I could turn back the hands of time and make everything right between me and Eli again, I'd even learn how to fix the pickled beets he likes so well.*

Laura glanced at her parents. They sat in their respective recliners: Dad reading the newspaper, Mom working on Christmas cards. They didn't seem to have a care in the world. Didn't they know how much she was hurting? Did they think this was just another typical Christmas?

A sudden knock at the front door drew Laura out of her musings. She looked over at the mantel clock. Who would be coming by at nine o'clock at night, and who would knock rather than use the doorbell?

Dad stood. "I'll get it."

Laura strained to hear the voices coming from the hall. She couldn't be sure who Dad was talking to, but it sounded like a woman. *Probably one of Mom's lady friends or someone from Dad's office.* She leaned against the sofa pillows and tried not to eavesdrop.

"Laura, someone is here to see you," Dad said as he entered the living room with a woman.

Laura's mouth dropped open, and she leaped from the couch. "Martha Rose! What are you doing here? Is Eli with you?" She stared at the doorway, half-expecting, half-hoping Eli might step into the room.

Martha Rose shook her head. "I've come alone. Only Amon knows I'm here. I left him plenty of my breast milk, and he agreed to care for baby Amanda and little Ben so I could make the trip to see you."

She smiled. "The bus ride took a little over twenty-seven hours, and Amon knows I won't be gone long. Besides, if he runs into any kind of problem with the kinner, he can always call on Mom."

Laura's heart began to pound as she tried to digest all that Martha Rose had said. "What's wrong? Has someone been hurt? Is it Eli?"

Martha Rose held up her hand. "Eli's fine. . .at least physically." She glanced at Laura's folks, then back at Laura. "Could we talk in private?"

Laura looked at Mom and Dad. They both shrugged and turned to go. "We'll be upstairs if you need us," Dad said.

"Thanks," Laura mumbled. Her brain felt like it was in a fog. Why had Martha Rose traveled all the way from Pennsylvania to Minnesota if there was nothing wrong at home? Home—was that how she thought of the house she and Eli had shared? Wasn't this her home—here with Mom and Dad? She studied her surroundings. Everything looked the same, yet it felt so different. It was like trying to fit into a pair of shoes that were too small.

When Wesley and Irene entered their room, Irene took a seat on the end of their bed and released a sigh. "I wonder what Martha Rose wants. I hope she's not here to try and talk Laura into going back to Pennsylvania with her."

"If she is, it's none of our business." Wesley leaned on the dresser and stared at her.

"You don't have to sound so snippy. I only want

what's best for our daughter."

His defenses rose, and he marched across the room. "And you think I don't?"

"Calm down, Wesley. It's not like you to shout like that."

"I'm not shouting. I'm speaking my mind, which is something I should have done a long time ago."

Irene's chin trembled, and tears shimmered in her green eyes. The old Wesley would have succumbed to that pathetic look, but not anymore. He was tired of saying things just because they were what she wanted to hear. It was high time he stood up to her and said what was on his mind.

He took a seat on the bed beside her. "I love you, Irene, and I have ever since we met in college."

"I–I love you, too."

"But just because I love you doesn't mean I always agree with you or will do things your way."

"What are you trying to say?"

He tucked his thumb under her chin and tipped her head back so she was looking into his eyes. "I'm saying that I don't agree with you where Laura's concerned."

"What do you mean?"

"I think Laura's place is with her husband and baby."

Her eyes widened. "You can't mean that, Wesley. Laura's baby is handicapped, and he will need special care."

He nodded. "I think Laura is capable of giving David whatever help he needs."

"But she doesn't want to care for him; she's said so many times."

"That's because she thinks she can't, but I believe she can."

"What makes you so sure?"

He smiled and reached for her hand. "She's her mother's daughter—full of courage, determination, and strength she doesn't even know she has."

"You–you think that about me?"

"Sure do."

She leaned her head against his shoulder. "That's the nicest thing you've ever said to me, dear."

He kissed the top of her head. "Laura's place is with Eli, just as much as your place is with me."

"Laura, are you okay?" Martha Rose asked, placing a hand on Laura's trembling shoulder.

"I. . .uh. . .sure didn't expect to see you tonight." Laura motioned to the sofa. "Please, have a seat. Let me take your coat. Would you like some tea or hot chocolate?" She was rambling but couldn't seem to help herself.

Martha Rose took off her coat and draped it over the back of the couch. Then she sat down. "Maybe something to drink, but after we talk."

Laura sat beside her. "What's so important that you would come all this way by bus?"

"My brother has been so upset since you left. He told me he wrote a letter asking you to come home."

"Did he also tell you that I've been lying to him all these months?"

"About being a believer?"

Laura nodded.

"Jah, he mentioned that, too."

Laura swallowed hard. "Then you understand why I can't go back."

Martha Rose reached inside her coat pocket and pulled out a small Bible. She opened it and began reading. " 'If any brother hath a wife that believeth not, and she be pleased to dwell with him, let him not put her away.' " She smiled. "That's found in the book of 1 Corinthians."

Laura's eyes widened. "Are you saying Eli could choose to stay with me even though I'm not a believer?"

Martha Rose nodded. "It doesn't have to be that way, though."

"What do you mean?"

"You could give your heart to Jesus, Laura. He wants you to accept His death as forgiveness for your sins. First John 3:23 says, 'And this is his commandment, that we should believe on the name of his Son Jesus Christ, and love one another, as he gave us commandment.' "

As Martha Rose continued to read from the Bible, Laura was finally convinced of the truth in God's Word, and soon tears began streaming down her face. "Oh, Martha Rose, you have no idea how much I've sinned. I did a terrible thing, and now God is punishing me. How can I ever believe He would forgive me?"

"Romans 3:23 says, 'For all have sinned, and come short of the glory of God.' If we ask, God will forgive any sin." Martha Rose clasped Laura's hand.

"When I first found out I was pregnant, I–I didn't even want our baby."

"Why, Laura?"

"I was afraid of having a child. I know it's a vain thing to say, but I wanted to keep my trim figure." She gulped. "Even more than that, I wanted Eli all to myself." Laura closed her eyes and drew in a shuddering breath. "God's punishment for my selfish thoughts was David. I believe that's why He gave us a disabled child."

Martha Rose shook her head. "God doesn't work that way. He loves you, just as He loves the special child He gave you and Eli. God wants you to ask His forgiveness and surrender your life to Him."

"I–I want to change, but I don't know if I have enough faith to believe."

"All you need to do is take that first little step by accepting Jesus as your Savior. Then, through studying His Word and praying, your faith will be strengthened. Would you like to pray right now and ask Jesus into your heart?"

Laura nodded and bowed her head. After surrendering her will to God and asking His forgiveness for her sins, the peace she so desperately sought flooded her soul. When she went to bed that night, a strange warmth crept through her body. She felt God's presence for the very first time and knew without reservation that she was a new person because of His Son, Jesus. Martha Rose slept in the guest room across the hall, and Laura thanked God that her special friend had come.

Chapter 28

Laura clung tightly to Martha Rose's hand as they stepped down from the bus. She was almost home, and even though she still had some doubts about her ability to care for a disabled child, it was comforting to know she would have God to help her. She scanned the faces of those waiting to pick up passengers. There was no sign of Eli or Amon.

"Are you sure they knew we were coming?" Laura asked Martha Rose, feeling a sense of panic rise in her throat.

"I talked to Eli at the furniture shop where he works, so I'm certain they'll be here." Martha Rose led Laura toward the bus station. "Let's get out of the cold and wait for them inside."

The women had no more than taken seats when Amon walked up. He was alone.

Laura felt like someone had punched her in the stomach. "Where's Eli? Didn't he come with you?" *Maybe he's changed his mind about wanting me back.*

"Eli's at the hospital," Amon said, placing a hand on Laura's shoulder.

Her stomach churned like whipping cream

about to become butter. "The hospital? Is it the baby? Is David worse?"

Amon shook his head. "There was an accident today."

"An accident? What happened?" Martha Rose's face registered the concern Laura felt.

"Eli cut his hand at work, on one of those fancy electric saws."

Laura covered her mouth with her hand. "How bad?"

"He lost part of one finger, but the doctor said he should still be able to use the hand once everything heals."

"Oh, my dear, sweet Eli," Laura cried. "Hasn't he already been through enough? If only I hadn't run away. If only—"

Martha Rose held up her hand. "No, Laura. You can't go blaming yourself. Just as David's birth defect is no one's fault, this was an accident, plain and simple. In time, Eli will heal and be back at work."

Laura looked down at her clasped hands, feeling like a small child learning to walk. "Guess my faith is still pretty weak. I'd better pray about it, huh?"

Martha Rose nodded. "Prayer is always the best way."

Eli lay in his hospital bed, fighting the weight of heavy eyelids. Against his wishes, the nurse had given him a shot for pain, and now he felt so sleepy he could hardly stay awake. Amon had left for the bus station over an hour ago. What was taking so long? Maybe Laura had changed her mind and stayed in Minneapolis. Maybe. . .

"Eli? Eli?" A gentle voice filled his senses. Was he dreaming, or was it just wishful thinking?

He felt someone touch his arm, and his eyes snapped open. "Laura?"

She nodded, her eyes full of tears. "Oh, Eli, I'm so sorry!" She rested her head on his chest and sobbed. "Can you ever forgive me for running away. . .for lying about my relationship with God. . . for wanting you to change when it was really me who needed changing?"

Eli stroked the top of her head, noting with joy that she was wearing her covering. "I've already forgiven you, but I must ask your forgiveness, too."

She raised her head and stared into his eyes. "For what? You've done nothing."

He swallowed against the lump in his throat. "For not being understanding enough." He touched her chin with his uninjured hand. "I think I expected too much, and sometimes I spoke harshly instead of trying to see things from your point of view. If I'd been a better husband, maybe you would have found your way to God sooner."

Laura shook her head. "It wasn't your fault. I was stubborn and selfish. That's what kept me from turning to God. I believed I could do everything in my own strength. I thought I could have whatever I wanted, and it didn't matter who I hurt in the process." She sniffed deeply. "When I finally found forgiveness for my sins, I became a new creature." She leaned closer, so their lips were almost touching. "I love you, Eli."

He smiled. "And I love you. Christmas is only a few days away, and I'm convinced that it's going to be our best Christmas ever." He sealed his promise with a tender kiss.

Epilogue

Laura stood at the kitchen counter, about to open the jar of pickled beets she would serve with the stew they'd be having for supper. She gazed out the window at Eli and their two-year-old son as they romped in the snow. David was doing so well, and she thanked God for him every day. He was such an agreeable, loving child. How could she have ever not wanted him? Eli had been right all along. David was special—a wonderful gift from God.

A soft *meow* drew Laura's attention from the window. She turned toward the sound, and her lips formed a smile. Foosie ran across the kitchen floor, and their nine-month-old daughter, Barbara, followed in fast pursuit.

Laura chuckled at the sight of her perfect little girl, up on her knees, chasing that poor cat and pulling on its tail. No wonder Foosie preferred to be outdoors these days.

"Life couldn't be any better," Laura whispered. Not only had she made peace with God, but her parents had also moved to Lancaster County, where her father practiced law at a small firm during the week and tinkered in his garden every weekend.

Laura had finally come to realize that Eli's folks really did care about her, and she'd even made things right with Pauline, who had written her a letter not long ago, apologizing for her bad behavior.

As Laura poured the beets from the glass canning jar into a bowl, she looked up. "Lord, I thank You for the two wunderbaar children and the husband You gave to me, and I especially thank You for turning a fancy, spoiled English woman like me into a plain Amish wife who loves You so much. You have truly blessed me, and I ask for Your blessings on each one in our extended families."

Recipe for Laura's Pickled Beets

Ingredients:

- 3 quarts small beets
- 3 cups cider vinegar
- 2 tablespoons salt
- 4 cups sugar
- 1½ cups water
- 2 cinnamon sticks

Cook the beets in a large pan until tender and put into clean, hot canning jars. Combine the rest of the ingredients in a separate pan and boil until it becomes a syrup. Pour the boiling syrup over the beets, then seal. Cold pack them for 10 to 15 minutes.

About the Author

Descended from Anabaptists herself, Wanda E. Brunstetter enjoys writing about the Amish because they live a peaceful, simple life. Wanda's interest in the Amish and other Plain communities began when she married her husband, Richard, who grew up in a Mennonite church in Pennsylvania. Wanda and Richard have made numerous trips to Amish Country and have many Amish friends, living in several communities. Wanda hopes her readers will learn to love the wonderful Amish people as much as she does.

Wanda and Richard have been blessed with two grown children, six grandchildren, and one great-grandson. In her spare time Wanda enjoys beachcombing, ventriloquism, gardening, photography, knitting, and having fun with her family.

Wanda has written over 60 books, as well as hundreds of stories, articles, poems, devotionals, and puppet scripts.

To learn more about Wanda, visit her website at www.wandabrunstetter.com.

Also Available in This Series. . .

A MERRY HEART

LOOKING FOR A MIRACLE

THE HOPE CHEST